Remembering Wheatfield Bridge

Joni VanNest

For Jim: my husband, friend, staunchest supporter and biggest fan. He has been there for me ever since the first time I said, "Hey, I want to be a writer!" and has encouraged me throughout the many incarnations of this book. Without him, these pages would never have been born.

A great big thank you also to my children, Jim and Justin, who frequently remind me that it's never too late to dream.

I also wish to thank the Writers of Light, the initial test subjects for the stories of Wheatfield Bridge. Their belief in me, along with their kind words, gave me the courage to keep writing.

Mary J., grammarian-in-chief and woman of sound logic, I thank you for assuring the finished product was fit for print.

And to God, the Author of all things – thanks for the words. May they bring you glory.

JONI VANNEST

CONTENTS

Prologue   vii

1	CONNIE ANDERSEN	1
2	THE ROAD TO EMMAUS	11
3	CONNIE ANDERSEN	27
4	PASS IT ON	33
5	CONNIE ANDERSEN	45
6	A LONG WAY FROM HOME	47
7	CONNIE ANDERSEN	61
8	JODI'S BRIDGE	65
9	HE WHO BEGAN A GOOD WORK	75
10	CONNIE ANDERSEN	107
11	ON BECOMING	115
12	CONNIE ANDERSEN	123
13	WHITMIRE'S GENERAL STORE	131
14	CONNIE ANDERSEN	171
15	MUCH WILL BE REQUIRED	179
16	INTO DARK CORNERS	199
17	PATRIOT WOODS	223
18	CONNIE ANDERSEN	239
19	39½ RIVER ROAD	241
20	CONNIE ANDERSEN	269
21	ALL GOOD GIFTS	271
22	CONNIE ANDERSEN	283
23	CHAIN OF LOVE	285
24	A LESS THAN SILENT NIGHT	303
25	ANGEL BRIGADE	309
26	CONNIE ANDERSEN	341

PROLOGUE

Have you ever wondered where literary characters go when you are done with them, when they are left to the devices of what remains of their own reality? You probably think it an odd question to ponder as heroes and villains are merely contrivances of someone's vivid imagination, not born of flesh and bone. How could they go anywhere or do anything? Their existence is solely at the behest of the one experiencing the story, and when the story is over, THE END become final words on the subject.

Rhetoric asks, "If a tree falls in the woods and no one is there to hear it, does it make a sound?" Philosophy and science both attempt to answer the question, however unsatisfactorily to the other side. Truth is parochial. We believe what we want to or are able to believe.

And I am no different. I, too, weigh the great themes of life, occasionally to much success. Other times, not so much. Like with the sound of the tree, or lack thereof, it is a quandary that will haunt each new freshman academic until thought is no more. But, of one thing I can vouch for with unwavering certainty: that now and some other time aren't the only planes of existence.

JONI VANNEST

1
CONNIE ANDERSEN

The alarm sounded, an annoying high-pitched repetitive beep. The first time I heard it, it sent an already weakened heart into an overtime it could scarcely afford. Was something wrong? "Nurse, NURSE." Back then the words came out much stronger than they do now. I hit the call button too—appropriately, the big red cross in the middle of the speaker clipped to my pillow—like I was going for a world record on the panic button. My heart jumped from my chest to my throat where I felt it pound out my life's rhythm. Shallow, rapid-fire respirations failed to produce the consolation of a refreshing breath.

A second alarm sounded, followed by a woman in flowered scrubs who appeared in the doorway. Her first glance was at me—conscious—her second glance at the monitors.

"What's up sweetie? Your bp is through the roof."

Did I really have to tell her? Couldn't she hear? Her calm approach and relative comfort with my predicament did little to still my nerves. Between breaths I managed, "Lots - of - beeps. What's - wrong? Make it - stop."

"Just the IV monitor telling me your drip is done." She hit a button to silence the initial squawk. I must have visibly exhaled a sigh of relief. "Is that what has you all stressed out?" The hint of a southern drawl was evident in how she turned stressed into a two-syllable word: stray-essed. She also couldn't hide a small, yet perceptible smirk at my ignorance. I tried to manage a conciliatory smile as my breathing came into a more regular pace, quieting the second alarm. She placed a diamond laden hand on my arm, probably the promise of an overworked doctor. "Don't you worry about that alarm sweetie; nothing bad is going to happen to you because of a silly old bell."

The next time it happened a different nurse took her leisure to check in on me, as it was only one alarm and obviously not an urgent matter. I had no choice but to wait. Of course, I'm sure she had more than her fair share of patients. They do seem vastly outnumbered, a nurse/patient ratio designed to make sure employees do not have a moment to waste corporate healthcare dividends. The diagnosis the second time: "Oops, a little snag in the line. Nothing to worry about." After that: "Battery's low. Someone forgot to plug it back in."

So it was that my life had become a series of bells and beeps.

Betsy (bless her heart) came in to switch out my drip. "How are you doing, Miss Connie?"

It surprised me she would really ask that question. As if the answer would ever be different, more positive or hopeful. Still, I suppose they have to keep tabs on changes, good or bad.

In truth, I was tired, cold, in pain, struggling for air. The prongs of the cannula were annoying me. I tried wriggling my nose to make it better only to feel a trickle of mucus make its way down the chute. My arm, like lead, barely budged when I tried to adjust it. I resigned myself to live with a soggy nose for the time being. "Couldn't be better."

There must be some innate trait in good nurses deep in their DNA that allows them instinctively to know their patients' needs. Betsy's diamond studded hand reached for a tissue, wiped my runny nose as gently as she would a newborn's, then reset the oxygen tube back in place. She patted the y-joint for good measure. "There."

I was not a child being tucked into bed, I was a grown woman; yet that was how her actions made me feel – placated, dealt with. I'm certain she meant only to comfort me. That knowledge did little to appease my spirit. I closed my eyes and tensed, opened them again. "Thank you." The breathy exasperated word moved off my tongue and dissolved into thin air like cotton candy.

"Anything I can do, even little things like that, you just let me know." She approached the bed and tilted her head toward me as if in confidence. "I know a lot of women relate to Ellen Steele or Kelly Loggins, maybe some even prefer Jodi. But I have to be honest, I really liked Jack Priestly; he was my favorite. I hope you don't mind my saying, but I see a lot of him in you." She thought about that for a moment. "In a good way, that is. A woman needs to be a little sassy from time to time, don't you think? Where I'm from most folks appreciate the Melanies rather than the Scarletts. So I say, you go girl."

My lips formed a weary smile. It would have been hypocritical to take offense. There was a lot of me in the character of Jack Priestly. It's like bits of me flecked off and landed on the page comingling with his personality. I didn't plan it that way, it just sort of happened. Nevertheless, it worked. Jack came to life sharing a small part of my soul.

Betsy pulled the blanket up to my chin. "You rest now, Connie."

As if there was another option.

After she left the room I took her advice and sank my head deeper into the pillow. Bill came to mind. I think about him often, of the years together and the years missed. There was so much we looked forward to in growing old. Traveling. Experiencing new things. Enjoying grandchildren as they came along and grew. Even just sitting in rocking chairs on the front porch like a couple of fuddy-duddies. It's funny, sometimes I have a hard time conjuring up a clear image of him in my mind, but I can still hear the sound of his voice, mellow and reassuring. I loved that voice. When he sat at the piano and sang a ballad just for me, peering into my heart with his song, there was no question we were meant to be together through all time. But alas, dreamy reflections have no bearing on life. And now I'm on the edge of that same deep dark river he crossed without me, long before my personal schedule called for it. If I could, I'd employ the old deus ex machina and add several more chapters giving myself the opportunity to do some of those things, for Bill's sake. But this book is already bound with no possibility to add any pages.

I watched the sun move quickly across the autumn afternoon painting long bands of faded light that crept up the wall, barely cheering its sedated neutral color. Greenish gray. Maybe a pale shade of blueish green. The debate kept me occupied until my eyelids failed me and I lay in darkness of the temporary kind, not yet ready to give in to a more permanent one.

William walked in right behind the kitchen worker who was carrying a dinner tray. Still in his suit, he hadn't even taken the time to remove his tie after leaving the office. He looked so much like his father, reaching 6'2", with a lean build. Blonde and fair, there was no mistaking his Andersen heritage. William. He always did go in for the formal rather than colloquial Bill or Billy, even when he was a boy. We knew we had an accountant on our hands when, as a child, he'd squirrel away most monetary gifts he'd received, saying, "Someday I'll have enough money to buy whatever I want. Until then it stays in my pig." The pig account ultimately grew into his first car – an old wood-paneled minivan with more miles than a Greyhound bus that earned him the nickname, Soccer Mom. He wore the title with grace and good humor.

"Hey, Mom."

The attendant nodded a greeting and placed the tray on the wheeled bedside table then left without uttering a word.

"Hi. Where are…" I didn't have to finish my sentence, airy as it was; he knew exactly what I wanted to ask and chimed right in. Thank goodness for small blessings.

"James is running a slight temp, so Molly thought it best for her and the kids to sit this one out."

My head bobbed, I see.

He leaned in to give me a peck on the forehead then pulled the lid off the dinner tray. "Let's check out the du jour. Shall we? Mmm. Something brown and squishy over tiny white pellets. A little green pile. Something in the corner that wiggles, presumably Jell-O. And tepid water pretending to be coffee. A meal fit for a queen."

He certainly inherited my sardonic sense of humor. I suppose there's still time for him to outgrow it. I made a face to match the food.

"Come on, Ma. Just a little?" He spooned a glob of the brown stuff and held it, pausing in reverence before delivery. "Father, bless this food to Mom's body to make her strong.

"Now, open wide."

I assumed he was no longer talking to the Lord at that point; heaven help him if he was. I stuck my tongue out and he couldn't help but laugh. He was supposed to. I meant for him to do just that, while also letting him know I was not interested in the pabulum. He tried again, despite my best effort to the contrary, so I sneered.

"You're not making this easy for me." His frustration at my noncompliance resounded in his voice. We both stopped and met in each other's eyes. No, I wasn't making it easy on him. It was no picnic for me either, but he remembered that a little too late and looked away, ashamed at losing his patience. I suppose I should have been more careful not to inflict guilt for which I may not have the opportunity to ask forgiveness. Life gives us a finite set of days, hours, minutes, seconds in which to accomplish all the things we are meant to do and there are no leftover days beyond those necessary to achieve them. Moments left to random chance cannot be retrieved. Hitting restart, not an option. The Creator gives us one chance to get it right.

I have failed at this. There is too much left undone, unsaid. My story remains unfinished. The clock ticks marking my time, and I want more.

The spoon still hung in mid-air, so I opened my mouth and ate what I could.

I awoke with a start.

"Frannie, no." Molly reached out to thwart the leap that was already in progress, without success. Five-year-old Frannie landed on the foot of the mattress sending tremulous waves across the bed. Her unruly blonde curls bounced right along with her, falling where they would. Chubby little hands pushed the long golden strands out of her eyes. Only then did she offer her beautiful gap-toothed smile to me.

"Hi, Grandma."

I melt every time she does that.

I worked at drawing in enough air to give my reply strong and clear. The last thing I want is for the kids to be afraid of me. As it was, tiny James stood partially behind his mother clinging to her leg, still unsure if I really was his Gama.

"Hi, Frannie. Hi, James. I missed you guys yesterday." It came out better than I'd hoped, but James didn't buy it. He stuck his thumb in his mouth and moved even further behind Molly. Frannie on the other hand crawled up the bed and cuddled next to me. I leaned in and kissed her. The tender skin, still unmarred by sun and age, tasted sweet against my lips, reminding me of younger days when I still believed tomorrow was a promise.

"Hi, Mom. I guess William told you James was running a slight fever yesterday. That's why we couldn't be here."

"He's all better now," Frannie piped in with her two cents worth.

Molly bent over and placed a kiss on my forehead just as her husband had done the night before. So many women have nothing but complaints about their daughters-in-law, but I am blessed. Our common love makes us friends not combatants. She picked up James and tried to lean him in to me. He wanted nothing to do with it; instead, he turned away and drew himself into his mother's embrace. Molly knew it was hopeless to try convincing him otherwise, so she just rolled her eyes in acceptance and hoisted him up into a more comfortable position on her hip. "You look good today."

It was an observation, I noted, not a question. She tactfully avoided the how are you feeling today? inquisition in favor of small talk with a positive twist. Molly knew what she was doing. I bobbed my head in confirmation. And it was true. My spirit buoyed when I was with the kids, even if my body didn't. I guess today it was obvious.

"Tell me a story, Grandma."

Frannie cuddled in a little closer waiting for story time to begin. It was not an unusual request. Many were the times I would sit her on my knee or tuck her into bed with a story. Even James had been starting to show interest in hearing the stories, although his attention span waned quickly. When that happened, he would slide off my knee and toddle nearby with a raised hand to support the inevitable bottle in his mouth. But Frannie listened intently, soaking in every word. Speedy and Slowpoke, the mischievous chipmunks, were by far her favorite. Somehow those critters always seemed to be having grand adventures right in her own backyard.

Molly pulled Frannie's hair out of her face letting it drop over her shoulder. "Oh, honey, I don't think Grandma is up to telling you a story today."

"Is that because you're sick?" A pudgy hand stroked my face, no doubt a learned response. Molly was the mother to Frannie and James I always pretended to be to William, although I'm sure he knew the truth. Molly offered a charitable suggestion before I had the chance to reply.

"Frannie, since Grandma can't tell you a story, why don't you tell her one?"

She bolted upright, her face radiant. "Really? This time I get to tell the story?"

Her mother smiled. "Don't you think that would be fun?"

There was no doubt she thought it was the next best thing to getting extra dessert after Sunday dinner, which rarely, if ever, happened. A change overcame her expression, as if she was trying to wipe away all traces of the little girl she was. She sat straighter, held her head up high, even pursed her lips. No doubt she felt she was being granted honorary membership into the grownup world. She was just about to begin when her eyes suddenly grew wide. "I almost forgot," she half whispered. Then she got up and tucked the blankets snug all around me like I always did for her on those nights I'd put her to bed. Molly put a hand to her mouth either to cover her smile or in admiration of her daughter's loving actions.

"Thank you."

Frannie sat back down again on the bed and placed her index finger aside of her chin, pushing it in so that two mounds of soft cheek puffed up on either side of it. "Now where was I?" Molly nearly lost it. I could see her body tremble trying to hold in the laughter. "Well…" There was a long pause. "A long time ago there lived a person named Derla Duck. Of course, she wasn't really a person if she was a duck, but we'll just pretend for the story. Anyway, one day while…"

She regaled me with the tale of Derla Duck—the

animation in her voice so much like my own it was almost eerie. I was impressed that she was able to do this on a moment's notice. I wondered if it was a story she had already concocted in her mind long ago or if it was fresh and off the cuff. Either way, I was proud, glad the torch was being passed, not extinguished.

The fairytale took me away, out of the hospital and into her world of make-believe where there was no sickness and the worst that happened was someone losing a webbed flipper then finding it again at the bottom of her messy closet.

I guess that is why I like stories and books so much. They let us step outside ourselves for a short time, to forget our own longing and live vicariously through others' hopes and dreams. A different Opium for the Masses, so to speak. I doubt if the Wheatfield Bridge series in all its incarnations of books and short stories even vaguely amounted to anyone's drug of choice, but it did allow me to walk where this world could never take me. I guess it did for others as well.

Soon Frannie's voice faded like an echo traveling in the distance, and I found myself forming words in my head, words belonging to a world that has no form, where life is as I want it to be. To Wheatfield Bridge. It was as familiar to me as my own small three-dimensional universe, filled with people living mundane lives who touch us in ways we long to be touched. It is a cozy hamlet that exists somewhere between western Connecticut and my imagination, filled with woods and wild animals, a temperamental river, winding roads where you 'can't get there from here' but nonetheless get where you want to be; hardy New Englanders who take life as it comes and are stronger for it; more good people than bad, though none non-redeemable; homes that have withstood more than a century of storm and sun; a place you would want to call home. It is a place where good overcomes evil. At least it always had.

And that was the problem. Jack Priestly's fictional cancer came into being before my illness struck and now suddenly I was faced with two diagnoses needing outcomes. In other circumstances, it would not have fazed me one bit to write him off. Characters are dispensable; I cause them into being and can cause their demise. But Jack and I are too closely related. How could I do to him what I did not want to happen to me? I wanted Jack to survive. The words had churned in my head seeking release to a page, the story tumbling and circling in all directions never finding conclusion. It felt as if any movement in Jack's life would have a profound effect on mine, the two being inexorably joined. If he died, my own story, I feared, would end. Yet making him well would not bring me hope, only sorrow, as our lives broke apart. I realized this made no sense. Fiction has no bearing on reality and certainly a woman of faith should not be thinking this way. God is in charge, not fate. A pleasant sentiment to be sure, yet one which is sometimes hard to hold onto.

Faith. My pastor always said that we should never use feelings to verify our faith. Feelings are fleeting, faith is constant, based in knowledge and wisdom. So if I couldn't break from the idea that Jack and I are somehow entwined, then where is my faith, my assurance of God? Was my reality in Him? I never wanted to stop long enough to dwell on the questions. I didn't think I'd like the results. Sometimes I just wished He would prop up a big billboard in front of me with a giant arrow. Here you go, Connie. Here I am, this way. Well, it never happened, so I could not let the feeling of my entanglement with Jack go. It ruled every plot decision. The story went nowhere.

I thought back to the first time I met Jack Priestly. Ellen Steele briefly introduced us in The Road to Emmaus. I never really thought about her even having a father before then. It all started with that radio preacher...

2
THE ROAD TO EMMAUS

"It has gotten to the point where there is a great chasm separating us; so much so, that I am finding it increasingly harder to recognize the other side as Americans."

Ellen pressed the car radio's scan button, anxious to tune out the political propaganda.

"Hey, I was listening to that."

Brad's smirk and raised eyebrows told her he didn't really care that she'd changed the station. After all, he knew how she felt. Still, she had to make her point. "No, you were arguing with Haggerty and you know it makes me crazy." Ellen was tired of listening to her husband yell at the radio talk show host. Samuel Haggerty had a way of making her husband's blood boil and for some reason he would rather have a one-sided argument with the radio than turn it off.

"But I like listening to him, he's entertaining."

"Well that kind of entertainment's going to give you a coronary someday."

Brad glanced at her. Maybe it was his deep-set hazel eyes with long lashes that any woman would envy. Or maybe it was his broad shoulders and strong arms just right for giving comfort. Or the way he would toss his socks on the floor instead of carrying them to the hamper just so he could hop into bed with her quicker. Perhaps it was his sense of humor and the way he teased her just to get her riled. It was probably all of the above but, even at his most incorrigible, she had every reason to love him. She considered herself lucky. Brad could have married someone a lot prettier, or at least someone who kept herself better. She was never one to pile on the make-up or wear the latest fashions, and would rather spend more time reading books than getting her nails done. She had a standing appointment at the hair salon every two months to trim and perm her hair, which she kept short and manageable, making it easier to get herself and three kids out the door every morning.

Brad opened his mouth to say something when Ellen raised an eyebrow in return, daring him. It was an argument he would never win. He went back to looking at the road ahead, defeated.

The radio continued to scan through the dial, stopping and starting on assorted commercials, songs, conversations.

"Ladies and gentlemen, I mislead you not," a voice professed with great enthusiasm. "The Lord God will return." Ellen pictured a preacher with his hand high in the air, a finger pointing up to heaven, at once both rebuking and evangelizing. The voice's excitement level grew, rising to a fevered pitch. "And that time is coming soon!" A roar of "Amens" sprang forth from the on-air congregation. "We know not the time. We know not the day. So friends, do not, I repeat, do not let yourselves be caught unprepa..." The scan moved on to a new station.

"Now there's something worth listening to," Ellen teased, knowing Brad had more disdain for charlatan TV and radio preachers than he did for conservative talk show hosts.

Brad grinned. "I'll make you get out and walk."

She smiled and turned off the radio, ending the debate.

"It's so nice to have this time to ourselves, isn't it?" Time alone with Brad was always at a premium. A great job comes with high demands and usually included extended periods away from home at business functions. Add in the kids' needs and that did not offer a lot of individual face time with her husband.

"Sure is. We should have my parents take the kids every weekend, at least when I'm home."

"What, and not do things with your children on the weekend? That statement has allusions to my Dad in it. Do me a favor, don't go there."

"You know I'm joking, Ellen. You and the kids are my life." He placed his hand on her knee. "Everything I do, I do for us." She squeezed his hand. In her heart, she knew there was no comparison. Brad and her father were worlds apart when it came to parenting. Jack Priestly was seriously old-school; child rearing was a woman's domain. He saw his job as the breadwinner and superintendent of the house and yard. And he was good at it. Ellen always felt safe and secure in her childhood home. Her father's lack of paternal instincts had never been an issue until her mother passed away when she was a young girl and single parenthood presented him problems he did not know how to overcome. His logic and practicality replaced the warmth of her mother's love. Intellectually, Ellen knew he loved her. She just didn't always feel it. As a parent herself, she took comfort in knowing that Brad was capable of filling her shoes, if necessary. He didn't even shy from helping Brielle practice her ballerina poses. It was one of the many reasons she loved him.

Whitmire's General Store came into view. The plan was to pick up the newspaper before heading over to the diner for breakfast. As Brad slowed down to make the right hand turn into the parking lot, he had to wait to let a couple on foot cross over to the sidewalk. "Hmm. I haven't seen those folks around here before."

Wheatfield Bridge was a small town hiding in the western woods of Connecticut, not even big enough for its own zip code. And whereas not all the locals knew the names of each one of its citizens, they came close to it. Still Ellen didn't recall seeing the couple before either and wondered if they were new in town. "Maybe they're the folks who bought the old Wheeler place."

Brad pulled into a spot and put the car in park. "Maybe."

He held the door open for her to enter the store where she greeted the clerk with familiarity. "Morning, Joe."

Joe Whitmire ran the shop longer than anyone could remember, and his father ran it before him. It was comprised of three aisles of I-just-need-to-pick-up-this-one-thing variety of dry goods, a short bank of coolers on the side wall and a pizza oven and counter in the back for takeout. Joe was also the father of her best friend, Kelly Loggins.

"Brad, Ellen." Joe acknowledged them with a smile then went back to waiting on his customer, an elderly woman wearing a print dress that had seen better days. Ellen recognized her as Kelly's neighbor, Helen. Almost daily, she walked along Bridge Street with her metal shopping cart, toting the provisions she bought at the store. They didn't know each other well, just a wave across the yard if she happened to be out in her garden when she visited Kelly.

Brad picked up the paper from the stack by the door and together they stood in line to wait their turn.

Joe placed the last item in the bag. "That'll be $10.75, Helen."

The woman counted out a five-dollar bill, three ones and some change and laid it on the counter.

She began to dig in her purse. "I'm sure I have a couple more bills in here somewhere."

Ellen noticed the groceries on the counter were nothing more than basic staples: bread, peanut butter, jelly, two cans of spaghetti. The woman was clearly embarrassed at not having enough to pay for the food. "I just, I just don't know how this could happen." She looked from one item to the other as if trying to decide which to do without.

"You know, we could..." Joe did not get a chance to finish his sentence. An elbow in Brad's side prompted him to speak up, cutting the shopkeeper off.

"Here, let me help." He offered Joe several dollars. "For the newspaper and for the rest of this nice lady's order."

The woman turned toward Brad and Ellen, not quite able to look them in the eye. "I thought I had enough, really I did. It seems prices just get higher and higher." She paused and humbly added, "Bless you."

"It's my pleasure."

The three of them walked out together. Brad and Ellen got in their car and watched as the woman headed home, pulling her groceries behind her.

"You're a good man, Brad Steele."

"Even if it takes a woman to make me so?" he asked, still feeling that elbow.

"Especially then." She kissed him on the cheek to confirm it.

Wheatfield Bridge slid by on their way to breakfast. Modest homes, many built long before the concept of planned neighborhoods, lined the road. Meandering New Englanders and simple capes stood as sentries to the passing decades, some still housing decedents of the original owners. Ellen noticed the fresh growth on all the trees and the abundance of pink and purple phlox on lawn after lawn. Spring, in her estimation, was always a promise. A promise that life goes on, even after the darkest nights and that goodness will always overcome evil. Very naïve, she knew, but it worked for her.

The Parkside Diner was straight up the road, the last bastion of civilization before reaching Emmaus State Park farther up, a favorite for picnics and swimming in summertime, cross-country skiing in winter. This time of year it barely saw any visitors, but in a couple of weeks the day-trippers would be hiking its many trails and summer would bring out family campers by the score. As Ellen and Brad headed in that direction, they once again noticed the couple who had been walking through the store parking lot, still on foot, headed the same way. Ellen thought she noticed a slight limp as the woman walked. They drove on and she put the couple out of her mind.

Ellen always felt like she was spying on her

daughter, Jodi, when they came to the diner during one of her shifts. Like most teenagers, Jodi dreamed of owning her own car, and her desire for a car outweighed her desire for free time. So she got a part-time job at the diner to save for an old clunker. Ellen and Brad were not onboard at first, as they didn't want anything to interfere with her schoolwork, but she was relentless in her pleading. "Please? I've just got to get a car. Everyone else has a ride but me. I'll be really responsible with it. I'll even run errands for you. I could take Brielle to dance class. I could pick stuff up at the store for you after school. Of course, that's after I get back from the mall... And I promise to keep my grades up. Pa-lease?" They gave in with the understanding they would take the car away if her grades suffered. It wasn't long before Jodi realized the cost of ownership didn't end with the purchase; she had to keep working to support it. Life lessons such as that were hard for Ellen to watch her kids go through. Hard, but necessary. They always left a great tip for her on the table after they were finished.

As it happened, Jodi was off that day, having stayed with a friend the night before. With all of her kids safely in other places, Ellen was enjoying a morning of empty nest. She scanned the menu for something light. The angel on one shoulder was currently keeping the devil on the other at bay. Brad knew what he wanted and was ready when the server came by. "I'll have the Big House Breakfast with coffee." The server, Claire, whispered the order aloud as she carefully wrote it on the pad.

Ellen looked at Brad with wide eyes, then closed her menu and placed it on the table. "What the heck, I'll splurge and have the same thing." The devil won.

"I'll go tell Mr. Jordan right now that you both want a Big House Breakfast."

Ellen admired Claire's determination to do her job well. Even if her round face, widely spaced eyes and slowness of speech didn't give it away, being familiar with the staff, Ellen and Brad knew the waitress had Down's syndrome. Claire gave them a big smile and headed back to the kitchen to place their orders. On the way, she passed a group of teenagers coming in.

"Please be seated. I'll be with you in a minute."

One of the boys mimicked her and his friends laughed as they took their seats. Claire either didn't notice or chose to ignore them. The teens' raucous behavior drew attention to themselves from other diners who looked up to assess the commotion. Ellen could see the disdain on some of their faces as they turned back to their private conversations, ignoring the unpleasantness of the rowdy kids.

The server returned with mugs of steaming coffee, then moved on to the next booth where the teenagers sat. Ellen kept her eyes and ears open as she sipped her morning wake up. She had a feeling Claire's day was about to turn sour.

"What would you like to order?"

"I'd like pancakes," the smallest boy among them said. "Maybe put a flat smiley face in the middle of it. You can add it to the menu, call it the waitress special." The boys howled while Claire wrote it on her pad, doing her job with dignity and courtesy they did not deserve.

Ellen looked deep into her husband's eyes. They were dark and unblinking. No words crossed between them. Brad's quiet demeanor belied the anger she knew was roiling inside, an anger to match her own.

One boy in particular escalated the fun they were having at Claire's expense. Slurring his speech and holding his hands and fingers up at skewed angles, he gave his order. "I'll have my eggs sunny-side downs."

Brad sprang from the booth, his rage a steam pipe that had blown, and confronted the youths. At 6'1", he towered above the young men, who remained seated. A sudden sense of alarm squelched the boys' amusement. Their laughter went silent.

"You think that's funny?" Brad barked at the last boy who spoke, while staring him down with his hands on his hips.

The boy did not answer right away. Brad's unrelenting stance and forceful, "Well?" prompted him in time to reply.

"No."

"Then why did you do it?"

"I don't know," he muttered with a trace of defiance in his voice, although looking uncomfortable at being challenged. The boy's friends were shrinking further into the booth as if to disown him. Had the encounter been out on the street, certainly they would have deserted him. As it was, they were a captive audience.

"Then I think you owe this lady an apology, wouldn't you say?"

Claire stood off to the side and stepped from one foot to the other, appearing embarrassed at being the center of the disruption.

The teenager looked around as if searching for a possible response to the question or maybe a little backup from his friends. The latter did not materialize. Ellen was glad he was sitting on the inside of the booth. It assured her of the limited potential for physical confrontation. She saw the tension release in his posture when he realized he was outgunned and on his own.

"Sorry," he finally mumbled almost inaudibly.

Brad tilted his head, leaned in as if to hear better. "Excuse me, did you say something? I don't think Claire heard you."

He yelled loud enough for Claire and most of the nearby patrons to hear. "Sorry."

The server took a step forward and admonished her tormentor with gentle words. "You shouldn't be mean like that, you know, or you won't have any friends."

Ellen was stunned. A genetically gifted innocence allowed Claire to see beyond herself, to be truly concerned for the boy's wellbeing. Ellen watched as anxious worry lines slipped from the girl's expression to the point where she was able to add, "I forgive you."

Such dignified words and so full of grace.

Ellen bent her head and thought of her father. Someday. Maybe. With God's help.

As they were driving home after breakfast they noticed that same couple walking along the road. Because they were driving in the opposite direction this time, they were able to see the couple head on. Ellen figured them to be in their fifties, looking weary from their journey, the woman leaning on the man for support.

"Brad, that couple walked all the way out here from town. Where could they possibly be going? There's nothing in that direction for miles except the park, and of course the diner."

"Do you think we should offer them a ride?" he asked.

She wasn't so sure that was a good idea. "We're not going that way." She hoped that would be the end of the discussion.

"We could be. They've been walking an awful long time, and it doesn't look like they're just out walking for pleasure."

"What if they're dangerous?"

Brad shot her a look that would inflict guilt into

the most piously self-righteous and turned the car around. Pulling over, he hit the button to roll down the window on the passenger side of the car.

"Hi there," Ellen called out to them. "We couldn't help but notice you've walked all the way out here from town. Could you use a lift somewhere?"

The woman looked to the man as if to ask, "Do you think it's safe?" At the same time her eyes also betraying, "Please say it is."

"It's not too far up the road from here," the man replied. "But it sure would be nice to get off our feet."

"Sure, hop in," Brad called from the driver's side.

As they settled in the car, Ellen turned around in her seat to get a better look at their guests. She believed her initial evaluation of their ages was pretty near on point – mid-fifties, maybe a little younger. He wore a faded tee shirt and jeans, she had on a blouse missing a button and stretch pants. Their sneakers looked as if they got a lot of use.

The man told them they were staying in the campground at Emmaus State Park and asked if Brad knew where it was. He assured him he did.

The man went on to explain how they had just come from a trip to the hospital. "Needed to get something for my wife's arthritis. Her hips been giving her a bit of trouble these days. The docs fixed her up with some pain killer and here we are."

Ellen and Brad glanced at one another, sharing unspoken thoughts. They knew the hospital was a good hike even from where they had first seen the couple walking.

As they drove through the campground, the man led them to a small pop-up camper that appeared to have traveled its share of miles. The pick-up truck parked in front of it, littered with dirt and pollen residue, also looked weary from the journey. The couple had staked an open-air kitchen to one side of the camper around a fire pit. An outhouse stood in the distance.

"It's not much, but it's home. For now. When the truck gets fixed we'll be on our way again."

Ellen took in the situation and could see their needs were great. Brad did too. "You know, I'm no mechanic," he said, "but I'm kind of handy with a wrench if you'd like some help getting her up and running again."

"Well, Mr..." The man was at a loss for a name.

"Brad. Brad and Ellen Steele." He reached back to offer his hand. It was met with gratitude.

In a slow, tired voice the man replied, "Well then, Brad, I'm Dan Deaton. This is my wife, Susan. And that'd be mighty kind of you."

Ellen thought Dan's soft voice and the gentle manner in which he spoke contradicted their circumstances, as there was a serenity about the couple that seemed out of place. Another example of grace under fire.

"You know, Susan was just saying as we were walking there - 'Dan,' she says, 'the good Lord provides. You just wait and see. When He sees fit, He'll provide.' So I guess that kind of makes you folks an answer to prayer, huh?"

*   *   *

Brad was pensive in the car heading home to get the tools to work on the truck. "You know I never thought of myself as being a blessing to others, and I'm pretty sure the thought never crossed your mind either."

"No, not really." They tried to live their lives as best as they could, doing good where good was needed. Dan's words offered them a new perspective.

After driving a while in quiet thought, Ellen clicked the radio back on. The scanner landed on the same Christian station it had before, but a different preacher was speaking to an unseen congregation.

"And in Luke 24 we read, 'when suddenly, it was as though their eyes were opened - they recognized Him!'"

JONI VANNEST

3
CONNIE ANDERSEN

The BP monitor buzzed and I felt the pressure cuff tighten around my upper arm in its recurring schedule of ebb and flow. I listened as it clicked and let out some air, then clicked again letting out a little more. The machine did this several times until its internal brain was satisfied it had a valid reading. I didn't want to look at the numbers, already knowing they were nowhere near where they should be. William looked without comment. He took a breath.

"So, did the doctor see you today?"

I nodded in the affirmative.

"And?"

"No more marathons for me." I coughed. It was a common occurrence these days. Short ones like that weren't a bother. The ones that refused to give up took a lot out of me. William ignored it, as if it was just a part of who I was now, as ubiquitous as my age spots and thinning hair.

"And I was so looking forward to spending Patriot's Day in Boston. Seriously, what did he say?"

He was anxious, almost annoyed; I could hear it in his voice. These visits were starting to wear on him. Maybe it was fear or sadness. Maybe he was just plain tired from adding one more commitment to his schedule. It was hard to tell with him. Love manifests itself in all kinds of ways in situations like this. At least I hoped it was love and not a sense of obligation that brought him here every day. I remembered all those times when I should have been there for him. A sick thought ran through my head - that he was only trying to show me how it should have been done. I readjusted myself on the bed, uncomfortable with that thought, then reached for his hand. It was so easy to comfort him when he was a boy. Bear hugs and holding hands healed all wounds back then. If only it was that way now. His grasp was firm and warm. He laid his other hand on top of mine so that it was sandwiched between his. It had to be love. I just couldn't understand why. I gave him his answer, though not the one he wanted to hear. "Not on top yet."

To be on top was the dream of all who waited, even knowing at what great expense one's name moved up the list. Those before you checked off one by one, either by ascension or attrition. A game of beat the clock: tic toc, tic toc, always hopeful you'll beat the buzzer. William tried to be hopeful for both of us. Lord knows, I didn't have the strength to do it. The disappointment of still having to wait hung in the air between us, an intangible object almost too heavy to bear.

That night I had the TV tuned to Letterman. As usual, he took a cheap shot at someone who was there to plug a new movie or a new CD. I wasn't sure which. The guest was one of those crossover entertainers, like Will Smith, a performer who did a little of this and a little of that. I never heard of the guy. The audience seemed to enjoy him, though, and the laughter was a pleasant enough pastime until I fell asleep. I laid on my side facing away from the door so that the sounds from the hall, what little there were that late at night, would not bother me. The guest was trying a comeback at Dave when I heard the faintest of sounds behind me - a sugary-sweet giggle, high-pitched and shy, not boisterous and bawdy. I could tell it belonged to a child, which was odd because visiting hours ended much earlier. Even those families that tended to push the envelope were gone by then. I rolled onto my back to see what was going on. The maneuver was easier than when I rolled onto my side, taking little effort.

A small shadow in the doorway quickly moved from view. I did not see the child it belonged to, but I heard the giggle again revealing she was still there. Shadows, mimics of our every move, stretch and shrink with the light that creates it, so that we do not get an accurate view of the subject, only its essence. The hospital's overhead fluorescent lighting in the hall should have cast a short shadow, if any at all, on the marble floor. However, when it came back into view the shadow was elongated, as if backlit, stretching across the threshold of the room. I would not have been able to determine the child's gender if not for the outline of a ballerina tutu. The little girl jumped, I could see, and clapped her hands.

"Look at me. Look at me." The imploring voice beckoned to someone I could neither see nor hear. A soft hum wandered in from beyond the room and I noticed the shadow begin to dance as the girl serenaded herself. Tiny leaps and pirouettes performed for the unknown audience entertained me from afar, followed by a deep curtsey at its conclusion. There was no applause, no one offered praise for the solo recital. The little girl's shadow clasped its hands to its face. Another giggle filled the air. Then the hands came down, one resting at her side while the other gave a side-to-side wave. "Goodbye," the soft voice cooed through the hall as the shadow drifted out of sight.

As I closed my eyes waiting for sleep to overtake me I thought about the shadowed ballerina, and how she was probably around the same age as Frannie. It's funny how it seems I always appreciated that age group, as if five years old was the perfect time in a child's life. Brielle, Ellen and Brad Steele's little girl and Tara, Kelly and Bill Loggins' little one came into being at age five. They were best friends, and always would be, that relationship forever depicted in print. When Frannie came along and eventually grew to that age it was like the icing on the cake. I could have my little girl and play with her too. Until now.

It was very early in the morning, when the day was new and the nurses changed shifts that Betsey came in to check on me before going home for her well-deserved rest.

"Hey Miss Connie, just here for the daily draw before I head out." She rubbed an alcohol swab on the port in my IV before hooking up a tube to get the blood sample, a much more humane way of doing it than in the old days when you got poked all the time. I stared away from the action anyway out of habit and once again thought about the tiny dancer.

"Who was the ballerina?" I asked Betsey, figuring she must have seen the performance earlier. The nurse cocked her head and looked askance.

"The who?"

"Little girl in… tutu. Earlier. Dance. Hall. " I made my staccatoed point through intermittent bouts of coughing and shortness of breath.

Betsey waited until I had stopped coughing before plugging a new vial onto the needle. "Sweetie, if there had been a little girl dancing in the hallway I surely would have seen it. Sounds to me like you had yourself a dream about being at the bál-let." Her drawl once again stressed the wrong syllable, at least it was wrong on this side of the Mason-Dixon Line. "Tell me, was it The Dance of the Sugarplum Fairies? I just love that one from The Nutcracker."

I shook my head.

"Swan Lake?" She laid the dark red tubes on the table to put the labels with my name on them. I told her the only thing I knew for certain. "Twinkle, Twinkle Little Star."

She quickly stood up straight. "What?" She laughed at the thought. "You mean there were ballerinas dancing to Twinkle, Twinkle Little Star right here at St. Luke's and I missed it?"

When she put it like that it did sound ridiculous. Maybe

it was just a dream after all, albeit a nice one. Although it certainly felt like it was real. I shrugged my shoulders and left it at that, while secretly wondering if I'd started to lose it. I didn't want people to say of my last days that I had gone nutty as a fruitcake, seeing and hearing things that weren't there. I mean, what if I started to have conversations with invisible people? Like Helen Boudreau. Well, at least deep down Helen really knew she wasn't talking to anyone. Those one-sided conversations just helped her get through the lonely days. That is much more acceptable than really believing something is there that isn't. I think. I hope.

Perhaps, I thought, I was jumping the gun. Just because Betsey didn't see the little girl didn't mean she wasn't there and that I was dreaming or imagining the whole thing. Someone else may have seen her. I would probably never know that, of course. So I had to satisfy myself that Betsey was not the target audience and hope that I'd see her dance again.

It was while I was eating lunch, or more appropriately while my lunch was sitting on the wheeled cart uneaten, that she showed up. As previously, I heard the giggle before she popped her head in the door sideways. A cherub-like face with rosy cheeks and blue eyes smiled at me. Wild red ringlets dangled in mid-air. She giggled again.

"Hello," I said.

The little girl put her thumb between her teeth and wiggled her fingers at me.

"Come in. Don't be afraid." The breath behind each word grew stronger as I spoke.

She took a few hesitant steps into the room. She was wearing a poufy pink tutu and ballerina slippers. I sighed at the sight of her. I was not going crazy. Here she was, in the flesh. She came a little closer. "What's your name?"

The petite ballerina did not answer, but she must have felt comfortable enough with me for she climbed up on the guest chair next to the bed and took a seat. My uneaten lunch sat between us. "Do you like Jell-O?" She bobbed her head enthusiastically. "You can have mine, if you'd like."

She looked at the tray as if trying to decide whether to take me up on the offer. It didn't take her long before she was kneeling up to the tray with spoon in hand. Who would have thought eating Jell-O was a two-handed proposition, but apparently it is for kids that age. I had seen Frannie do it that way as well, using one hand to scoop it up to her mouth and the other to make sure it got in.

She never spoke. When she was done, she slipped out of the chair and skipped to the door to leave, though not before turning back to give me a tiny side-to-side wave good-bye. I waved back. When she spun around to exit, she nearly ran into the lunch attendant who was coming in to retrieve my tray and scooted past her into the hallway.

The attendant picked up the tray and assessed it. "I'm glad you ate a little something today."

I smiled weakly at her and thrust my chin toward the door where the little girl had scooted past her. "Cute tutu, huh?"

"Excuse me?"

"The little girl's tutu. It's cute."

She looked confused. "Oh, I must have missed it. Sorry. See you at dinnertime." With that she was out the door.

My mind must have run through a dozen scenarios of how the woman could have missed seeing the little girl. If I had been writing it as part of a story, I never would have been able to come up with a viable explanation that would satisfy an intelligent reader. The idea that I was losing it came back to slap me across the face. Then I remembered what the woman said about being glad I ate some of my lunch. That is when I knew I was not losing my mind.

I did not eat the Jell-O.

4

PASS IT ON

"Henry, did you see what that nice young man did? He paid for my groceries when I didn't have enough money. What a sweet thing to do. It's encouraging to see there are still good people in the world. Of course I never really doubted it, but every now and then it's good to get confirmation."

Helen Boudreau conversed aloud as she pulled the two-wheeled shopping cart behind her walking home from Whitmire's General Store. Her print dress, a birthday gift from her Henry long ago, and now more threadbare than not, flapped around her legs with the breeze. She had long since given up her driver's license, relying on both the store and the cart for her daily bread. On days like this when the morning sun warmed her face she enjoyed the walk. Sometimes Kelly Loggins would take her to the Stop and Shop. But on the whole, Helen rarely imposed on the good will of her neighbor. Thus, she lived a simple life, gleaning fulfillment from those people and things close to home.

"You know, Henry, my Social Security just doesn't go as far as it used to. Over two dollars for a loaf of bread. Can you imagine?" The sidewalk curved off Bridge

Street and onto River Road where she lived. She walked it at a steady pace, chattering as she went.

"Oh, look, there's Kelly and her little girl."

Kelly and Tara were digging holes in front of the boxwoods that grew beneath the bay window of their home. Several small flowerpots stood at attention nearby. Helen thought they were just the cutest little family. Kelly worked at Wheatfield Bridge High School and her husband did something or another, she never could remember what, but was a Marine on the weekends, just like her Henry was during the war. Their daughter, Tara, would soon be in kindergarten.

"Good morning, Kelly. It looks like you have a little helper there today."

The two turned to greet their neighbor. "Hi, Helen." Kelly got up and pushed some flyaway hair out of her face with the back of her hand, that had escaped from a ponytail. She had on polka dot gardening gloves that left a smear on her cheek where her hand had touched it. The lettering in Tara's pale green Princess shirt sparkled where it was not covered in dirt. "Actually, I'm helping Tara plant some flowers she's been growing from seed."

"It was my science project at daycare. I got a sticker for it."

Helen bent down to speak to Tara, careful not to get in a position she couldn't get out of. "My Henry and I used to mix coffee grounds in the soil when we planted flowers. Helps them grow, you see."

Kelly smiled. "My mother used to do the same thing."

Tara scrunched up her face as if Helen and her mother had just uttered the most ridiculous things she had ever heard.

"Give it a try, you'll see." Helen winked at the girl then stood straight again, placing her hand at her back to work out the creak. "Well, I should be going. Nice talking to you. Good luck with the plants."

As Helen started toward home, she turned away from the Loggins's and began to take up a different conversation. "Those folks are such nice people, always something pleasant to say."

Then, from behind, she heard Tara's small voice call out to her. "Mrs. Boudreau?"

She turned to answer. "Yes, dear?"

"Why do you talk to yourself?"

Helen froze. No one ever asked before, although she supposed many people wanted to. It started shortly after Henry died. For decades he had been there to carry on his side of the conversation, and suddenly she found empty space where the love of her life had always been. It was natural, in its own strange way, to continue talking to him. It took a while to get used to having no reply, but once she did, it seemed perfectly normal to continue as if he were still there. She did not know how to reply to the child's question, how to explain loss and loneliness to one of such innocence. She began to stumble over her words. "I, um... well..."

Kelly ran up to Tara and grabbed her hand. "Honey, we should let Mrs. Boudreau get back home." She followed up the statement by mouthing the words I'm sorry to Helen.

Tara persisted. "But who is she talking to, Mommy? There's no one there."

Kelly looked into Helen's eyes as if seeking permission to answer her daughter truthfully. Helen gazed back and swallowed hard. Permission granted. Kelly squat down so that her face was level with Tara's. "You know Mrs. Boudreau lives alone; her husband died a long time ago. Well, sometimes she gets lonely. So she'll talk to Mr. Boudreau as if he's still here. It makes her feel better."

"Does he ever talk to her?"

Kelly looked up at Helen and back to Tara. "I suppose in her heart she still feels his love. So I guess he does in a way."

Discernment was never Helen's forte, but from somewhere inside, Kelly had withdrawn a response that made sense and even surprised her with the young woman's insight. Helen's grew moist. It was a good answer.

It was a good enough answer for Tara as well. Her child's attention span quickly changed the subject. "Maybe we should get some coffee grounds too, huh Mom?"

Kelly smiled at her daughter. "Maybe we should."

Tara looked up at the old woman. "Goodbye, Mrs. Boudreau."

"Goodbye, Tara."

As Helen again headed for home again, she heard little Tara call out one more time. "Goodbye, Mr. Boudreau."

Helen stopped. Still looking forward, she smiled and went on her way.

"Henry, I so enjoy our daily walk, but I think my arthritis is starting to act up again. We may have to sit it out tomorrow." She walked in silence the short distance from the Loggins's home to her own, acutely aware of the pain in her big toe. An inner dialogue kept pace with her steps. I don't know what I'll do if I ever become so feeble I can't get to the store anymore. I don't want to end up like Louise. I'm a grown woman. I should be able to take care of myself. I just hope that I can still do it until this old body gives up. Poor Louise.

Her sister Louise moved in with her son and his family shortly after she was widowed. Her son had to work hard to convince her, claiming the house was too big to take care of alone. Helen was certain other arrangements could have been made that would have allowed her to stay in Wheatfield Bridge. She hoped her own son would never try that with her. She would have to refuse to go. The last thing she wanted was for someone else to be telling her how and where she should live.

"Here we are."

Helen opened the unlocked door, which had rarely seen the tumbler engaged in the 45 years she lived there. She wasn't expecting any trouble and trouble had never found her. She stepped up and through the kitchen doorway, turning around to pull her cart in as well. She remembered the days when Henry would help carry the groceries in the house and put them away. The chore was solely hers now.

As she placed a jar of peanut butter in the pantry, Helen could not help but reflect, once again, on the kindness shown to her that day.

"I still can't get over how that nice young man helped me. People are so disconnected these days. Oh, they think they're 'connected,' what with their electronic gizmos they carry everywhere. But personally relating to those in the same room? Ha! They just can't be bothered." She waved her hand for emphasis, a visual display she'd almost forgotten no one would see, and felt silly for it.

"Anyway, I think more people should be like that young man today. The world would be a better place."

The sun-catcher threw early morning rays on the walls of her bedroom, inviting Helen to welcome the new day. As always, she spent the first few minutes of the morning thanking God she was still on this side of the grass, then immediately set about planning her day. The first order of business, post-breakfast, would be to deadhead the late bloomers in the garden, then she would write a letter to Louise. Of course, she would have to straighten up the house before the ladies came over in the afternoon for cards. Her work was cut out for her before even stepping out of bed.

Dear Louise,

I trust you are well since my last letter. My arthritis is flaring up again, kept me from my walk and finishing work in the garden today. Maybe I'll be up to completing it later. Other than that, I haven't anything to complain about.

The girls will be over this afternoon. You will not believe what Myrtle did. She dyed her hair blonde, of all things! She says it makes her feel young. I think it makes her look like a hussy. But to each her own. The gals sure miss you at the card table. Especially since there's no one else who can catch Edna at cheating quite like you. Of course, I miss you too, more than you can imagine.

I have to tell you, I was mortified at the store yesterday. I ran out of money and couldn't afford to pay for all my groceries when this nice man offered to pay the difference. Truly, being in that situation I don't know if I felt more embarrassed or like a damsel who'd been rescued by her shining knight. (And he was handsome!) It was such a nice affirmation of the general goodness of people. Every now and then (not too often, thankfully) I get dismayed and think the world is going you know where in a you know what. Who knows, maybe someday I will be able to repay the favor, though not if the Social Security Administration has any say in it.

I hope Gil and his wife are treating you like a queen down there. I hate to think of you downsized to a spare room. Well I expect that's better than one of those nursing homes.

Give the grandkids a hug for me.

Your loving sister,
Helen

"Three of a kind, an Ace on your run and I'm out."

Helen slapped her cards down on the table in disgust. "Honestly, Edna, sometimes I think you're pulling cards out of your sleeve."

"Probably is; we just haven't been able to catch her at it yet." Myrtle was just as upset as Helen with Edna's winning streak. "Edna, give us a chance to win too."

The women began counting their points, subtracting their losses. Edna collected the cards and started to shuffle. "Now ladies, there's no need to blemish my fine reputation. Lady Luck is with me today."

"She's probably hiding somewhere up your sleeve." Myrtle's comment got the women laughing. Helen used the downtime as an opportunity to slip into the kitchen and prepare refreshments. She put the kettle on to boil and then pulled a quart-sized container from the refrigerator. It felt mostly empty.

"Oh dear, there's not much milk. Henry, I wish you had reminded me. I could have gotten it at the store yesterday. Of course, I wouldn't have had enough money to buy it. Well, we will just have to make do and hope the girls don't use too much. I do so need it for my tea in the morning. I never could tolerate tea without milk."

The women relaxed with their snacks and used the time to bring themselves up to speed on the latest news.

"So tell us, Helen, what do you hear of Louise these days?" Edna lifted the silver creamer and poured, her attention fixed more on her friend than her cup.

Helen eyed Edna helping herself to a generous serving of milk for her coffee and grew concerned there wouldn't be any left for tomorrow. "Yes, well a, she's um..." Distracted by the sight of the dwindling milk supply, Helen stumbled over her answer and quietly said, "Enough."

"Pardon me?"

"Enough," she said a little louder, still off in her

thoughts. Helen was considering the possibility of being without her cup of tea in the morning. It wasn't just a morning wake-me-up, it was more of a ritual, like praying and bathing. The day couldn't start without it. As irrational as she knew it was, she couldn't do without her morning tea and her morning tea couldn't do without milk. However, overriding the need for her daily fix was the sanctity of social graces: she could not and would not say a word to her friend. At Edna's tapping of her spoon against the lip of her cup, Helen came out of her fog, slightly embarrassed by her own inappropriate behavior. The others were looking at her with odd expressions on their faces.

"Oh, Louise is fine but misses us dearly."

Myrtle shook her head bewildered. "Helen, I think you may be spending too much time out in the sun. I love you, but sometimes you're as ditsy as a schoolgirl."

Upon cleaning up after the ladies left, Helen was relieved to find enough milk left for her morning tea. All was right with the world.

"I think I'll try to finish up in the garden if my aching bones will cooperate. It's times like this that I really miss you, Henry. You loved those roses as much as I do." She grabbed her hand clippers and stepped outside to the yard. The air was fresh with the fragrance of blossoms as she deadheaded the stems.

"Mew." A faint noise came from somewhere

behind her. "Mew." Helen saw movement near the phlox. A pair of green eyes peaked out from behind some of the blooms.

"Meooow."

"Well, what have we here?" Helen very carefully moved closer so as not to scare the cat, which upon further examination, appeared to be still a kitten.

"I don't recall seeing you around here before. Of course my memory isn't what it used to be, but I'm pretty sure you're new to the neighborhood." She slowly bent down to pick up the kitten whose watery eyes and sad cry were impossible to ignore. A sharp pain shot up her leg and dissipated just as quickly as it came on. She sighed, then turned her attention back to the mewing stranger.

"Now, let's get a look at you." She held it out so they were face to face. The kitten splayed its arms and legs in fear, so she pulled it close into a cuddle reducing it to a tiny ball of fur in her hands. Helen believed its ribs were far too pronounced as she gently stroked its side.

"Oh poor baby, you must be hungry." She looked around to make sure there were no other furry friends who had wandered into her yard. Satisfied this was the only one, she brought it inside and placed it on her kitchen counter while she reached into the cupboard for a saucer.

"If only my Henry could see this – a cat on the counter. He'd have kittens!" She giggled at the unintentional pun. "Now, you stay there and I'll grab the mi–" The word stuck in her throat "–ilk. Oh dear."

It was the last of the milk. The milk she needed for her morning tea, the milk whose use she so staunchly monitored when her friends were visiting. The quandary in which she found herself gave her pause.

In spite of her aches, her troubles and losses, she knew her life was blessed. God was good. It was then Helen realized she would be able to do for one of His creatures what that young man had done for her the previous day. Silly though it seemed—after all, it was just a little milk for a homeless cat—it was as if fate had given her the opportunity to repay his kindness by passing it on to another.

She filled the saucer, threw out the empty carton, and watched as the hungry kitten lapped to contentment.

5
CONNIE ANDERSEN

The phone rang, making its way into my subconscious and waking me from a dreamless sleep. The little nap seemed to have done some good, but I wasn't quite ready to wake up yet. Two rings, three rings… I wasn't sure how long it had previously rung, only that it was about to sound for the fourth time since I had become aware of it. I closed my eyes again and hoped the caller would go away. Five, six… So persistent. "Ugh. All right, all right."

It was a struggle to reach the phone where it dangled behind my head from its chord as it laid over the raised hospital bed. Just as I grabbed it and hit the answer button it slipped from my hand and fell onto the plastic bed guard with a loud crash. I paused a moment then picked it up again, securely this time, and brought it to my ear answering with an obvious irritation in my voice. "Yeah."

"Is that any way to greet your favorite sister?"

"You're my only sister."

"Well, if you're going to get picky about it, maybe I'll just hang up."

"Your choice."

"Haha. You always could make me laugh, Connie. How are you sweetie? Are they treating you well in that place?"

"It's a hospital. Cardiac unit, to be precise. Waiting my turn for the grim reaper to do my bidding to some poor unsuspecting stranger."

"Now Connie…"

"It's true." There was no way to put a positive spin on it, and if she had tried again I really would have hung up. "Speaking of being held captive, how are they treating you in your garage makeover accommodations?" I hated how every word took such effort.

"You know it's not that bad, fairly roomy even. I'm used to it by now and we're long past the adjustment phase. As the grandkids say, it is what it is."

"Didn't have to be."

"It was my choice."

"They coerced you."

"That's harsh. Why are you being so grumpy?"

"Maybe because I'm dying." There was silence on the other end. Uh oh. You always hear of people who bear up to adversity with grace and courage. I'm not one of them. A moment later my sister recouped from the sting.

"I suppose William has been there to see you every day."

It wasn't a question. William had always been a sensitive child and it carried through to adulthood. He was a good son and everyone knew it. "Yes." I thought about him sandwiching my hand yesterday and how comforting it was, and thought again how I didn't deserve it. "Why?"

"Why what?"

"Why does William do it? Why. does. he…" My chest hurt and I ran out of breath to push out the words. I was wheezing in earnest as William walked in the room and held the phone to him. I felt so alone; I always did when this happened. There could have been one hundred people in the room at that moment and I still would have felt as if I was in a dark bubble with no escape.

"Hello?" He covered his ear with his free hand so he could hear better over the coughing. "Oh, hi. Yeah, I just got here. Listen, let me go so I can see to Mom. Yeah, I will. Take care." He put the receiver on the hook.

6
A LONG WAY FROM HOME

Dear Louise,

How wonderful it is the seasons rotate so that just as we tire of one, a new one comes along for our enjoyment! God certainly knew what He was doing when creating this world of His.

The leaves are turning a bit early this year; bound to upset some of the tourists who planned their New England foliage tours long ago. Honestly, I look forward to that time just after the leaf-peepers go home, before the snow falls and the skiers return. I always feel that's when Wheatfield Bridge becomes ours again, at least for a little while.

Myrtle and Edna had a bit of a row at cards the other day. Seems Myrtle wasn't sure how an extra king came into play that won Edna the game. She wasn't able to prove any impropriety, but the accusation was enough to cause sparks to fly. I hope they are able to make up before our game next week at Myrtle's house. I'm so looking forward to having some of her coconut cake.

It appears my arthritis is in check these days. Praise the Lord!

My new little kitten, Rusty, seems to be taking over my life. So many of my daily activities now revolve around a cat, and not all of them are pleasant, if you know what I mean. But he does offer affection, even if it is frequently on his terms rather than mine.

I hope you and the family are all doing well. The grandkids grow so quickly don't they? You are lucky to be able to spend so much time with them. I wish my Jason lived closer. Thankfully, the holidays are just around the corner. I'll see him then.

Storm clouds appear to be gathering. I should head over to Whitmire's store before it rains. Give the young ones a hug from their long-distance great-aunt, and give one to yourself as well.

Your loving sister,
Helen

Louise sighed. Her wrinkled hands slowly folded the letter in half and placed it back in the envelope. She took off her glasses and let them dangle on the lanyard around her neck.

"So Mom, is anything exciting going on back in Wheatfield Bridge?" Gil asked between bites of a sandwich he was eating on the run. Louise knew his trips home for lunch most days were more about checking in on her than grabbing a bite to eat. It was all part of his plan to take care of her in her golden years. She believed she was quite capable of taking care of herself, despite what he thought. Still, she enjoyed his company at lunchtime.

"No, just the ordinary." She sighed again. "You know, it's funny, but those are the things I think I miss the most." She looked out the window, seeing beyond the flowers and the yard into a place that was no longer hers, separated now by time and distance, trying to remember the musty smell of dying maple leaves as they lay upon the earth.

Gil looked out the window, making no comment.

Everyone agreed when she came to live with Gil and his family in Georgia that it was the best thing for her. They could still be a part of each other's lives and, yes, Gil and Abby would get to keep an eye on her as she got on in years. Her recent memory lapses were confirmation enough that it was the right decision, but she didn't think he needed to watch over her like a mother hen the way he did.

Gil drew his attention back into the room and redirected the discussion. "Abby is taking Hailey shopping tonight. Why don't you go with them – have a girls' night out or something?"

"Oh, they don't want an old fuddy-duddy like me intruding on their time together," she said with a wave of her hand.

"Ma, we keep telling you, you're part of the

family; it's not intruding."

Although Gil, Abbey and the kids did their best to make Louise feel at home, after all these months she still felt a bit like an outsider, a voyeur observing the private goings-on of their nuclear family. "Well, they should have some mother-daughter time. Kids her age need that sort of thing. Besides, I'm sure I'd slow them down. I don't get around like I used to, you know." She did not intend to admit to her own body's betrayal. She hoped Gil wouldn't read too much into the statement, hoped he didn't notice her tendency these days to shuffle her feet rather than raise them to take steps, or the way she had difficulty getting in and out of a chair.

"Well, it's up to you. I have to get back to work. See you tonight." And he was out the door.

* * *

"Louise, it's your turn." Eura Mae Higginbotham thrummed her fingertips on the table and peered out over her long hooked nose at Louise, waiting for her to play her cards. Theirs was one of many games in play at the social hall of the Barrow County Senior Center. Louise regularly took part in the center's activities since moving to town and enjoyed her weekly game of 500 Rummy. "My ride will be here before you ever play your hand." Eura Mae's patience was wearing thin.

"Eura Mae, you're always trying to rush me," Louise countered, trying not to sound annoyed.

"This is a game; we should be playing, not

meditating."

Wallace Ernst reprimanded Eura Mae while scanning from his cards to those in play on the table. "Keep your pants on. The van won't be here for another fifteen minutes." Wallace was a good-natured man who tended to be blunt without being offensive. His wife Philomena always said it was his what-you-see-is-what-you-get characteristic that drew her to him ten years prior. They met at the senior center. Some say it was love at first sight, others say it was the harmony. Either way, they both knew whatever time they had left in this world, they wanted to spend it together. And that they did. They married within months of meeting and since then one was infrequently seen without the other.

"Well I never..." Eura Mae was the exception; she always took offense.

"Yes you have, Eura Mae. Now stop fussing and let Louise play without you pressuring her."

"Just wait Wallace. One of these days you won't be driving anymore and you'll have to depend on someone else to get around."

"Probably be dead by then," he said dryly, provoking her further.

"Wallace Ernst you are so aggravating... Ooh!"

It was long understood at the Barrow County Senior Center that Wallace and Eura Mae had "a thing" going on. It was neither love nor hate, something more in the mid-range of mutual tolerance. If it came down to it though, they would probably each admit the other was a friend - incognito.

Louise finally played her cards, which pleased Eura Mae. Changing the subject, Louise asked Wallace and Philomena, "Are you two going to sing again on Friday?" The senior center's monthly Golden Café provided a spotlight opportunity for members who liked to, and could still, strut their stuff. Louise had only attended a few of the cafés. It took a while for her to be comfortable in asking Gil or Abby for a ride at night after they had worked all day, as the senior but didn't run in the evening.

Philomena was quick to answer, patting her hand on Wallace's as she did. "We've never missed a Golden Café since it started. Have we dear?" Wallace was distracted, planning his next move. He never took his eyes off his hand when answering, "No-pe," making a deliberate popping sound with his lips on the letter p.

"That last song you sang, what was it now?" Louise squeezed her eyes trying to remember.

"Phil and Wallace have been closing the café with Scarborough Fair since they started singing in it. You'll get to know the routine the longer you're around," Eura Mae explained to Louise. "I just hope Patsy doesn't try to do a soft shoe again. She looked ridiculous last time, pretending her walker was Fred Astaire."

Louise tried to hide a chuckle at Eura Mae's comment in case Patsy was nearby, yet she knew how right she was.

Dear Helen,

I was glad to hear in your last letter that Myrtle and Edna have made up with each other. Your description of Myrtle's coconut cake left my mouth watering.

Summer seems to drag on down here in the south. I'm sure autumn is hiding somewhere in all this heat. Imagine, here we are heading towards Thanksgiving and it's still hot enough to go without a sweater on some days. I'll never get used to it. I need a crisp, sunny afternoon with the smell of a warm fire in the chimney, and a Macintosh right off the tree! Of course, I'd have to peel it and cut it up or risk losing my dentures on the first bite. My, we are old, aren't we?

The kids are being so good to me, really they are, but I miss my independence. If I want to go somewhere either Gil or Abigail have to drive me, and I hate to impose. The van picks me up to go to the Senior Center, so at least I have that small freedom. I so appreciate it, but again, it's on someone else's schedule.

I'm sorry, it seems all I'm doing is complaining.

Hailey and Aaron have a busy social calendar - what with after school activities and all. And they are so good looking! It must be in the genes.

The family was invited to a friend's house for barbeque tonight (which, by the way, has a totally different meaning here in Dixie, more of a noun than a verb). They insisted the invitation was for all of us; however, I declined. They have their own lives to live and they don't need to drag me along. I stayed home and had a peanut butter sandwich (the kind without the little crunchies). I got to feeling sorry for myself all alone in the house. It's just so hard restarting one's life, you know. There I go again – complaining.

Let's see... something positive... I know. I am going out tomorrow evening to a cabaret of sorts at the Senior Center. It will be an early evening of course, as we old fossils tend to tucker out shortly after dark. It should be fun, though.

Oh, have Myrtle and Edna made up yet? Scratch that last sentence. I just reread this letter; guess I forgot.

Well, take care and give my best to the girls (yes, even the cardshark).

Louise

The kids bounded into the house from the barbeque all excited. Aaron, plopped into the recliner and stretched out. Helen couldn't believe how big he was getting – a teenager already. Certainly with that broad smile and long-lashed eyes he was bound to start breaking hearts soon.

"Hey Grandma, you should have come with us. The Burkes have this awesome new in-home movie theater set up now. We watched James Bond." Aaron was clearly impressed with the Burke's remodeling.

Hailey had to have her say as well. "That's just because the boys out-numbered the girls. We wanted to watch something else."

"Yeah, a stupid chick flick."

"Grandma, if you had been there it would have at least been a tie and the girls would have had a shot and something better than Bond, James Bond." She tried to mimic the famous 007.

"All right, enough of that. Get to your homework." Abigail broke up what could have become a shouting match. The kids grimaced at the mention of homework. "Come on, that's what happens when we go out on a school night. The work catches up eventually." Turning to Louise, she added, "We really did miss you tonight. The Burkes were asking after you."

Abigail's pleasant mannerisms and soft voice made anything she said sound warm and sincere. Louise felt a pang of guilt for turning them down earlier and wondered if she would have really fit in.

*   *   *

The banner stretched high above the stage.
The Golden Café

Barrow County Senior Center's Movers and Shakers

Louise noted many of the people seated in the audience were Senior Center regulars. However, some of the patrons were quite a bit her junior, many still with their natural hair color and God-given teeth. They came to watch their favorite senior citizen perform, allowing them to pretend for just a little while that he or she was young again.

As performers came on stage, the crowd let out a lot of hootin' and hollerin'. The larger the cheering section, the louder the yelling. And none was louder than those who came out to cheer on Wallace and Philomena. Her three children and assorted grandchildren from her first marriage tried to make it for every show, going out of their way to make it a family event. Louise observed the tight-knit family and noticed how they were enjoying this night together. She thought about the previous evening and wondered if her own family had had as much fun at the Burke's.

"Did you hear about Patsy?" Eura Mae slid into the chair next to Louise. She didn't give her time to respond. "Fell and broke a hip. They say she won't be coming back; her family is putting her in a home when she's ready to leave the hospital. They say Patsy is really distraught. She doesn't want to go." Eura Mae shook her head, adding a little, "tsk, tsk," suggesting how terrible she thought it was.

The news about Patsy stayed on Louise's mind throughout most of the night. After all, wasn't that why she was with Gil – to have someone take care of her? He tried to put a spin on it, saying that they missed her after moving from Connecticut to Georgia for his job. "If you move in with us," he had said, "we could be with each other all the time." But she wasn't born yesterday. She understood the reality that, like Patsy, she was getting older... and more forgetful. It was just a matter of time and he wanted to keep an eye on her.

"Go Gram and Gramps!" Philomena's grandchildren were loud enough to be heard across town as the couple took the stage. The evening's entertainment was pleasant enough, but everyone waited in anticipation for Wallace and Phil. Their voices blended in such harmony, like living sound from the same organic chord. The crowd always hushed to listen while they performed. Traditionally they sang two karaoke songs at the café, the last one always being Simon and Garfunkel's Scarborough Fair/Canticle: two songs brilliantly intertwined as one - as was their love. For in similar harmonious union, their two hearts were forever bound. Tonight's performance, even by their own standards, was exceptional. The room exploded in applause when they were done.

The news came unexpectedly, Eura Mae once again being the harbinger of bad news, this time via telephone. "Philomena's dead, went to sleep and never woke up. Funeral's on Tuesday."

Louise, still reeling from personal revelations after hearing about Patsy the night before, was surprised at her own reaction to the report of Philomena's death: she locked herself in her room for the rest of the day to mourn in private. True, she didn't know Philomena very well, but weren't they all facing the same journey? Louise believed her friend was at least blessed to have spent her last hours in the presence of her loving family, surely a precious gift for each one of them.

*   *   *

There are moments when, above and beyond anyone's expectation, someone holds himself together with such poise in the face of adversity that it leaves an indelible mark on those who witness it. In the loss of his second wife, it was Wallace who so affected all who attended the final farewell for his beloved Philomena. As is common at funeral services, the presiding minister invited anyone who knew her to come forward and share special memories with all gathered. There were stories of kindness, much laughter, and an abundance of love. However, no one present, except for a select few, expected the service to end the way it did.

With what appeared to be great difficulty, and at one point needing the support of a nearby arm, a lone figure rose from the pew and walked to the front of the chapel. The initial unsteadiness of gate improved with each step. He turned to face the assembled group, paused and took a deep breath, then gave a small pre-arranged nod indicating it was time. The subtle introductory notes of Scarborough Fair/Canticle started to play and hung in the air moving about the room as if on a breeze. The familiar melody reinvigorated Wallace as he stood before his family and friends to sing in a steady, rich tenor voice.

"Are you going to Scarborough Fair? Parsley, sage, rosemary, and thyme. Remember me to one who lives there. She once was a true love of mine..."[1] Unbound from one another, the emptiness of Scarborough Fair without Philomena's Canticle left a void needing to be filled. Wallace sang in spite of it.

After the funeral, Louise sat alone in her room preparing to write a letter to her sister when there was a knock at the door. She took off her glasses, letting them dangle around her neck, stood and answered the door. A determined looking Abigail and Hailey stood before her. "Grandma," Hailey said, "we're going shopping at the mall. We're kidnapping you and we're not taking no for an answer."

Louise was stunned. She turned to look at her writing desk then back at the resolute women. They smiled satisfied grins when Louise replied, "Let me get my sweater."

JONI VANNEST

7
CONNIE ANDERSEN

Next to Jack Priestly, I always did like Louise. "She's a plucky old broad," I used to tell people. "Didn't start out that way, but she grew into it the more we became comfortable with each other." It was nice thinking about her again.

The squealing metal of the dinner cart's wobbly wheel screeched through the hallway. You would think a hospital, where peace and quiet were mandatory, wouldn't allow that caterwauling to continue as it did. No such luck; it had been like that for days. At least it announced dinnertime, even before a savory aroma filtered into my room. I wished the food tasted as good as this particular meal smelled. Maybe that would bring my appetite back. So far, nothing on the hospital's menu ever seemed worth the bother of expending energy to eat it.

An attendant who appeared to be in her late seventies, maybe even early eighties, breezed in through the doorway carrying a tray. She was a little on the plump side and even through the hair net I could tell she had a standing appointment with a hairdresser, as she had that helmet head thing going on. She had a round face with laugh lines outlining smiling eyes, the kind that made you want to go out of your way to be friends with her. A pair of eyeglasses hung on a lanyard around her neck. "Hel-lo." Her cheery, singsong voice was not surprising. The woman compared the tray identification slip with the info written up on the wall. "3-A. Connie Andersen, right?" I nodded. "Not the Connie Andersen?" The woman feigned astonishment, obviously already aware of who I was. I nodded again, suppressing the urge to roll my eyes, and played along. "Oh my, I just love your books." She placed the tray on the bedside cart so her hands could animate my praises. "Your stories make me feel good all over," she said giving a little shiver. "Why I almost feel as if we're old friends. And that Louise, isn't she just a hoot?" She waved her hand to emphasize her assessment.

Louise. That got my attention. I sat up straighter, without much effort. It felt good for a change. The attendant pressed the button to adjust the bed so that it would provide support. I took a closer look at the woman. There was something in the way she moved and acted that seemed familiar. Had she been at one of my book signings? Or maybe at a reading? Maybe she was someone I met long ago at one of the many writers' conferences where I gave keynote addresses. I couldn't put my finger on it but felt certain our paths had crossed at some other time. "Funny you should say that. I was just thinking to myself about how much I admire Louise." The words spilled comfortably off my tongue without the need to stop for a breath.

The attendant lifted the lid exposing a bowl of what appeared to be pumpkin bisque, my favorite. I was surprised that my mouth watered in anticipation. She then ripped the plastic off the spoon and dipped it into the bowl to stir the soup around. To my amazement, she scooped a spoonful and held it up for me to taste. The first time that had happened during my current stay in hospital. Pumpkin and nutmeg filled my nostrils, making me feel warm inside. It smelled wonderful, too good not to try. I opened my mouth and allowed myself to be fed. The soup's texture teetered appropriately between liquid and puree and swirled around my mouth in a gentle explosion of flavor before gently making its way down my throat. By far the best bisque I had ever tasted. "Oh my gosh, that is so good." The woman offered another taste and then another, diminishing the contents of the bowl.

We looked at each other across steaming spoonfuls. I could not get the strange feeling I had about the woman out of my head. "Have we met before?"

The woman giggled, a pleasant soundtrack to her laugh lines. "You know old ladies, we're all the same – wrinkled, overweight and with too much time on our hands." She paused, sighed. "Oh to be young again." She spooned another taste to my lips. "Say, wouldn't it be nice if we could be young again? I tell you, there are so many things I'd probably rethink, you know, do a little differently. How about you?"

A small dribble of soup pooled on my chin. I tried to suck it in to no avail. It was gone with a quick move of the attendant's hand. I thought about her question. Of course there were things I'd reassess, things for which I would love to have a do-over. Like the time I backed the car into my husband's motorcycle, his pride and joy, totaling it. I would be sure to check my rearview mirror in a do-over instead of just assuming the coast was clear. And like William, for instance. But hindsight is 20/20 as they say. There was no going back. "I suppose. But what's the point in thinking like that? What's done is done."

The woman thought about that. "True enough. Luckily we can learn from mistakes even if we can't correct them, right?"

If only I had. All those times spent locked in my study writing, or on the road promoting my latest book. So involved with myself, failing to see the disappointment in William's eyes each time he asked me to be at a school play or an important track meet and I declined with an, "I'm sorry, I have to work." No, I did not learn. William always said he understood. "It's OK, Mom. Really." My husband,

Bill went alone and always told William that I would have loved to have been there.

"I wish I had learned. Then I wouldn't have kept repeating the same mistakes." I didn't know what prompted me to share. Normally, I kept my private thoughts to myself, but here I was spilling my guts to a complete stranger. Still, there was something about her that felt so comfortable, even safe.

The woman scraped the bottom of the bowl for the last bit of bisque. "Oh, I see. Well, it seems to me you learned at some point because you understand that now."

"Yeah, but it's too late."

"Sweetie, it's never too late. Take it from me"

"I can't undo the past."

"No, but you can make amends."

"You mean ask forgiveness?"

"Yes. That and offer forgiveness."

I was taken aback; I was the one at fault. "Offer forgiveness? To whom?"

The woman placed the lid back over the tray and lifted it to return to the cart in the hallway. Stepping away from the bed toward the door she said, "Think about it. You know." And she was gone.

8
JODI'S BRIDGE

It was quiet at the dinner table when Jodi got there after finishing her shift. She kicked her shoes off under the table and felt instant relief for her aching feet. Her hair was still pulled back in a clip, standard server protocol at the Parkside Diner, leaving feathery tendrils to frame her face. Working weekends at the diner gave her money for car repairs and insurance, but the unexpected benefit— the impetus to work hard at school so she could someday have a cushy desk job off her feet—was a surprising byproduct.

Avery and Brielle played with their food and sulked. Probably mad at each other again. Her younger brother was forever taunting their little sister. Jodi noted, however, that whatever was bothering Avery did not keep him from filling his plate beyond reasonable human consumption. Her dad was mixing peas into the mashed potatoes on his plate. It was so different from the way her mother made sure that no two things on her plate touched. Jodi looked at the mashed concoction and shook her head. "Gross."

"Hey, don't knock it 'til you've tried it." He took a huge forkful and made a big production out of making sure she witnessed its thorough enjoyment. The younger kids giggled at their father's antics. She laughed in spite of herself.

Her mother came in from the kitchen with biscuits rescued from the oven just before the smoke detector went off. It was her usual MO. As precise as she was in all other aspects of her life, she had an uncanny mind-block when it came to baking. The biscuits were dark brown and more than likely hard as rock. It still beat the greasy stuff they served at the diner though. She took one to be polite, with every intention of making it look nibbled at without ever tasting it.

Her father was just about to take another bite of his green spotted potatoes when he remembered something and stopped, leaving the fork hanging in mid-air. "I almost forgot to mention I heard from Uncle Mike today."

Avery mumbled through the chicken in his mouth, too eager to wait until he'd finished. A tiny piece of meat sailed through the air and landed, unnoticed, near Brielle. "He's weird – in a cool sort of way."

Their mother scolded him. "That's not nice, and don't talk with your mouth full."

Her father continued, oblivious to forgotten manners. "He says he'll be returning to the states soon and would like to come home for a visit."

"That's wonderful Brad" her mom said, trying to slice a biscuit. "We can put him up in Avery's room and Avery can camp out on the living room rug."

"Awesome." Her brother was all about it.

Jodi liked Uncle Mike but Avery was right, he had his moments of weirdness. Like on his last visit. He slept out in the backyard in a three sided lien-to he had erected for that purpose. "It will help acclimate me to being out in the field," he said at the time. It convinced her how passionate he was about his work, which at the moment had him serving as a missionary in Africa.

It was a couple of weeks before Uncle Mike arrived looking pale and thin but happy to be home. Despite his sunken eyes and shaggy hair, the family resemblance was still obvious. He had broad shoulders and a ski slope nose, just like her dad. He brought everyone gifts and told stories of places and things much different from the world Jodi knew in Wheatfield Bridge.

"And one time I got deep into the jungle. It was there I met up with a ferocious, wild and, I might add, very hungry lion. Now believe me when I say ferocious, I mean FEROCIOUS. He had claws out to here." He gave a visual for those supposed claws by placing one hand about a foot apart from the fingernails on his other hand. "I tell you, he came running toward us with his mouth wide open and dinner on his mind." Uncle Mike was so excited by his own story he had to stop and catch his breath. Then he coughed. It lingered a few moments before he could go on. When he did, it was with just a little less enthusiasm. "Well I thought we were goners."

There was one thing about Uncle Mike's stories - that somewhere between the first and last words you could always find a small grain of truth. For instance, he was in Africa.

"If it wasn't for a vine that I was just able to grab on to and swing awa..." He started coughing again and wheezed in between outbursts.

Her mom went into action. "Why don't you kids let your uncle rest for a bit. The long journey has probably worn him out." She ushered the younger ones along like a shepherd leading sheep to pasture. Jodi remained seated and watched Uncle Mike lean on her father as he helped him up to Avery's room. Her mother's claim that it was only jetlag was losing steam.

Uncle Mike didn't put up a fuss when her parents insisted on taking him to the doctor, who prescribed enough drugs to fill a pharmacy and told him to rest. Again, he didn't argue. He told us it was a respiratory thing the clinic doctors started to treat before he came home. That evening as her dad was propping pillows behind him, Uncle Mike must have figured it was time for the truth. Neither one knew Jodi was listening beyond the door.

"You know, Brad, I just loved being over there. The people, oh the people are just so amazing and so receptive to the Word. Their lives are in tune to creation." He stopped to cough and catch his breath. "I got to eat with them, pray with them, learn their customs. I treated their illnesses in the clinic while the Lord healed their hearts."

"We are proud of you, Mike. Not everyone just drops everything and heeds the call to missions. It takes a special person."

"Nah, I'm not special. Just blessed to be given such an honor."

"Well, modesty aside, you did a great thing."

Then Uncle Mike told of his carelessness and the needle prick that sealed his fate. His own body was now turning against him.

Jodi held her breath, shocked by the implication of his words. She stole a peek at her uncle and father through the open space near the door jam. Her father was sitting on the edge of the bed, his head hanging in sorrow. As her uncle grew silent, his story told, her father leaned in to embrace him. They held each other for a long time, each one stifling a sob trying to be strong for the other.

Without warning, Jodi's eyes began to burn with tears from a fiery well deep inside. She ran downstairs and out the door, and did not stop until she reached her "thinking spot" on the grassy bank beneath the covered bridge. More than a century old, it spanned the Housatonic River joining Wheatfield Bridge to River Mills, and was still in use today. Many were the times she sought solace in the shade of its ancient wooden timbers. She gained comfort from the rugged, sturdy structure as from a wizened friend. It was a place where time stood still, a place where she could step outside of her problems or concerns and look at them from a new perspective. And she knew it was where she needed to be at that moment to think this through.

"Why God? Why would You allow this to happen to such a good person as Uncle Mike? He's one of your best followers." Her voice raised in anger and confusion. "Why?" It wasn't often she went to Him with questions, usually it was just the rote prayers said on Sundays when she accompanied her parents to church or during youth group. She waited for some kind of revelation but God didn't offer any answers. His silence was infuriating. She took a stone and whipped it out over the water. Like a perfectly aimed rocket, it splashed into a small logjam of leaves and twigs. The debris dislodged, spun around and quickly moved downstream. Here one minute, gone the next. The fragility of life was becoming clear; everything can change in the blink of an eye.

That evening she brought a cup of tea up to Uncle Mike, her mother's cure for everything, even the incurable. She placed it on the night table and noticed a Bible lying open in his lap. She believed in God, but not like him. For Uncle Mike it was more than believing, it was almost like a cult. Or a friendship. She wasn't sure which. She always thought it odd that he was practically on a first name basis with his deity, but she had to respect someone who lived what he believed. So many kids she knew from school wouldn't even have the nerve to stand up to their own friends if they thought it would make themselves look bad.

She decided to probe. "What are you reading?"

"The story of grace."

Her Biblical knowledge was limited. It was not a story she recalled. "Who's she?"

Uncle Mike gave a wry smile. "Not who, what." He saw that she fell for the bait and started reeling her in. "Grace..." He tried to take a deep breath, settled for a couple of shallow ones and continued. "Grace. It's the best kind of love there is. It's God's way of saying, 'Here, I'm giving you all of my love. I freely give it to you, and there's nothing you did to earn it.' Pretty great stuff, huh?"

"Yeah, I guess. But how do you know it's for real?"

"Well, the Bible tells us, but I also feel it...here." He lightly tapped his hand over his heart. "When God is in your life, there's a feeling, a love, that has no comparison. God has great plans for our lives and only wants the best for us."

"He sure seems to have forgotten you." The words had slipped out of her mouth without thinking them through and she let out a gasp. "Oh my God. I'm so sorry. I didn't mean that." She had been stupid before but never like this. She wanted to run and hide, wanted to run to her thinking spot. No. She wanted to crawl into a hole and never come out. But Uncle Mike got to her first.

Their eyes met and he looked at her for what felt like an eternity. It was as if he knew what was in her soul, recognizing it and forgiving it at the same time. By far, it was the longest single moment of her life.

"I know you didn't."

He coughed, cleared his voice and continued. "But God hasn't forgotten me. That's what faith is all about - trusting God knows the whole plan from beginning to end and has it all under control." A small tear welled up in the corner of his eye. He firmly believed what he was saying but, apparently, that didn't make it easy.

He coughed and brought up some phlegm. She passed him a tissue and wondered about truth and trust and eternal plans with such dire consequences. Gazing down at the floor she said, "I have to go," and headed for the door.

He didn't let her get off that easy. "Jodi," he called through thin breaths. "It's a love worth dying for."

She breathed deep, nodded as if in agreement, as if she understood, but it was beyond comprehension. She turned and left the room.

In time, her uncle's condition got worse and he was admitted to the hospital. Each day his breathing became weaker and more hollow sounding until it was barely an audible wheeze. Finally, if he could, she supposed he would have said he went home.

After the funeral the house was much quieter than she could ever recall. The stillness in the hallways and the emptiness in the rooms reflected the sadness of the whole family. Jodi spent a lot of her free time by the bridge trying to make sense of it all.

Until the rains came.

A week of heavy rain and flooding turned the normally tranquil river into a raging torrent. The Steele family stood on the porch and watched as the old wooden bridge struggled vainly under the brutal attack to keep its hold on the shore, eventually losing the battle. When the rain ended and the waters receded, they went out to the riverbank to look at what remained of the Wheatfield Bridge. There were all sizes of planks sunk here and there in the mud. For years, the pride of the town, and now her beloved bridge was just a memory in timbers.

Looking at the wreckage, Jodi asked out loud to no one in particular, maybe to God, "How could this happen?" A reminiscent thought, she realized.

Her father, ever practical but not without emotion in his voice, simply said, "Everything has its season."

She couldn't help but feel that his answer was more complex than it first appeared. For that matter, maybe her question was as well.

She noticed a piece of splintered wood carried by the storm up to where they stood laid near her feet. She picked it up and turned it over in her hand. At that moment Uncle Mike's wisdom spoke to her and formed a base of understanding: all things are temporary, gifts that God gives us for a little while until they have served His greater purpose. The only unchanging thing in life was God Himself.

Jodi decided then she would have to trust He knew the whole plan from beginning to end and had it all under control.

9

HE WHO BEGAN A GOOD WORK

Andrew lay in bed staring up at the water stains, stealing time with them like shadowy acquaintances. There were memories attached to many of them: nights waking up in soggy sheets from something other than well-earned sweat, moist carpet between his toes, slow to dry in the damp air, leaving behind a musty smell that lingered still. One stain, his favorite, resembled a joint, complete with swirling, hazy smoke. Some of the blemishes even predated his own residency. It was a time-acquired décor. Likewise, sheer curtains, having transformed over the years from white to their current shade of beige, gently moved with a breeze through the open window of his room flashing bits of light like a mantra, drawing Andrew's attention to a place of emptiness where everything and yet nothing made sense.

He rolled over and, once again, found himself connected to the memory he wished he could erase - the experience at the diner a few days ago that still pervaded his consciousness. He couldn't figure out why the waitress's reaction mattered so much to him, and why it unnerved him so. The intention of her words was clear, spoken not in anger but rather in pity. Hardly the response he was trying to elicit by his actions. And yet, understanding his cruelty, she forgave him in spite of it. That's why it bothered him and he knew it. He just didn't want to admit it, not even to himself. He didn't want to accept that someone like her could see through him, or for that matter would have the reasoning to do so. It's not my fault she's smarter than I thought. He was who he was. Andrew believed it was ok to mess with her as long as she didn't have the capacity to understand what he was doing. The fact that she did understand put the event in a whole new light, one that for some inexplicable reason, he didn't like. Damn. It wouldn't be bugging me if she had been normal. Somewhere inside a quiet voice suggested he may have crossed a line. It was a voice he'd never heard before, or perhaps never paid attention to.

He began to wonder about his friends, Sam and Eddie, who were there with him. He could swear he saw them looking like they wanted to slither under the table, like maybe they thought he had gone too far, even further than them. He was sure if they weren't all cramped in that tiny booth they would have split on him. He was also sure that if that guy hadn't made a big deal out of it, they would have been fine with it.

But even more troubling than his friends'

betrayal was the waitress. She pitied him. She said as much. "You shouldn't be mean like that, you know, or you won't have any friends." And that he couldn't deal with. He grunted and pulled the pillow over his eyes, wrapping his arms tightly around it in an attempt to make everything go away.

At seventeen, Andrew Steiff was the oldest of three brothers. His parents divorced when he was ten, leaving his mother, Mary, to raise a brood of boys on her own. This, she would maintain she did to the best of her ability. In reality, her abilities far outweighed her motivation, which generated his recurring waking nightmare.

"Mom, what's up?" Andrew would ask after coming home from school to find her in front of the soaps. "Why aren't you at work?" Her responses over time had become predictable, cycled and recycled.

"It didn't work out." That was the standard excuse. Followed by, "I can't work for that creep," as a close second. At times she would include a physical malady designed to evoke sympathy. "You know I have weak legs. I can't stand on them all day like that no more. Your momma's gettin' old."

For his mother, jobs lasted long enough to get them caught up on bills and back on their feet. Long enough so that Andrew and his brothers would start to believe there might actually be hope for the future. Then, without warning, she'd wake up one day and decide the job wasn't worth her time. The repetition of disappointment was something he never got used to. His absent father, a long haul driver, rarely played a part in the tragic drama that was Andrew's life.

On this particular morning he was pretty sure school had nothing better in store than the usual crap he put up with every day – boring work and teachers with low expectations for him. Like his mother and work, he felt school was hardly worth getting up for. But it's where his friends would be, so for that reason alone he climbed out of bed, showered, ignored his family over a bowl of cereal and walked to school at Wheatfield Bridge High.

Mrs. Loggins scrawled the words MARRIAGE PROJECT on the board in Andrew's first period Social Studies class. He tried not to look interested for the sake of an image he needed to preserve, but he actually liked Social Studies. There were no numbers or tedious facts to remember. The sly look on his teacher's face told him and the rest of the class that she was up to something. She clapped her hands together and held them in place as if forgetting to let go. As far as teachers went, she would do.

"Ladies and gentlemen, today we will begin the final and, I might add, most practical module of this class: the Marriage Project. Now I'm sure you just can't wait to find out how this is going to work, so let me get to it."

Sarcastic groans and whining came from several of the students. Andrew couldn't help but toss out,

"Is there going to be a honeymoon? 'Cause I left my condoms at home."

Everyone in the class laughed, but the teacher didn't miss a beat. "No Mr. Steiff, for everyone's sake, especially your project partner, it will be an unbinding and unconsummated marriage."

"That sucks." He tried to sound disappointed. Somewhere inside he was.

The teacher went on to explain how the module worked. "Everyone will be 'hitched' to a marriage partner." Turning to Andrew she said, "And yes Mr. Steiff, it will be a heterosexual partnership."

He never even got the chance to ask the question. Damn, she's good.

"Each partner will be randomly assigned a profession. The couple must make decisions together and learn to live within a practical budget based on their income. Like the game of Life, surprises and hardships will come your way, and you will have to deal with them. Just think of this as The Rest of Your Life 101." The teacher strolled through the aisles of desks as she spoke. She stopped to pull a pen out of a doodling hand, and took a math book from someone else who appeared to be doing homework for another class, all the while continuing with her explanation of the marriage project. "Now, your partners will be drawn from a hat, preferably one without lice. Who's got one we can borrow?"

Andrew appreciated how Mrs. Loggins was cool enough to get away with statements like that. No one would ever call her on it. One of the jocks offered up his baseball cap and she took it from him with a smile. Andrew squirmed in his seat. I shoulda wore my Metallica hat.

The wedding announcements began. Andrew sat with Sam and Eddie at the back of the class, snickering as the teacher called out the pairings, and occasionally offered unsolicited comments. "Must have been a shotgun wedding." Or, "I guess there's someone for everyone." They laughed among themselves at each announcement, and acted disgusted when Sam and Eddie each got paired with plain or unattractive girls. At one point Mrs. Loggins gave Andrew a stern look. He in turn got quiet and kicked the others under the desk the next time they spoke out of line.

"And last, but not least, congratulations go out to Andrew Steiff and Jodi Steele, our final couple now engaged in faux marital bliss." Andrew sat up upon hearing his name and without his permission, his face flushed. He hoped no one noticed.

Jodi Steele. Could have been worse. Not a babe, but easy on the eyes. He sort of liked the way she looked a little mysterious when her feathery hair hung loose at the side of her face as she leaned over the desk to do her work. Andrew looked at his friends and shrugged his shoulders then glanced in Jodi's direction. He saw her roll her eyes and shake her head. This is gonna be fun.

*   *   *

Jodi met Andrew in third grade when he first moved to town. Even then, like a bully in training, he used to pull her pigtails. Over the years he worked hard at perfecting his taunts and insults with little regard for his victims. Many were the egos damaged at his hand. He also lived in the trailer park. Jodi didn't have a problem with people who lived there, she just never went out of her way to be friends with anyone who did. Her dad always told her to judge people by their character not by their wallet. In her book, Andrew missed on both counts. She also believed him and his friends to be jerks of major proportions. Her judgment cast, she knew him for the intimidator he was.

The newlyweds were instructed to separate into their respective couples. Andrew made no effort to move so Jodi picked up her things and sat in the now-vacant chair next to him. This was not starting out well.

The teacher then reloaded the hat and passed it around the room allowing everyone to pick out their professions with corresponding salary info. Jodi pulled out a small piece of paper that read Teacher $28,000/year. Andrew showed her his, Carpenter $32,000/year.

Their first task was to set a budget, which they had to complete in class. The homework assignment required them to go shopping together for one week's worth of imaginary groceries and report back on how it affected their budget. Mrs. Loggins stressed they were going to be graded as a couple so teamwork was paramount.

Jodi looked at Andrew. "Well?"

"Well, what?"

He was being incorrigible. "Are you going to cooperate or am I on my own?" She was blunt and to the point. She had no intention of letting him bring down her GPA. With or without his help she was not going to fail this late in the game.

Andrew picked up his pen and began beating it on his books. "Yeah, whatever. We gotta, right? Can't graduate without it."

Jodi felt a small reassurance in his words. If he needed the grade then it may not go as bad as she first anticipated.

They struggled through the initial classwork. Planning for and living within a defined means was new to her, and Andrew's attitude made it even harder. It crossed Jodi's mind that God might have played an active role in their 'random' union. Certainly, no one else in the class would be able to deal with Andrew and actually get the work done. Lately she had been trusting that God could get her through anything, even this. She wasn't so sure all of her female classmates had that same confidence.

The bell rang signaling the end of class. Andrew and Jodi packed up their books and left without saying a word to the other.

*   *   *

Andrew headed to gym class with his friends, the

Marriage Project stricken from his mind the minute he walked out of the classroom. The boys were in a good mood. Gym was their release, the only place in school where they were not only permitted to let out their aggressions but strongly encouraged to do so. The quickest way to the gym was to cut through the door at the end of the east wing and cross the courtyard to enter through the locker room's emergency exit. The door was conveniently left ajar to allow for that traffic.

Home Ec and Special Ed ruled the east wing. Although the boys walked this way twice a week for most of the year, it wasn't until that day Andrew saw, for the first time at school, the server who waited on them at the Parkside Diner, the same waitress who felt sorry for him, the one who occupied his mind so frequently since that day. Right there in the halls of WFB High School, two worlds collided, the cataclysm of which nearly stopped him in his tracks. This was his world; she didn't belong in it. Mesmerized, his eyes followed hers to the point of turning his head to look over his shoulder as they passed. She recognized him as well. In spite of their untoward meeting earlier, she smiled, reminding him once again that he was forgiven. His Cheerios turned in his stomach. People never respond to him that way. Most people disliked him from the start and left him alone out of fear or hatred, or both. She was giving him a second chance that he neither asked for nor deserved. Somewhere in the deep recesses of his soul, he felt a small flicker of something he couldn't quite name, a feeling that was foreign to him. He turned back to his friends and quickened his pace to catch up. "Hey, how long do they let those people stay in school anyway?"

"I don't know." Eddie didn't seem interested in the question. "Who gives a flying leap."

"Twenty-one, I think." Sam was a wealth of useless knowledge.

"Andrew," his mother called to him from the living room, "get the phone." She had long ago stopped answering. Calls were rarely for her anymore. When they were, they were usually bill collectors. The boys had the task of blowing them off.

Andrew grabbed the phone while muttering under his breath about lazy brothers. He heard his mother lower the volume on the TV to have a better chance of eavesdropping on the conversation. She never wanted to take the calls but always wanted to know about them.

"Hello?" It was more of a question than statement.

Jodi Steele announced herself. He wasn't expecting her to call, had forgotten about the assignment and that he had given her the house number.

"Oh, hey." He lowered his voice to a softer level than he'd use if Eddie or Sam had been on the line.

"So, do you want to do that shopping thing today?"

Andrew shifted from one foot to the other. "Yeah, ok."

"I can pick you up at your..."

Andrew cut her off. "We can meet at Whitmire's, in the parking lot. I'll see you there in a half hour." He hung up the phone without a goodbye.

His mother jumped right in. "Where are you going, and when are you gonna be home?" A typical motherly inquiry.

"Out and I don't know." His typical response. He was not about to tell her he was meeting a girl, even if it was only for a homework assignment.

"Don't talk to me like that, I'm your mother! I have a right to know."

"Whatever." Andrew slammed the door behind him hard enough to make a point. He could hear the volume go up again on the TV before he was off the front steps.

Jodi's car was parked in front of Whitmire's General Store by the time he arrived. He was glad he'd arranged to meet here. It was okay that his friends came to his house, there were no presuppositions involved with them. They'd been friends for years and their stories were much like his. But he didn't want Jodi to see where he lived. Better supposition than confirmation he believed.

The passenger side window was down. She hit the button to unlock the door. "Hey, come on in.

You have to wear your seatbelt."

"Jeesh, just married and already you're nagging." Andrew half meant it as a joke, half because he was Andrew.

Jodi blushed, contradicting her stony response. "It's the law."

The trip to the grocery store was awkward. Andrew didn't feel the need to feign politeness and apparently neither did she. They pulled away in silence. The quiet made him uncomfortable so he turned the radio on to a heavy metal station. Jodi didn't object; but by the look on her face, she also didn't like it. She said nothing either way, which was fine with him. He looked around the car and decided it must not be hers. Leather interior, OnStar navigation. Not the kind of car a parent would buy for his kid, at least not in this town. Maybe in Hopkinton, those snot-nosed pedigrees got whatever they wanted.

Jodi noticed him giving it the onceover. "My mom's. Mine's out of gas, and I won't have enough money to get some until I get paid next week."

"That's right. You work at Parkside." He turned his head and stared out the window, ticked off to be reminded of that place again.

The Stop and Shop was in River Mills. Jodi followed the detour signs away from the small cliff where the bridge had washed out. The silent drive was longer because of it. In time, the grocery store came into sight. Jodi parked the car and grabbed a notebook and pen from the glove box and held them up. "Our shopping cart." Then she pulled a hand-held calculator out of her pocket. "So we don't go over budget." He gave a sarcastic laugh and got out of the car.

The giant carriages lined up in the entrance made it clear customers usually bought in bulk. The newlyweds bypassed the carriages and walked through the automatic doors to start their homework.

Andrew scanned the store. He didn't see anyone he knew, not even other students up to the same thing they were. He followed Jodi's lead.

"Did you ever notice how stores con you into spending more money?" Her question came out of nowhere like nervous chatter. "Look, see, the first couple of aisles have all the expensive fresh fruit and baked stuff you really want. Then they put the things you really need, like milk, butter, eggs and stuff in the last aisle. So you have to walk through the whole store to get to the things you need, and by that time you've already gone over your budget on the things you want. So we should be careful about that."

"What, are you some kind of Shopping Network freak or something?" Andrew was actually surprised by her knowledge but would never let on that she just scored a point on his 'maybe she's not so bad meter'.

She confronted him in self-defense that must have been pent up since 3rd grade. "You know, you don't have to be such a jerk. I was just trying to make conversation. Forgive me if I know my way around a stupid grocery store."

Points lost. Andrew's first thought was to turn around and walk home but for some unknown reason he stayed. They wandered from case to case picking up and turning over the produce, much more concerned about their avoidance of each other than the food. He could see her steeling glances when he stole his. Like steel to a magnet, they eventually made their way toward each other. Jodi spoke without the previous venom in her voice.

"I help my mom shop sometimes... Please don't be mean because I know how to do this."

Andrew needed out of this; he hated being advised of his faults. He grabbed a small, yet particularly stringy coconut and tossed it to Jodi as he quipped, "Hey look, Mrs. Loggins having a bad hair day." She was quick to reach for the nut but failed to catch it. It bounced off her palm and dropped to her other hand, rolling down her fingers before she could get a hold of it. Just before it hit the floor, she made a mad dive and grabbed it with both hands. "Excellent catch," he said with enthusiasm. She stood and smiled, causing Andrew to smile back - the first pleasant moment between them. The congeniality gave way to a clumsy self-consciousness. Jodi quickly turned to put the coconut back on the shelf.

"You know, my mom always makes a list. Why

don't we get a drink at the café up front? We can sit down and make a list, then get the prices afterward."

Andrew agreed. Point recouped.

They sat in the warmth of the sun-filled café in the bakery department, she sipping on a latte, he drinking coffee - black. Andrew realized how cliché it must look to passersby. Certainly, any shopper who saw them together would draw the conclusion they were friends or even hooked up. The possible misinterpretation of the scene made him uneasy. He scanned the area again to make sure no one he knew just happened by. After all, it was likely other kids from the class would be here at some point today.

"So." She picked the pen up and gave a small hint of a smile. "What's for dinner?"

They created a list through exchanged monosyllabic words. Andrew hardly looked at Jodi, focusing instead on the paper cup he rotated in his hands. When he did look up, he was amazed to see beneath softly cut bangs and those feathery wisps, how her brown eyes sparkled in the sun. He felt certain behind those eyes hid the contempt she no doubt held for him. At that moment he wanted to be someone else.

*   *   *

On the way home they were once again lost for words. Jodi was thankful this time Andrew left the music off.

He turned to her. "You were out for a while a few

months ago."

It was a statement clearly looking for a response. She was surprised he even noticed. Had she thought it was an attempt at friendly banter rather than just killing time, she might have expounded. Instead, she offered only basic information. "Death in the family."

"Oh... Sorry."

Jodi felt immediate remorse for her abruptness. Even if he was a jerk, she didn't have to be one as well.

Andrew fidgeted in his seat and started playing with the cross that dangled from her purse, a symbol of her new faith. It reminded Jodi of her missionary uncle. She used the memory of his strong faith as a catalyst for her own. After seeing what her uncle was willing to die for, she knew she couldn't hide her candle under a stone. Andrew's observation presented the perfect opportunity to share her faith and make up for being rude.

"It's OK. It was my uncle. He was a missionary in Africa and got AIDS from an accident with a needle. He didn't have access to some of the newer medicines available to fight it. His system was weak and it finally got him." She paused to get the courage to continue, afraid of any comments Andrew would come back with. "He died as he lived - serving God." There, she said it. The Lord would have to do the rest.

*   *   *

Andrew turned her words around in his head

trying to understand. God was no more real to him than Superman or the Tooth Fairy. His family never attended church. He never learned to believe in or be in awe of a power greater than himself, so the concept of dying for a god was more foreign than any distant country. That is not to say he never tossed around the idea of the existence of God. He remembered standing over an open pit in the ground at his grandmother's funeral, seeking answers from behind eyes moist with emotion. Did his grandmother just suddenly cease to exist or had she become some sort of ghost or angel, a spirit who now lives in that place called heaven? He was certain there could not be a hell, at least not for her. And if there was a heaven, did that mean there had to be a God? And if there was a God, how could he let this happen? The questions boiled in him for weeks. Eventually, time and distance moved them to the back burner, reducing them to a gentle simmer, not quite gone.

He felt the urge to ask Jodi her opinion but then thought better of it. Those kinds of conversations bonded people or made stronger friends of those who already had bonded. He and Jodi were not friends. Except for this project, they had never really spoken to each other. To ask would be breaking new ground, potentially creating a sort of intimate moment between them. He did not want that, but the question nagged at him as they continued down the road. He decided to take a chance. "Do you believe in God?"

Jodi smiled, as if she was expecting the question. "Yes. But not just some guy up in heaven somewhere who doesn't care about us. I believe that God knows and cares for me personally."

"Personally?" He sniggered at the thought.

"Yeah."

"Like you're friends or something?"

She spoke hesitantly and shrugged her shoulders a little. "Pretty much."

Andrew would have expected to feel claustrophobic held hostage in a car with a Jesus freak, like when the JWs come to the door. There were times he slammed the door in their faces, others when he could not bring himself to answer it. He didn't mind it so much in Jodi. Maybe because she was his age, and not some perv dressed in black and white with a backpack and a Bible trying to convert him. That didn't keep him from deciding to push her buttons though, despite having jumped into the conversation himself. "So, you guys hang out, or what?"

Jodi drew in a deep breath. Her face grew tight and she stared straight ahead. For a minute Andrew thought she was gonna blow but she kept her cool.

"Every day; mostly in the mornings and at night. Occasionally we get together for a meal on Sundays."

Andrew met his match. They didn't speak the rest of the way back.

*   *   *

The teacher stood at the front of the class.

"Differences of opinion, i.e., arguments, will happen. At some point as a couple you will find yourselves in conflict with one another; you can rest assured of that. As in everything, it's not whether you win or lose, it's do you have the skills to play the game without destroying what you have. Yes, I did say skills.

"A successful marriage is hard work. You've probably observed instances of couples who work at it and survive and those who don't. Chances are every one of you has been along for the ride in one or maybe even both of those scenarios. Since history repeats itself, some day you too will have to know how to have a disagreement with a partner and come out on the other side still intact. Therefore, today we're going to learn the rules of conflict."

Mrs. Loggins had Andrew's attention. He never considered the possibility there were rules of engagement. He sat beside a stoically silent Jodi as project guidelines required. He found it ironic that today's lesson was one they could probably use. The two hadn't looked at each other, let alone spoken since class began. He realized the button he had pushed yesterday in the car must have been red hot and started feeling a little guilty for his actions. Shame and regret seemed to be following him these days: first the diner, now Jodi. He nervously drummed a pencil on the desk wondering what was happening to him. Going soft, that's what. Without fanfare, Mrs. Loggins placed a hand on his, silencing the beat as she walked up the aisle and continued past his desk.

"So, what are these rules?" The teacher threw out the question and proceeded to lecture with no allowance for discussion. She talked of nurturing free and open conversation that remained respectful of the other partner; actively listening to the other side; if necessary, admitting error; and ending with addressing each other's needs until a satisfactory resolution is attained. Andrew listened intently, passing up opportunities for his usual offhanded comments. Neither Sam nor Eddie failed to notice his attention to the lesson. He saw that both looked to him for tasteless chatter at what they believed to be opportune times during the lecture. Their disappointment in him registered in spitballs and kicks under the desk. The class was quick to engage in lively dialogue when the teacher finally opened the floor for discussion. Andrew remained quiet throughout.

"Your assignment is on the board. It's due Wednesday."

The students copied down the homework just as the bell rang dismissing class. Andrew left without notating the assignment: Jointly put together a long-term plan for the future: hopes, dreams, realities.

*　　*　　*

"Don't you get it? It's about fostering a relationship, allowing it to grow." Jodi was getting frustrated.

"You mean Loggins wants us to hook up or something?"

Sitting in the library with Andrew, that question sent chills down Jodi's spine. Their time together was simply to get the assignment done, one more thing to do in order to graduate. But Jodi also believed she understood where his question was coming from, so she took only a minor offense at his rudeness. She was beginning to realize he had difficulty seeing beyond black and white, to read between the lines. Gray areas were difficult for him. "No, the idea is to learn how to be a member of a successful relationship. You can use her ideas not just with a boyfriend or girlfriend, but with anybody you're trying to relate to."

"Oh." He looked to be running thoughts around his brain. "Hey, ah..." he began reluctantly. "About the other day, in the car, I didn't mean to..."

Jodi felt an apology coming on. She didn't feel the need to put him through it nor to listen to it. "Nah, forget it. Sometimes I get a little uptight when I think someone is making fun of me because of my faith. Freaks me out, you know. I get kind of defensive." She couldn't believe she was sharing this much information with Andrew Steiff of all people.

"So, if you have to work at relationships, then what about you and your God? Do you work at that?

...Seriously."

Jodi was sure he added that last bit to make certain she knew he was for real. She looked at him and thought she saw something that wasn't there before, or perhaps she had missed, an honesty, someone looking for answers. She was afraid to open up again but felt a small inner nudge. She felt the Spirit's presence guiding her words.

"Well, yeah," She hesitated then went on. "It's like any friendship, you have to spend time with someone to get to know them."

"So you pray."

He seemed to know that much about religion. "Yes. That, and read The Word. The Bible, that is." Keep it black and white.

"You know, people are real hypocritical about that stuff. If someone has a problem, they'll tell that person to pray. But if that same person who then prayed to God says, 'God told me to do this,' everyone thinks he's nuts."

She couldn't argue with him on that point; hypocrites abounded in all religions, hers included. "I can't allow other people to get in the way of my relationship with God, because when it's all over, it's just going to be me and Him face to face. I can't blame or take the glory from anyone else."

"You're really into this, huh?"

"Into Him. He keeps me going. When the rest of the world let's me down, He's there to hold me up."

"How?"

Just as she was about to answer, Sam and Eddie stormed into the library and slammed their books on the table. "There you are, punkhead! We've been looking all over for you. You and Mrs. Punkhead playing house? Oh how cute, can we play too?" They pushed between Jodi and Andrew, forcing them to move to other chairs so they could take their seats. Jodi settled in the next seat hoping the boys would leave, although she was certain the opportunity to witness her faith had passed. At first Andrew didn't seem to care about the boys' intrusion and even laughed at their antics, that is until Sam went too far. He leaned in close to Jodi and raised his eyebrows in a suggestive manner. "Hey, Mrs. Punkhead, if you get tired of his lame ass," he said, punching Andrew's shoulder, "come see me. I'll show you a thing or two I'll bet you've never seen."

Jodi didn't have time to process the disgust she felt at Sam's implications before Andrew was on his feet pulling Sam up out of his chair. He was just about to throw a solid punch at his face when Mrs. Smith, the librarian, yelled from across the room and bolted over to where they were. "Andrew, Samuel and Edward, outside now." The librarian escorted the boys to the principal's office leaving Jodi alone at the table, stunned. She picked up her things and left, surprised at the tears forming in her eyes.

* * *

Andrew laid stretched out on his bed thinking about what had happened in the library earlier that day. He had taken part in similar scenes many times before with his friends, never thinking about the casualties. This time, being on the receiving end with Jodi present, it brought out an anger he had never felt before. Jodi was above that. The waitress was above that. Why do I keep coming back to that? He, himself, felt the need to be above that.

He heard the phone ring in the other room.

"Andrew." His mom was engrossed in Wheel of Fortune and not about to be bothered with answering.

"Yeah, yeah, I know." The caller ID told him it was Eddie. "What do you want?" Courtesies were unnecessary.

Eddie's news came out of the blue. Words, they were just words, Andrew told himself. Words he knew to be a lie, had to be a lie. Eddie continued to speak, but a soft ringing filled Andrew's ears and grew to overshadow his words, negating all other sounds except for the ringing. It surrounded him and pressed down on him like a living breathing thing, almost smothering the very breath from his body. He took the phone from his ear and stared at it. "Lies. Lies." He repeated the word, each time getting louder, eventually fending off the ringing and coming back to reality where the phone in his hand was the enemy, the messenger of death. Eddie was still speaking. Repulsed by his words, Andrew dropped the phone to the floor where it landed with a thud that got his mother's attention. He registered her nasty glare but stood motionless, frozen in a moment that only he possessed. Ever so slowly, he began to back away from where the phone lay on the ground as if it was a demon from which he needed to escape.

"Andrew?" his mother called. "Andrew?" She yelled louder. "What's the matter?"

Her voice grew more distant to him with each backwards step he took. Then without warning, he ran and burst out the front door.

"Andrew!" He kept going as if he never heard her.

Andrew bounded down the front steps and out into the road that wrapped around the perimeter of the trailer park. He was unaware of a decision to turn left or right onto the road and barely realized he had chosen as he veered toward the park exit. The decaying wooden sign declaring Bay Cove Homes was a mere blur in his periphery as he passed through the gate, the sign being even more questionable than a trailer park that was near neither a bay nor a cove. False promises filled his life.

Like the promise of tomorrow. They were the youth; their future was bright. Isn't that what the teachers and guidance counselors always tried to shove down their throats? Where was that golden tomorrow now?

Pound, stride, pound, stride. His feet repeated the cycle. Pound, stride. He ran not knowing where he was going. He ran because it was the only thing that made sense; he wanted it to consume him and he it, to be one with the movement. Pound, stride, pound stride. Breathe in, breathe out. One mile, two miles, three.

Andrew had never participated in any kind of organized athletic sport. His body was not used to the demands being placed on it. Young though he was, he was out of shape and much more used to running down the end zone from the comfort of his couch playing Madden. His breathing became labored, burning his lungs. He tripped on a piece of uneven pavement and struggled to maintain his stride. He went down in spite of his efforts to keep pace. The beat inside him did not stop. Pound, stride. He was back on his feet again, momentum and sheer will propelling him forward.

"Why, God? Why?" The age-old rhetorical question plagued him. The answer never exposed itself, keeping its distance in a vicious game of torment. He was keenly aware now that it was at times like this when God snuck into his vocabulary, and always with a question mark associated with it. Maybe there is a God – a God not of the living, but of the dead. His legs, malleable as rubber, no longer wanted to support him. His lungs afire with each breath, he felt the question seizing from within, writhing its way to the surface. "Why?????" The scream broke free from the temple of his thoughts causing him to drop to his knees and fall prostrate on the ground. He screamed until the hurt became a silent cry, a sound for only God to hear. His soul void, there was nothing more to convey.

"My God, Andrew, what's the matter? What happened?"

A soft, gentle arm lay across his shoulder like a warm electric current, soothing and comforting his worn body. Through tears, he turned his head and looked up into Jodi's eyes. He wanted to speak but found no words, longed to be numb but felt the pain. He reached up and embraced Jodi as if his life depended on it.

They sat on the hillside overlooking the Housatonic River making its way toward the Long Island Sound, the clear sky above reflecting blue in the waters headed downstream. Andrew's gaze transfixed on the flowing river. He whipped small pebbles in without taking aim, jerking his arm violently with each stone thrown. He was still digesting the words he had finally said aloud to Jodi.

Sam was dead, killed in a car crash. He'd never see him again.

Sam, he and Eddie – three people, yet one. Now it was just he and Eddie. Ever since the phone call, the world had been rushing by him as if he existed in another dimension whose only speed was slow motion. Two parallel worlds, by definition, never to be one. He longed for reality, wanted to reach into that other world to find a sense of normalcy, to find peace. What was left of reality was slipping away out of a gaping wound. The amputation, still raw, had yet to be cauterized.

He wasn't sure how he had ended up at Jodi's, what unseen force had drawn him here, but here he was and it felt right. Her presence calmed the tremors in his soul. He tried to understand this, the peace that engulfed her and by osmosis spilled into him when she was near, but it eluded him. He only knew he wanted more of it, needed more of it to get through this day.

*   *   *

Jodi sat quietly beside him. If she were to classify her role in the drama she found herself swept up in, it would simply be as a presence. She felt nothing more than regret for a soul that left this world without knowing the love of the Lord, and nothing more than sadness for his grief-stricken friend. She didn't know Andrew well enough to offer personal words of comfort, and pat generic phrases were not only inappropriate here, they were out of the question. Still, she knew there was more here for her to do, it just wasn't going to come directly from her. Ever since she found him in the road outside her house, through his embrace, through the spilling of his heart and subsequent silence, and now side-by-side on the riverbank, she had been praying for him – asking God to show Himself as the Great Comforter she knew Him to be.

She knew this was the right place to bring him. It

was her place. She used to sit here in the shadows of the old wooden bridge and ponder some of life's toughest questions. The bridge was gone now, swept away in a great storm. Its collapse notwithstanding, this is where God spoke to her, above the hum of the rushing waters, to sooth her troubled spirit when her world seemed out of control. It felt good to share this special place with Andrew in his time of need. She waited until he was ready to speak; it wasn't long.

"Where do you think he is? Did he just stop existing?" That was the question at the heart of the matter that needed an answer: Was there more?

Jodi felt the Spirit guiding her words. It was not a time to mince them.

"I can't answer that question without causing you pain or getting you angry." She paused a moment in anticipation of an outburst. None materialized. "I believe there is life beyond this world. I believe it's a place of unending peace and joy beyond our wildest dreams. Eternal life in heaven with God is His greatest gift to us. But like any gift that's given, you have to accept it." She was having a hard time keeping it black and white so she looked for a metaphor he might understand. She hoped he had paid just a little bit of attention in science class.

"It's kind of like in science class – the difference between kinetic and potential energy. Kinetic energy has action; potential is kinetic energy waiting to happen. That's how it is with God. He wants you to have eternal life with Him, but you have to ask for the gift; you have to take that action. He's not about forcing Himself into your life. He gave us all free will so we can choose or not choose Him. If you never take Him up on the offer, well... that's where the conversation gets dicey." She didn't want to go any further in that direction. She hoped he was smart enough to read between the lines.

*   *   *

Andrew picked up on the peace aspect of this other world - heaven. Certainly, it was better than the one he was in now, assuming it was real. Maybe that was the other reality, the one he wanted to reach out to. But if it was real and it was like she said, then Sam wasn't there. He had no doubt about that. A small tear escaped and slid down his cheek, stinging his skin along its journey. He couldn't tell if Jodi noticed and at that moment he didn't care. He lifted the hem of his tee shirt to wipe his face.

"How can you be really sure he's out there - God that is - in heaven? How do you know he really exists?" He knew Sam was beyond help. He continued to question Jodi purely for his own self-interest.

She let out a short breathy, "Hmpf," and looked out beyond the distant shore. "Funny, I asked my uncle the same thing. That's when I realized I needed to step out in faith. It allows me to believe in something I can't see and can only feel." She tapped her hand to her heart. "Here."

"Feel? You can feel God?" Andrew thought that maybe he wasn't getting this right. Had this conversation taken place at another moment in time, those words would have been spoken with great sarcasm. Jodi must have heard the difference in the tone of his voice since she went on to explain.

"Not like in a physical way, but inside. I can feel His presence with me all the time. He's right there with me in everything I do... It's actually pretty cool to know I don't have to do this world all alone. People let you down. God never will."

Hope for the future, peace for all time. He wanted it. Now.

Andrew would never be eloquent enough to explain in mere words what happened next. If he had asked Jodi the question on his heart she would have said you need to pray. But that never happened. There was no need to pray, words were unnecessary. It was as if God knew the intensions of his thoughts and that's what mattered to Him – a changed heart.

He looked across the river and noticed dark clouds foretelling of storms ahead. He was glad as never before that he wouldn't have to face them alone.

JONI VANNEST

10
CONNIE ANDERSEN

The blank I drew in reference to the meal attendant bothered me long after she was gone. I was certain I knew her from somewhere and was miffed for not learning her name while she was still there. The memory of that mouthwatering bisque lingered, as did the woman's words, which weighed heavily on my mind. I had to ask for forgiveness from William. She also said I needed to forgive myself. As if that ship hadn't sailed long ago. Some things were beyond reconciliation. But William. Maybe there was hope yet, even so late in the game. For once in my life I wanted to look him in the eye, one adult to another, and not feel shame. My pulse quickened just thinking about trying to make amends. Sweat formed on my brow having nothing to do with my heart. Like the cowardly lion, courage never was one of my finer attributes; I imbued all that I had into my characters, leaving a stark void somewhere in the corner of my soul. It's funny that in writing it is possible to create a whole universe of people with strengths the author himself is sorely missing. Ironic to be sure. Even in real life, the child I had birthed, blessed with wisdom beyond that which I could ever have genetically imparted, knew I loved him, in spite of all my failures and shortcomings. Although he was not oblivious. In retrospect I know his "It's alright, Mom" and "Next time, Mom," were just a farce, a brick wall he put up to hide his feelings. If only I hadn't been so selfish I would have seen that. Nothing can be worse than hurting your own child. I felt sick to my stomach just thinking about it. I was grateful now that he was an adult with a family of his own; I was no longer someone who could disappoint him. Ours was an adult relationship, beyond the pain of the past, and we got along fine. Which meant, I realized then for the first time, that even beyond our adult relationship - he forgave me.

Grace. Over the years the ministers had always brought their sermons around to it. Undeserved favor – God's specialty. It was a lesson included in all my books, and yet contrition, its human counterpart, could not find its way into my own life. William understood the concept from both sides and took it to heart. I knew I needed to tell him how sorry I was.

The rhythmic tapping of heals and shuffling of little feet broke the hush that frequently permeated the halls. In an environment where soft voices and quietude ruled, anything to the contrary was obvious. This time it wasn't monitor alarms or nurse call buttons but two sweetly high-pitched voices that further sought to interrupt the melancholy standard.

"Mine."

"No, it's not. You don't even know all the words."

Frannie and James burst into the room tugging the book between them in opposite directions. "Mine." James grunted a little as he gave one last tug. Despite his efforts, the book slipped from his fingers, spurring a small tirade. "Ahhhh." Molly was quick to try to quell his disappointment by explaining that the book was Frannie's, but logic rarely, if ever, works with a toddler. She resorted to retrieving a toy from her enormous purse that looked more like an overnight bag to assuage him. He turned his attention to examining the plastic toy and calmed down even as his tiny body still jerked with uncontrolled sniffles.

Molly rolled her eyes and sighed - another battle won.

As William pulled away from a quick peck, I saw worry lines on his face that seemed deeper and somehow sadder than in recent days. He appeared ready for a long vacation with no responsibilities and no worries, a time allotted simply to enjoying life. I wanted to grant him that and was pained I could not. Molly put an arm around his waist and gave him a loving smile, a yang to his yin.

Frannie got right to business and came closer to the bed. "Grandma, I brought a story to read to you tonight." She held up a book whose cover featured a cowgirl with a stethoscope around her neck wearing an astronaut helmet, the title I Can Be Anything I Want To Be displayed prominently across the top in an arc. She began to recite the book from memory, turning the pages in just the right places. I could hear Molly's inflections in Frannie's voice. Her mother must have read it to her a hundred times. Molly smiled from the teal vinyl chair where she sat with James on her lap. William held up the wall beside them, arms crossed, looking like he'd rather be resting somewhere tropical, sipping on a drink with a little paper umbrella.

I couldn't blame him. I didn't want to be here either. Alas, I was here for a reason and it soon reared its ugly head.

My back hurt from lying in the same position for too long – a small annoyance, really, when faced with a much greater obstacle to my wellbeing. Still, I wanted to be more comfortable if I could, so I pushed the button to adjust the bed angle. When that did not do the trick, I tried to press on my elbows to see if I could lift and rotate my back a little. You would think I was trying to move a mountain. My arms had no strength and they collapsed back on the bed. The effort it took, even to no avail, left me exhausted and winded. I wheezed, felt dizzy. My heart wanted to race but it could not. Electricity suddenly surged from my center core and emanated through my whole body. I heard an alarm.

"Mom? Mom, are you OK?" William leaped to my side, pushing Frannie out of the way. He raised his hands and moved them about, first toward me then toward the beeping monitor, not knowing what he could possibly do to help. Several nurses came in and took charge, rescuing him from his helplessness. One of them, with great authority, ushered him and the family to the door. I can still see little James burying his face in the hollow of his mother's neck and Frannie turning back to look at me, arm extended in my direction, as her father led her out of the room. I watched as the nurse moved the storybook from where it lay on the bed, closed it and put it on the nightstand. I Can Be Anything I Want To Be. I wished I had that option.

William was sitting in the ugly vinyl chair staring out into space when I awoke. He was wearing the same clothes as before, so I guessed I hadn't been sleeping long. I must have made a noise or sighed because he turned his attention to me, walked over and wrapped his hands around mine. His deep-set eyes looked nearly sunken from the dark circles around them. His right thumb brushed back and forth along the back of my hand and I found it very comforting, the parent/child roles reversed.

"You're here," I whispered.

"Where else would I be?" His masquerade smile feigned cheerfulness, maybe even with a touch of hope.

"I'm tired, William."

"Well it is kind of late; you had a rough spell and you've been asleep for…"

"No, not like that." I took a shallow breath. "I'm weary," and another breath, "of the struggle."

His eyes diverted downward. He moved his mouth to speak then changed his mind. There was nothing to say.

"D.N.R." Those three letters snapped him to attention – do not resuscitate. A medical directive was one of those things I put on the back burner, right along with cleaning the basement and going to the dentist. Maybe I was a little more than superstitious about it, so I never brought it up. Neither did he. We both always believed that somehow God would make everything all right. That was His job, wasn't it? I'd come to believe recently that maybe His plan was different from ours.

"Mom, maybe…"

Nothing he could say would change my mind. I'd been through too much. And nothing they could do short of a transplant would make me better. I didn't need extraordinary measures that would make my life even more miserable and a further burden to my family. I shook my head to the contrary of William's plea. "It's time. Please make it happen."

We didn't talk much after that for what seemed a long time. He pulled the chair up close to the bed and continued to hold my hand. I reminisced of younger days, eventually sharing those thoughts with William about a time when our roles were reversed.

"Remember when you had your appendix out and I sat with you for days until you felt better?"

William's mouth spread into a smile. "I couldn't move around much, so we sat on the couch and played video games every day. You hated it, but you played to make me happy."

Yes I did. Such a mind numbing waste of time. I should have made him read, instead. "Guess it's payback time, huh?"

He chuckled. "Yeah, I don't mind."

No, he wouldn't; it was not his way.

"Besides, I was having so much fun actually being allowed to play video games without being nagged, I faked the last day I was out of school just so I could keep playing."

"You didn't?"

"I did."

"Scoundrel."

"Sucker!" he proclaimed with a laugh.

God, I loved that boy.

"Hey, remember when I got the stitches out and the doctor promised me a sticker if I didn't flinch? I was scared silly. I made a squeaky noise when he pulled out the first stitch. You didn't want me to miss out on the sticker so you pretended you had sneezed so the doc wasn't any wiser. That was great."

I looked at him. I knew the story. He and his dad laughed hysterically when they told me all about it the next day. I heard a lot of things second hand like that when I was off at a book signing or holed up at a writer's retreat or at some other function that kept me away from those who should have been my priority. He must have seen it in my eyes, and knew there was something wrong with his story.

"Oh, wait. No, that... was Dad."

I pursed my lips and nodded. His disappointment that it wasn't me in his happy memory laid open like a fresh wound, my guilt just as raw. I hated myself more than ever at that moment. I so needed to ask his forgiveness. Time was running out.

I wondered how Ellen Steele would guide a patient in this kind of scenario. For a character pulled out of thin air, she exuded wisdom. She would probably say to look internally. Self-analyze where the dark feelings stem from. Only then will you be able to go forward and make amends for your past.

Screw therapy. I didn't have time for reviewing or amending. I was like the thief on the cross. There is only now. What I really needed was to find out how to make the feelings go away, how to scrub away shame. Will his forgiveness do that?

"William," I started to say, but stopped. How can I be remorseful for what I've done to someone else when I haven't even forgiven myself. A clean heart must come first,

I realized, and I was not ready for that.
    "I need to rest."

JONI VANNEST

11
ON BECOMING

Rev. Paul Hemphill spoke as one does of something that takes your breath away, an awe so inspiring it can barely be contained, yet in deference to it, the words are uttered in barely a whisper. His notes lay open on the pulpit with hardly a glance in their direction—he needed no prompting—for his sermon on this Palm Sunday came from the heart.

Kelly Loggins listened with just one ear; her mind was preoccupied with more secular thoughts about the holy season of Lent than the spiritual ones the minister was trying to convey. She had to make an appointment at the salon for a long overdue haircut, shop for Tara's dress, check to see if her own floral dress still fit, buy the groceries for Easter dinner and make cupcakes for Tara's spring party at school and somehow squeeze in entering the store's payables into the spreadsheet. It was going to be a rough week. She supposed she could forgo the haircut if necessary. Her long chestnut locks could be pulled into an upsweep for the occasion; it would draw attention to her high cheek bones. Add a nice pair of earrings and she would be presentable. Phew. One thing off my plate.

Her husband Bill sat stoically beside her as he did every Sunday, his eyes heavy from the jetlag of his recent trip to San Francisco. Traveling for work was hard on him but was necessary for a job well done. They held hands as they always did in church. They held hands whenever they walked together as well, a symbolic act declaring the two as one. It blessed Kelly's heart and brought peace to her soul.

The pastor, nearing the end of his message, closed with a probing question.

"So I ask you, my friends, what... are you... becoming?"

Kelly and Bill stood in the fellowship hall after the service talking with friends, the pastor's message already a distant memory. They were waiting for their daughter, Tara, to be released from Sunday School. The teachers always let the children out about ten minutes after worship ended so the adults could have time to mingle before getting run over by kids dashing through the hall to the snack table.

"Whoa there, speedster." Kelly grabbed Tara's arm to make sure she put the brakes on. "Walk, don't run or you might bump into someone."

Later, the little girl joined her parents with juice and cookie in hand. "I have a secret."

Kelly pretended to look askance. "A secret, huh? Can you tell me?"

"Nope."

"How about me?" Bill inquired.

"Nope." Tara dragged her fingers across her lips to zip them.

Kelly turned to Bill. "Well, I guess it's going to stay a secret."

"Just until Easte... Uh!" Tara drew in a quick breath. "Uh oh." She snapped her mouth shut, eyes darting left and right beneath her shaggy bangs as if looking to see if anyone noticed her slip of the tongue. "I almost told you."

"It's okay, sweetie, your secret is still safe. By the way, where is your artwork from Sunday School?" Most times the children made a craft representative of the Bible lesson they learned that day. It wasn't often Tara left class empty handed. Kelly noticed none of the other children had any artwork either.

"It's part of the secret and I'm not gonna tell." As if to prove her commitment to silence, she jammed the cookie in her mouth to keep it occupied, assuring there would be no more slip-ups. Crumbs dropped from the corners of her mouth as she smiled a knowing grin.

It was one of those years when Easter came early. Spring had officially sprung, but winter still had its grip on the landscape and in the air. Kelly looked at the bare trees through her kitchen window and wondered if indeed she was seeing branches pregnant with tiny buds waiting for their moment in the sun. She hoped so. New England winters were brutal, but they were almost worth experiencing for the joyful release basking in the warmth of spring, knowing you'd made it through the winter.

Kelly was sitting at the kitchen table icing cupcakes with Tara, who was in charge of sprinkles. So far there was more confetti on the table than the cupcakes. "Is Grandpa going to come to my Easter egg hunt?"

"I think so, honey. He wouldn't want to miss such a special day. Besides, he has no excuse not to, it's one of the few days he closes the store."

Whitmire's General Store had become her father's life after her mother passed away three years before. Joe Whitmire dedicated almost every waking hour to it and the customers he served, leaving precious little time to take care of himself. Of course, he always found a way to make time for Tara. She was his golden girl, the sparkle in his eye. Kelly made time in her days to help him where she could, but some days it felt like she was running on a treadmill of tasks that included work, family, shuttling between her father's home and her own, and of course, the store. She had taken on many of her mother's household and store related chores and had been doing them ever since. Kelly tried to remember if she had ironed a shirt for him for Sunday and drew a blank. Too much to do, so little time.

"Did you know butterflies like purple flowers?"

"Really? How interesting." Where did she come

up with these things?

"And did you know," Tara continued, so proud to be the dispenser of wisdom, "that caterpillars spend their whole lives eating and eating and eating and eating. That's all they do." She dipped her finger in the bowl of icing then stuck it in her mouth, pulling it back out with a satisfactory pop, leaving a trace of chocolate on her lip. "That and sleep."

Kelly loved how young children marveled at the world around them. She wished that same desire for knowledge would stick with them as they got older. Her high school students could use a dose of what the little ones had. "Now where did you learn all these interesting facts?"

Tara tipped the colorful tube of sprinkles on its side, spilling more candy on the table, and answered her mother without looking up. "I'll never tell."

Kelly giggled to herself. Her little girl was certainly full of secrets these days.

On the evening of Good Friday as Kelly and Bill tucked Tara into bed with a kiss, she told them that the caterpillar makes a "koo-koon" just before it dies. "But it doesn't really die," she explained with wide-eyed amazement. "it... becomes." Tara let the sentence hang on the air, before lying down and pulling the covers up to her chin.

Kelly turned toward Bill and squinted, trying to remember where she had heard that before. He only shrugged, just as baffled as her.

Easter dawned with promise of life. Crocuses

adjacent to the front steps boldly battled the remnant snow, peeping out just enough to offer hope of warmer days to come. Tara enjoyed an early morning indoor Easter egg hunt with her grandfather, who came by especially for the occasion.

"Would you like more coffee, Dad?" Kelly offered to top off his cup as they lingered after a hearty breakfast. She sighed at the sight of his wrinkled lavender shirt. A fidgety Tara answered for him.

"He doesn't need any more. We have to clean up so we can go." At that pronouncement, she stood and carried her plate to the counter, then scurried from the room leaving behind three befuddled adults staring at one another, questioning what had gotten into her.

Kelly raised her hands in wonder. "What the..."

"Perhaps you should worry less about me and a bit more about my granddaughter." Joe was teasing, but Kelly thought there might have been a little truth in it.

Before long, Tara was in the doorway asking, "Is it time to go yet?" Kelly laughed at the sight of her. She had tied her hair up in lopsided ponytails and put her shoes on the wrong feet. "Is it?" she asked again. It took some doing, but Kelly convinced her it would be okay to take the time to fix her hair before heading out to church.

The sun played upon their shoulders as they all walked the short distance to the First

Congregational Church of Wheatfield Bridge. Kelly was thankful she could start to feel a change of seasons in the air. Tara walked at a quick pace, the new stuffed bunny she found in her basket that morning in one arm, her free hand clasping that of her mother's. She was pulling her along, trying to get her to walk even faster.

Kelly looked back and saw Bill and her dad chatting away, paying no attention to how they were lagging behind. "Tara, slow down, wait for Grandpa." She was reminded of her father's words earlier that morning to worry less about him and more about her family. It was so hard not to worry about him. He depended on her and needed her to help around the house and to keep his and the store's finances in line. She wondered in her efforts to be a good daughter, was she overlooking her own family's needs. Kelly looked back again. He certainly didn't look like he was at a loss for anything at that moment so she quick stepped and caught up to Tara.

Bright sunlight shone in Kelly's eyes as she gazed up the street toward the church. She sensed something looked different but couldn't be sure for the glare. As they got closer, she noticed the trees in the churchyard were fuller, occupied. And something, many things actually, were dotting the outer walls of the building. In a moment of clarity she saw they were butterflies - hundreds of them – alighting all around the front of the church. Some were crafted of wood. Most were made of cardboard, each a beautiful splash of color, the obvious product of a child's creative endeavor.

Tara's words from Friday evening echoed in Kelly's ears. "It's becoming." She knew then where she'd heard the phrase before. The pastor had used it in his sermon when talking about the sacrificial death and resurrection to glory. He had asked the members of his congregation what they were becoming, because being stagnant while on life's journey was not an option.

Kelly came back to the present when Tara broke free from her grasp and ran pointing to a pink butterfly with orange spots tacked to a tree trunk.

"Look Mommy," she said. "See it's not a caterpillar anymore. It's brand new, just like Jesus!"

"Yes, I see," and she wondered, *What am I becoming?*

12
CONNIE ANDERSEN

When he walked in the door I had no doubt whatsoever who he was, despite knowing it was impossible. He was about 5'10" with a build that hinted at a previous life of manual labor, and a receding hairline that crowned an otherwise balding head. Deep diagonal troughs separated his cheeks from his pencil-thin mouth like animated parentheses. If I hadn't known any better I would have guessed him to be in his late sixties, but I knew full well he was in his mid-seventies. His voice even sounded raspy, just as I knew it would. "Hello, Connie."

I wanted to say, "Hello, Jack." If it was anyone other than Jack Priestly, a sad lonely character who started out as a side note and grew to be my alter ego, I would not have a problem at all saying hi. But it was him, which created an enormous problem for me.

"You're not real, are you?"

"Reality is a state of mind, don't you think?"

The twinkle in his eye didn't put me off. "That's not an answer to the question."

He shrugged his shoulders. "I never promised you one. Come, let's walk." He shuffled toward the door expecting me to comply and follow.

To my surprise, I swung my feet off the bed as if I knew I could, without question. I immediately felt the blood circulate through my veins as it hadn't in a long time, down my legs and back up again. Back up again! And my breath, my breath! I drew in a deep, long inhale, held it, savored it. It tasted like the salty sea air and a refreshing mountain breeze all at once, and moved in my being as if life itself. Then I felt it – the beating of my heart. Not a weak irregular pulse, nor the pounding of one gone out of control, but a stable rhythmic da dum, da dum, da dum. I was re-made, brand new. It made no sense, yet all the sense in the world. This is how it should be; my crumbling body was just a nightmare.

I was careful to let my feet touch the floor while leaning hard on the bed, in case my legs, which hadn't had much use in a while, gave out. They held with the strength and vigor of a twenty-year-old. I bounced up and down on them just for fun, because I could. I knew my body could do whatever I asked of it. I wanted to run. To jump. To shout with the thunderous voice of a thousand angels, "Hallelujah and Amen!"

Jack waved me along. "Come on, now."

I double-timed it to catch up and my logic kicked in as I drew up beside him. None of this was right. How could it be? Maybe this was all my imagination, a hallucination. Or maybe I was dead and in the presence of the Almighty and this was how He chose to present Himself, as someone to whom I could relate. I grabbed his arm. I wanted it to be real, to be solid and not some ephemeral vision. It was. I stood still so that he could go no further and had to turn to look at me. "Am I sleeping? Is this a dream? Or am I in some sort of drug-induced or oxygen deprived hallucination?"

"Full of questions, aren't you? Hmf." Without answering, he began to walk away again. After a few small steps during which he barely raised his feet, he stopped, turned back to me and spoke. "Do you ever think about how Jesus hardly ever gave a straight answer to a question? All those parables, every one of them designed to let the listener weigh the options. Sometimes you just have to figure it out for yourself."

Well, if the man before me was God then he was not averse to playing mind games. I took the bait.

"Are you God?"

He stopped dead in his tracks. "God? Do I look like the Creator of the universe, the One who moves the sun and stars, breathed life into humanity and set everything in motion?" A satisfied half smile stretched his lips and he allowed for a dramatic pause. "Thanks for the compliment but, no." He looked down and I thought he was going to walk off again. Instead, almost as an afterthought he said, "I'm Jack. You know me. We've known each other for a long time now." He looked off to the side, thinking about that. "It has been a long time. I was just added content in your first book, back when Ellen and Brad picked up those hitchhikers. But I was there, in the small print."

"They weren't hitchhiking." Had I just argued a literary point with one of my characters?

He raised his index finger in the air, remembering. "Oh yeah, that's right. Picked them up along the side of the road. Not so sure that was a good move either. I never really was very good at pointing out things such as that to Ellen – 'Don't pick up hitchhikers' – and the like. There are lots of things I failed to do as a father. But it worked out in the long run, I guess – for Ellen, as well as that time with the hitchhikers."

I ignored his determination to label the walking couple as hitchhikers. If I could get over the fact that I was actually conversing with Jack Priestly, I could get over the fact that he had the story wrong. Which begged the question, how was this even happening? It was like I had stepped outside of reality clear into the Twilight Zone, and Jack was not forthcoming about any of it.

He didn't walk very fast, so we moved through the hall at a gentle pace. At this late hour, in between rounds and when most patients were asleep in their beds, the staff hung out at the nurse's station. They were hovering over someone's photo album, presumably of a vacation, based on comments I heard about the clear blue water. We walked past them unnoticed. Even though I was feeling much better, I suddenly realized I was pulling the IV stand along with me as we walked. I was curious. "How come I'm still hooked up to this thing?"

"You're in a hospital; it's their MO. Besides, you haven't been eating much lately, you need the nutrients."

"You're different, Jack. I wrote you as an irascible fellow, not an even-tempered conversationalist. Heck, you're not even grumpy."

He stood back and placed his hands on his hips, scowling in mock anger. "Are you complaining?"

"Well, no. It's just…"

"Oh, don't worry," he said much softer. "I've still got a good deal of that grumpiness in me too. Hang around with me a while and you'll see. Everyone has a generous helping of versatile characteristics in them. Think of it this way. An object, scientifically speaking, contains every color under the sun but our eyes only see the color that it reflects back. It's the same with people. We are all built the same but reflect back in different ways, depending on the circumstance."

There was comfort in our easy pace and conversation. It felt like home, a place or time to which I'd always want to return. I wanted to hold his hand; somehow, the notion seemed right. Like I used to hold my grandpas hand as we strolled on the beach when I was a kid. But I refrained.

"Why are you here, Jack? How is this all happening?"

"Questions, questions. I guess as a writer you can't help yourself. Attention to detail is what makes a good story."

It was an effortless diversion in the gift-wrapping of a compliment. But again he did not answer my questions and I was not going to let it go. I raised my eyebrows and stuck my chin out in expectation. "Well?"

This time I sensed some of his endowed cantankerousness. "The here and now and some other time aren't the only planes of existence, you know."

That answer, as unsatisfactory as it was, would have to do.

The hallway wrapped around the nurse's station and adjacent storage closet in a large rectangle. My friend Nurse Betsey, from somewhere in the Deep South, was on duty pulling a night shift and nibbling on a donut as she looked at the photos with the others. She laughed at something and a bite of food flew out of her mouth onto the floor. She bent down to pick it up just as we walked by.

Jack and I moved past darkened patient rooms on our left where only occasionally the blue light of a TV glowed from within. Monitor beeps and blips were our constant background soundtrack.

"So, Connie, why didn't you talk to William when you had the chance?"

I stopped, snapped my head around to face Jack. It never occurred to me that my character who could probably tell me anything I would ever want to know about the fictional town of Wheatfield Bridge would know anything at all about my real life situation. This was getting too bizarre. But then, why wouldn't he know? We were as one. With that thought, I realized I was accepting this whole situation a little too easily for my comfort. "Jack, help me understand what is going on here."

His face went a vaguely ashen shade. He held his midsection and veered off toward the family lounge. "My stomach is bothering me a little. Would you mind if we sit for a moment?" Somehow, in this strange Twilight Zone universe, this too was acceptable. I supported his elbow and escorted him into the empty room where a dim table lamp was the only light. He set himself heavily upon a sofa and I joined him. The color seemed to come back to his face after a few minutes.

"Connie, you've made some unwise decisions in your life which haunt you to this day." He took my hand. I wasn't wrong about the comfort that action would bring. I felt good all over, like embracing sunshine after a terrible storm. "And you've many regrets. Lucky thing humankind an eternal God sees the past as well as the future and offers forgiveness of those regrets. He created tomorrow so there is always hope."

My eyes began to burn from holding back the tears that wanted to flow.

"I thought they were the right choices at the time."

"Did you?"

Jack was challenging my memories and my integrity, and rightfully so. He was no longer just my character or my alter ego. He was now my confessor, and I obliged our new roles hoping to crawl out from under a long-shouldered burden.

"That's what I told myself. 'I'm doing the Lord's work so sometimes sacrifices have to be made.'"

"But it wasn't all about the Lord's work, was it?"

I hung my head. It was a rhetorical question; he knew the truth. "No. Sometimes it was all for the glory, not God's, mine." Well, there it was. I was called out on the carpet. I stood convicted.

He scrunched his face as if in pain and took a deep breath. "The world can be pretty seductive. It makes honor so hard to preserve."

"I'm sorry." I offered the words up to the universe. They seemed so petty. I was a person who lived for words, the beauty and harmony of how they ebbed and flowed, bent to my will and sometimes bent me to their will as a story came alive and into its own. Yet all I had to offer were those two overused and underrated words. There needed to be something more, that clean heart that was nowhere to be found when I was speaking with William. Yet, in all my naked guilt and apology, the shroud still covered my heart. I could not disown it.

He nodded. "Yes, I know you are sorry, and God forgives you, you know that. Now here's the hard part." He raised my hand in both of his, and in a flash of drama released it and withdrew his hands with splayed fingers. "God has dealt with it. Let it go."

JONI VANNEST

13
WHITMIRE'S GENERAL STORE
"For, lo, the winter is past, the rain is over and gone."
Solomon 2:11

The sign appeared marked by time. Whitmire's General Store – Serving Wheatfield Bridge Since 1883

The building stood alone as a place of commerce amid residential houses on Bridge Street, the store being there much longer than zoning ordinances had been in place. In decades long gone, the general store served as the place to shop. Somewhere along the line between urban sprawl's growing lack of sidewalk communities and the increasing number of multi-car families, it unknowingly cleared the path as a prototype for the now popular convenience store chains. However, in this small New England town residents still relied on their local homegrown establishment and the familiar face of a shop owner who not only recognized them by sight but knew their names and family members as well. Rush hour shoppers, a thriving pizza business and lack of competition kept the store relevant to the community.

Out front, a raised flower bed where the gas pumps used to stand caused drivers to choose which side of the flower box to park when pulling up to the store. A rusty oval Esso sign hung beside the front door, an echo of another time still present for ambiance and old times' sake. Inside, shelves of groceries about four and a half feet high enabled the proprietor, Joe Whitmire, to see from behind the front counter clear to the back where the pizza oven stood. Assistant Manager Preston Smith ran the store's thriving pizza and deli business, aided and staffed by several local teens after school let out in the afternoons. Currently, his crew worked rotating shifts throughout the summer months. Customers regularly filtered in and out of the store keeping Joe occupied from the time he opened in the morning until he closed at night.

*   *   *

Kelly Loggins' hand smarted from the door's sun baked metal handle. She should probably talk to her father about putting up an awning for shade over the door. The burning handle was a lawsuit waiting to happen. She didn't always think about things such as that in relation to the store. It started after her mother died, when she began to try to fill the empty space left behind and didn't want to miss anything that would adversely impact the business. She motioned for little Tara to enter the store as she held the door for her. The girl, oblivious to good manners, cut between two customers waiting to pay and ran behind the counter into the arms of the cashier.

"Grandpa!" She wrapped her arms around Joe's neck and planted a kiss on his cheek.

"Hey, how's my girl?"

Kelly observed the affectionate moment and noted her father had a lot more gray hair these days mixed in with his sandy color, and it was just long enough to prove he leaned a little toward the radical side. A little bit longer and he'd need a haircut. His unshorn hair, jeans and a collared shirt with sleeves rolled to just above his wrists could deceive the eyes into seeing a more youthful person than the years actually counted. His boyish grin was something that no doubt would have bothered him as a young man trying to look older, but as an older man it washed the years away. The slender build of his youth was now filling out with age and his face looked worn with time. Kelly thought about the ways he was changing as he got older and decided she just wasn't sure she was ready for it. He rang up purchases one handed as he held Tara in his other arm.

"I got brand new swimmies. We're going to the river so I can try them out." Tara was so excited about her new swimmies, she had her mother put them on before they left the house. Beads of moisture now clung where the plastic tubes wrapped around her upper arms.

"Sounds like fun." He tapped her on the nose and she scrunched up her face. "Thank you; come again," he said, handing the last customer his change.

Kelly strode to the coolers to pick out a soda and juice box to keep them hydrated while out in the sun. Soon enough she would be back at school. For now, she wanted to take full advantage of what was left of the days of summer before heading back to the routine of periods one through nine. She walked to the front of the store and placed the drinks on the counter. She was deep in thought as she rummaged through her change purse for money.

"That will be fifteen dollars, please," her father said with a straight face.

Taken aback at first, she quickly picked up on the familiar dry humor and played along. "That's outrageous." She slapped her hand on the counter. "What kind of a rip-off joint is this? That's it, Tara, we're never coming back here again."

"But Mommy..."

Kelly and Joe burst into smiles and laughter. Tara looked from one to the other. "Mommy's just being silly, sweetheart," Kelly assured her. Then Tara smiled too.

They were alone at the register now, so Kelly took a minute to chat. "Bill and I are having a barbeque on Saturday - nothing big, just a couple of friends, a few neighbors and some of the guys from Bill's reserve unit. Why don't you come by? Of course, if you have better prospects..." Kelly added the little tease as a small nudge. She had been dropping hints like that for a while now. She didn't know how to come right out and say she was okay with the idea of him moving on. At least she hoped she was. Three years. It was well past a respectable time of mourning. Only time would tell if she'd be able to look at him with another woman on his arm and not be uncomfortable, or worse, jealous because of it. He needed to move forward and she needed to let go.

Kelly believed the store took up too much of his time, not leaving enough for a life beyond it. Of course, she knew after her mom died it was the store that kept him going, that and Tara. His sense of responsibility to his customers helped to make the months following her death bearable. The store was closed for a respectable but brief time, then he reopened and had been working ever since keeping the people of Wheatfield Bridge supplied with their must have emergency items.

Even though her mother's absence in the store was palpable, it was where her father felt closest to her. Whenever Kelly suggested that he cut back a bit, maybe bring on someone else to help, he always had the same reply. "It was where we spent most of our days together for thirty-two years. I need to be in the store just as much as I hate being here without her."

He used a different version of the same old excuse to avoid the barbeque. "Oh, I don't know.

Someone's got to run the store."

"Come on, you can leave the store with Preston. He can handle it." Preston Smith had been with Joe since he took on Whitmire's as his first after school job, just before LaRue died. He had graduated right into the first full time employee Whitmire's had ever hired.

"We'll see."

Even Tara saw through his dismissive answer. "Grandpa, that means No. If I ask Mommy for something and she says, 'We'll see,' it always means no." Kelly turned to her daughter in mock surprise. "Rats, you're on to me."

"Well, little miss smarty pants," Joe conceded as he placed her on the counter. "How about this? I'll come if, and that's a big if, I can get someone to cover the store."

Tara wrapped her arms as best she could around her grandfather's chest. "Yay!"

*   *   *

She came into the store and his life when he wasn't looking.

Joe had heard the bell above the door jingle as she entered but his head was beneath the counter rearranging items in the glass display. "Howdy," he called from below grade. "Welcome to Whit-mire's." His voice noticeably slowed down as he finished the sentence and stood upright, cutting his last name into distinct syllables. He was more preoccupied with the person standing in front of him than in his normal greeting.

She was young, younger than Kelly, which caught him off guard, and beautiful. He never felt right taking notice of women young enough to be his daughter. Nevertheless, in this case he made an exception. Her hair was dark like LaRue's used to be, and long. She wore it straight, parted on the side and it bounced on her shoulder as she tilted her head and smiled. Her eyes, brimming with youthful effulgence, completed the work of art before him. Joe was quick to realize he had been bordering on gawking and worked to regain his composure before it became obvious. "H-how can I help you?" he stuttered.

"Hi, I'm Karen Tanner," she said, extending her hand to him. "I'm looking for the owner."

"Guilty as charged." She looked pleased. He shook her hand. It was warm and soft.

"Great. I'm new in town and was wondering if you needed any additional help in the store. I have retail experience and I'm looking for some part-time hours."

Joe hung on her every word like an enamored schoolboy, pleased to hear she was potentially going to be, hopefully, a regular visitor to his store. He noticed she was looking at him a little funny, and realized it was probably because he still held her hand. He snapped it back and quickly went on as if it hadn't been awkward at all. "Oh, did you buy the old Wheeler place?" She nodded her head in confirmation as she drew her hand back and clasped her other one in front of her. "I heard someone finally bought that house. Well in that case, welcome for sure; welcome to Wheatfield Bridge. So, what brings you to our neck of the woods?"

Karen told him she and her mother purchased the house together. "My mom was getting on in years and needed someone to keep an eye on her. I was looking for a new beginning after my marriage fell apart. It was the right place at the right time."

To Joe's delight they talked for a long time, conversing as if old friends, even when interrupted by customers. Finally, he had to tell her what she'd originally come in for in the first place. "I'm sorry to say I don't have any job openings at this time. But if you'd like to fill out an application, I'd be happy to keep it on file should there be one."

Disappointment registered on Karen's face, but she completed the application anyway. She shook his hand again as she got ready to leave. "Joe, it's too bad things couldn't work out, but I'm happy to at least have made a new friend."

Joe felt a small piece of him melt as she left the store and attributed it to a touch of heartburn.

"Hey Mr. W," Jim Hemphill called out as he came in and headed to the back of the store. Joe waved. He liked Jim. He was a little on the shaggy side with long hair, scruffy stubble on his face and tended to sport jeans and old tees. But he was clean and pleasant and showed up on time. And he was the preacher's son, which gave Joe a little comfort that he probably wasn't going to steal from the till. Best of all he made a mean pizza. His only downfall was that he had a tendency to get bored easily.

The boy had a long shift today – 10:30 AM to closing. Joe watched him get busy prepping the dough Preston started the night before. By 11:30 he was steadily turning out pizzas for a hungry lunchtime crowd. Around mid-afternoon a quiet lull had settled in. He used the time to clean the counter and refill topping bins. In spite of his best efforts to stay occupied, sometimes there just wasn't enough to keep him busy and thus, out of trouble. This was one of those days. However, it didn't come back to bite him in the rear until later that evening, near closing time.

The overhead bell rang and Elvin Griffin walked in for the second time that evening, this time holding what appeared to be part of a pizza box.

"Elvin."

"Joe, we have a problem."

As Joe listened to the man's story he could feel the anger rise from within. He snuck a peak at Jim, who looked innocent enough, wiping the counter. Joe apologized to Elvin and offered him a free pizza on his next visit. The two shook hands and Joe locked the door behind the man as he left. He then walked back to Jim with the vestiges of the box in his hand. Even from a distance he could see Jim's

Adam's apple slide up and down.

"Oh, crap!" Jim seemed to know where this was going.

"Jim..." Joe felt like planting his foot on Jim where the sun didn't shine. Instead, he shook his head repeating, "Jim, Jim, Jim."

"Look, I know what happened Mr. Whitmire and I just want to say how sorry I am. Really sorry. I got bored this afternoon. I totally forgot that I had done that, and just loaded his pizza in the box without thinking."

Joe slammed the box remnant on the counter. Somewhere inside - very deep inside - he could sympathize with him, although he could never let on. Certainly, this was the kind of thing he and his brother might have done in days gone by. But here, today, in his store, it was another matter.

They both looked down at the white cardboard, which had previously been the bottom of Elvin Griffin's pizza box. Drawn flamboyantly, in great detail, were a variety of both male and female body parts, the by-product of idle teenage hands in the middle of the afternoon. It had, apparently, raised many uncomfortable questions from Elvin's little girl as they were cleaning up after dinner. Jim blushed with the evidence staring up at him as it was, while apologizing profusely.

"I'm sorry too, Jim," Joe responded to the boy's pleas for mercy. "I like you, but you offended a customer and I just can't have that. I have to let you go."

Joe wished Jim luck as they went their separate ways. On his drive home, Joe remembered the application he had taken in earlier that day. It had previously slipped his mind. Now, in light of recent events, he believed his earlier encounter to be quite fortuitous and his gloomy mood transformed into one of great expectations.

*   *   *

Joe walked Karen behind the counter to learn the fine art of pizza making from the resident expert. "Now, don't work her too hard Preston. We don't want to scare her away on the first day."

Karen rubbed her hands together, ready for work. "Don't worry Joe; I'm tough. I got this."

He was sure she did. Joe thought her confidence made her eyes shine even more brightly than they did the day before. "Well, if he gives you any grief just let me know." He winked and went up front to take his place at the cash register, sorry he wouldn't be the one to train her. But that was on Preston. Pizza was his domain.

Joe went about his business that morning taking care of customers while keeping one eye focused on the activity in the back. He overheard snippets of conversations and embarrassed laughter as Karen tried and failed—as most did—on her initial attempts to make an appetizing pizza. He trusted Preston would have her turning out acceptable pies, if not great ones, by the end of the day.

As expected, the first day with Preston by her side went well. Her second and third day with him saw even greater improvements. On her own, day four was another story. At one point around lunchtime, a small line started to form, working its way from the pizza counter up the bread and snacks aisle. Knowing that a customer's patience, much like his lunch break, was limited, Joe decided to look into the hold up. Karen's back was to him as he approached.

"So, how are things going?" he asked stepping behind the counter.

Hearing Joe's voice, Karen turned to face him. Her hair and face were dusted with flour and there were oceans of sauce splattered on her apron and the prep area. She pushed her lower lip out to blow away some loose strands of hair that dangled in her eyes. Joe chuckled at the site of her. "Looks like we have a run on pizza today. Let's see if we can't get these fine people taken care of, shall we?" He hated abandoning the front register, but he could ring up purchase in the back as well. With his help, and assembly-line-like efficiency, they were able to catch up on the orders in no time at all.

After the last customer of the rush left, Joe washed his dough-covered hands and dried them on a towel. "Sometimes that happens. Guess it must mean we serve the best pizza in town."

"You're being kind. Thank you. The job is harder than it appears." Karen removed her dirty apron and replaced it with a clean one.

"It'll get better. Time does that you know, makes things better." He winked at her for the second time that day then went back to his post at the front register.

Things ran smoothly the rest of the day. As they were getting ready to close, Karen approached him about the afternoon's logjam. "I'm sorry things got so out of control at lunchtime. I'm sure I'll get better with practice."

"Not to worry. You'll get the hang of it." Then with a crafty smile and a stern look, Joe added, "Hopefully by tomorrow." He saw the flash of a worried expression on her face, as she nearly missed the drollness of his humor. A shaky moment later, the light bulb seemed to go off in her head and the tenseness dissipated. In that revelation, she teased back and softly fist-whacked his arm, immediately regretting it.

"Oh, I'm sorry, I shouldn't have done that." She still had the cleaning rag in her hand and began wiping his arm as if she had somehow soiled it, making things even more awkward.

"Haha. It's OK, it's OK." Joe moved to indicate she shouldn't worry about it and accidentally brushed his hand against hers, causing a strange and uncomfortable, yet pleasant feeling to wash over him.

Then Karen, with both hands, pointed over her shoulder to the door. "I... think I'm... going to go now." She laid the cloth on the counter, picked up her purse and said in a meek, almost mousy voice, "Goodnight." Then, taking a couple of backward steps, she turned and left for the evening.

Joe thought Karen's self-conscious actions could only be described as charming, and his own reaction plain weird. Still, the pleasure of her company, he decided, was something he could get used to.

He stocked a few more things on the shelves while replaying the day's events in his head. It brought to mind times when he and LaRue would spar back and forth like that. Later, after the lights were out and he was locking up, he almost felt as if he could feel her presence again. A new buoyancy in his step marked his walk to the car.

The next day Joe discovered that, without his consent, Karen was invading his thoughts, taking up residence in places previously reserved only for LaRue. This disturbed him. Aside from the obvious betrayal of heart, she was young enough to be his daughter. That alone was a boundary he felt ill at ease crossing. He told himself he was not ready for this sort of thing. And what would Karen want with an old man like him, anyway?

At one point when no customers were around, he stole a moment from the store to utter a small prayer. He always felt better after going to God when he had concerns. "God, I am so confused; my feelings are all mixed up. Please help guide me between what is right and what is wrong, and what would be your will."

Still, the issue tumbled around in his head all day. Kelly had been hinting the time for mourning his wife was over, but how could he set aside so many beautiful years together – just turn away from them like they didn't matter anymore. Was that what she was asking him to do? He did not think it was possible to split his life like that, to compartmentalize his emotions. And yet, here he was starting to have feelings for someone else. Joe's puzzled thoughts kept him actively trying to distance himself from his new employee. He stayed behind the cash register as much as possible, going so far as to send David, another part-time worker, to the storeroom for him just so he wouldn't have to walk near Karen. His efforts worked for a little while. He was able to go about his business taking care of customers without disruption. Then Kelly showed up.

"Dad, I hate to have to tell you this, but QuickMart submitted a request to the zoning board to open a convenience store with a gas island out on Route 7."

A thousand thoughts plagued Joe at once so that he remained frozen in place, overwhelmed, his slack jaw void of words able to express his surprise.

"It was approved."

Why hadn't he known? Had he been looking the other way when all this was coming about? He spent every day in one of the most public places in town and yet he didn't have a clue, no one had told him, not even hinted that his livelihood, and his world was about to change.

"Sorry to be the one to break it to you. I figured it was better coming from me than reading it in the paper. It was sort of a back room deal. The zoning board kept it hush hush until they were ready to approve it. But look, you've got a strong customer base, people come here to shoot the breeze with you just as much as to shop. I suppose you'll probably lose some business, but in the end I'm sure things will work out."

Kelly's unusual chattering told Joe she did not wholeheartedly believe her own words.

"Well now." Joe coughed to clear his throat, using the pause to gather his thoughts, choosing his words with great deliberateness. "You know, time doesn't stand still. Sooner or later the rest of the world was bound to infiltrate the likes of Wheatfield Bridge." A brave front did not ease the effect of this new reality. The future of the store was now in question.

"Yes, Dad, but the impact..."

Joe saw Karen approach from the corner of his eye and Kelly's voice faded away like a mist even though she continued speaking. His heart beat a little faster as she neared. She stopped just short of entering their circle of conversation and waited. Joe turned to her and smiled, temporarily pushing aside his new worries. They weren't going anywhere, they would wait until later.

"Karen, this is my daughter, Kelly. And this little one," he said swinging Tara up in his arms, "is my granddaughter, Tara."

"It's nice to meet you. Especially you," she said tickling Tara's side, causing her to break out in a riot of impish giggles.

Kelly welcomed Karen to the store as one who had a stake in it. "Glad to have you aboard. Try to keep this guy out of trouble, if you can. And don't worry; his bark is worse than his bite."

"Thank you and I'll have to keep that in mind," she said turning to look at Joe with squinting, teasing eyes.

Standing between Kelly and Karen, Joe felt like a child who just got caught sneaking a cookie from the cookie jar. He sensed an unexpected warmth rush up his neck and face. He looked down and shuffled his feet hoping neither woman noticed.

Karen quickly got down to business, letting him know they were running low on sausage then headed back to her post.

Kelly watched her walk away. "Seems like she'll fit in well around here."

"We'll see," he replied looking after her as well. "We'll see."

It was later that afternoon, between the lunchtime and rush hour crowds, when the same lull that had gotten Jim Hemphill into trouble with his artwork snagged Joe and Karen. Certainly, if the devil had a playtime it was then.

The store was empty except for the two of them, David having long-since ended his midday shift. Joe had been rearranging inventory on the bottom shelf in the first aisle, which ran from the front to the rear of the store. He had been at it a while. He stood to work out a kink in his back and as he did, his gaze took him to the pizza counter where he stopped to watch Karen at work. It was a mindless stare at first, progressing to one that insidiously moved in pushing reason aside. His eyes remained riveted on her. She was unaware he was staring until she looked up and saw him from across the room. As if drawn into a world in which only they existed, they held each other's gaze. Outside of place and time, they remained transfixed on one another, communicating a lifetime of thoughts without the necessity of words. The spell broke with the jingling of the bell above the front door as a customer came in, and they quickly looked away. Joe eagerly greeted the customer and rang up the purchases, but Karen was never far from his thoughts.

Later, amid organizing shelves and dusting box tops, Joe's thoughts frequented on the loneliness of the last three years. Picking up and going on after an amputation of the heart was hard enough, but the exile from the rest of life that he placed on himself only added to his grief. He hadn't wanted to be anywhere without LaRue, didn't want to pretend that everything was okay. The days and weeks following her death were some of the darkest of his life. Even after all this time, the light was still dim. Yet somewhere inside he knew it was time. LaRue had always been so effervescent the world could hardly contain her smile. If she was looking down on him from a place on high, he knew she'd be unhappy for him. LaRue, much more than he, was able to see the big picture and, he was certain, would not want him to be alone forever. So out of respect for her eternal happiness, a justification he found necessary under the circumstances, he was willing to take a chance on playing the fool. He just had to find the right moment.

Conversations were limited and tense between Joe and Karen as the day wore on; the elephant in the room was staring them down, challenging them to ignore it. They were both embarrassed at having been caught doing something usually reserved for wildly hormonal teenagers. Joe dared to breach the invisible wall as they were closing up for the night. He hardly looked at her as he spoke and used a lot of hand gesticulations to aid his cause. "Karen, uh, Kelly and Bill – Bill, he's my son-in-law - well, they're having this thing, this barbeque on Saturday and I was wondering... Well, I was wondering if you didn't have any plans, that maybe..." His ovation wasn't evolving nearly as well as he'd hoped and he felt stupid. The whole idea seemed out of left field. She was so much younger than he was and they hardly knew one another. In the midst of his nervous stumbling Karen seemed to recognize his efforts for what they were and interjected, "I'd love to," while placing her hand on his, rendering it motionless. It was then he allowed himself to look into her eyes and knew the darkness was fading into morning.

They decided to meet at the store, trying to avoid implications that the barbeque was anything more than a friendly outing but each was keenly aware, if only by their own actions, that it was much more.

Joe thought Karen looked great in her tan capris and V-neck peasant blouse, believing they accentuated her features without looking inappropriate. "You look nice," he offered, in understated approval.

"Thanks, I went through half my wardrobe before settling on this." She blushed as if having shared something she hadn't intended.

He, on the other hand, had rifled through several short-sleeved shirts before finding one that worked for him. He put on the clean and pressed shirt and stopped to think about it as he buttoned up. His clothes, his house, his finances were all in order because of Kelly. For the last three years she had been quietly moving in the background to make sure his world did not fall apart any more than it already had. Much like his lack of observation regarding the QuickMart, he didn't know why it took so long for him to notice, but he did know that it needed to change. From this day forward, his life would be his own to manage. Not that he didn't appreciate all Kelly had done. It was just time. He splashed on a little cologne and felt silly doing so, causing him to doubt everything – his new emancipation, his feelings, the pseudo-date. This was all so strange. He even wondered again why Karen would agree to accompany him in the first place. They were from different worlds. A feeling of dread overcame him. *What have I gotten myself into?*

Joe gave final instructions to Preston before he and Karen left for the barbeque. Preston assured him the store would be in capable hands during his absence.

Bunches of Shasta daisies smiled up the couple from the flower box as they exited the store, their bright yellow cores simulating sunshine. Joe picked one for Karen who promptly savored the fresh scent then slid the bloom behind her ear. Joe was off on the first date he had been on in over 30 years. The terrible uneasiness he feared might come between them as they headed out did not materialize. Conversation came easy as they walked up Bridge Street on their way to the party.

Kelly and Bill lived in a small saltbox on River Road, a short distance from the store. The modest home may not have boasted many a fine decor but it did see a wealth of friends who warmed the front door. Cars lined up on either side of their normally quiet street were testament to the good life Joe's daughter and son-in-law had built together. As they walked up the driveway, a small knot formed in the pit of his stomach. He never told Kelly for certain that he was coming and surely she'd never guess that he wouldn't come alone. A small voice inside his head told him to turn around and leave before they were spotted. He was just about to apologize to Karen and tell her he just couldn't do it when Tara came running out the door. "Grandpa, you're here, you're here!" There was no going back.

Kelly and Bill were close on Tara's heels. The look of astonishment on Kelly's face was no surprise. Bill's expression registered something more along the lines of, "You sly old dog, you." The 'friendly outing' rouse had bombed.

"Kelly, you remember Karen. Bill, this is my new associate, Karen Tanner. Karen, Bill."

"Welcome." He extended his hand. "I'm glad somebody was able to get this guy out of the store. Come on back, we have burgers on the grill and Kelly's potato salad is not to be missed."

"Y-yes," Kelly added, still in shock and stumbling over even just that one word. She gathered herself together and smiled, although Joe wasn't sure if it was authentic or just politeness. He knew his daughter well enough to see she was stunned he brought along a guest, let alone a much younger woman. He was thankful he could count on her offering a gracious welcome to Karen without passing judgment. Kelly echoed Bill's words. "Yes.

Come on back."

They walked across the lawn and joined the others in the crowded backyard. Joe recognized most of the people there. Even though he hadn't been to one of Kelly's parties in a while, he had seen most of them from time to time over the years. Friends, Bill's relatives, neighbors, co-workers. Kelly's best friend Ellen Steele and her husband, Brad. The men from Bill's reserve unit were easy to spot with their muscular builds and close cropped hair. They were all there, everyone who held a warm place in Kelly and Bill's lives. It did Joe good to know the kids had built a network of support and love around them.

Card tables laden with every kind of summer salad, vegetable or dessert imaginable were set up under a white canopy that provided shade from the sun. Kids of varying degrees ran around the side yard playing tag; while older "tweens", too young to be left home and too old to play with the little kids ("I'd rather die than be seen with them!"), stood off at the far end of the yard trying not to be noticed.

"Can I get you a drink?" Joe was reaching into an ice filled cooler to pull out a couple of sodas when someone slapped him on the back. "Joe! How's it going?" Brad Steele offered a handshake and pumped his arm as if they hadn't seen each other in months. In truth, in addition to being a close friend of Kelly and Bill, he was also a regular customer who came in every morning for coffee on the run. "I haven't seen you at one of these soirées in a long time."

"Ah, you know how it is, keeping busy with the store." Joe couldn't help notice Brad eyeing Karen inquisitively, with a Well isn't this interesting look on his face. "Brad, I don't know if you've met my newest associate, Karen Tanner."

Brad reached out his hand to Karen and shook it in a friendly though less enthusiastic manner than with Joe. "Now I know why you look so familiar. Nice to meet you. I suppose we'll be bumping into one another at the store then, huh?"

"I suppose so. That is, if you're ever in the market for a pizza. Best in town, hear."

Brad laughed. "Look at you, already plugging the business. Keep her around, Joe, and you won't have to worry one bit about the new QuickMart."

There it was again. The QuickMart seemed to be on everyone's mind. Joe wondered if it was just this little town or did people everywhere have strong reactions to change. Like it or not, he would have to deal with it soon enough.

Joe and Karen moved about the yard, making introductions and small talk. Each time he introduced Karen, the reaction was the same, the only difference was a change in character and the response based on gender. Without exception, the males gave Karen the once-over and nodded their heads in silent approval, while most of the women gave reprimanding glances to the dirty old man.

Through it all Karen stayed bright and cheerful, staying close by his side and winning the approval of all she met.

"Burgers are up!"

Bill flipped a sizzling burger onto a bun and placed it on Karen's plate. Joe watched her pile on the condiments and fill her plate with a variety of side dishes. Healthy appetite, I like that. They pulled up a patch of grass and sat down, side by side, to eat. As she took a bite of the sandwich, a cascade of ketchup dribbled down between her crossed legs. "Oh, sorry," she said with a mouthful, and put her hand up to cover her mouth. She threw her head back and laughed when she was able. "You must think I'm a glutton." On the contrary, Joe thought her unpretentiousness admirable. She held the burger away from her, letting it drip into her plate and said, "I look at it this way. Life is short. And if something good comes along, such as this wonderful picnic, take advantage of it while you can. Enjoy it. You never know when your luck may run out."

Joe thought about that. "It sounds as if you speak from experience." It wasn't his intention to squelch her happy mood with his statement. It just sort of happened.

Karen took a deep breath. There was regret in her voice as she spoke. "Yeah... Yeah, I had a good thing once. It didn't stay good. We discovered too late that we wanted different things out of life." She was quiet for a moment, wrapped in memories. "Anyway, like Shakespeare said, 'It's better to have loved and lost.' Right?" She was back to her perky self.

As bad as his own loss was, he would go through it all again in a heartbeat to be with LaRue one more time. However, he'd never thought to put that kind of positive spin on it before. "You amaze me, the way you can take a negative and turn it around."

She looked directly at him. "It'll kill you if you don't."

In short order they were joined by Kelly and her friend, Ellen Steele. "Mind if we join you?"

"No, not a'tall." Joe could have kicked himself for saying it like that. I sound like an old man.

Kelly held her plate with both hands and plopped down in front of him, while Ellen held her plate with one hand and used the other for balance as she set herself down on the ground with care. She opened her napkin on her lap and placed the plate on top, then primped her short cropped golden hair before biting into a chip. Joe always wondered about the contrast between those two, friends since childhood yet so very different. He inquired after her daughter. "Ellen, is Jodie at the diner today? I don't see her."

"Yeah, working the lunch and dinner shifts. I suppose she's not too unhappy to be missing the BBQ. She's at that age when it's best not to be seen with the family."

Joe remembered those days when Kelly would rather be dead than seen with him and LaRue.

Several times he spied her and Ellen trying to hide unnoticed among their group of teenage friends if their paths had crossed while they were out and about.

"I knew a couple of girls just like that once upon a time." Ellen froze mid-bite and Kelly snorted, both looking rather sheepish.

Kelly abruptly changed the subject. "Ellen, I can't believe how Avery is growing like a weed." Ellen jumped on the conversation redirection. "Sure is. I can barely keep him in clothes he's growing so fast."

"Well I'm glad I don't have to feed a growing boy. I think that child of yours has a hollow leg. You know, I have to fight with Tara sometimes to get her to eat. She can raise a fuss when she wants."

Touché, thought Joe. He looked among the guests in the yard. "Speaking of fussbudgets. Where's your dad, Ellen? I thought I saw old grumpy earlier." Jack Priestly had a well-earned reputation for being ornery and didn't care what anyone thought of it. He and Joe went way back.

"Yeah, he's here. Just sitting inside out of the sun for a while. He says it gives him a headache." She took a second napkin and wiped a crumb from the corner of her mouth.

Joe turned to Karen, who was licking the side of her burger to stop some ketchup from spilling again. Even as she was waylaying another condiment drip, her eyes were attentive to him. "I've known Jack Priestly since before these girls were in grade school, and I'll give you this, he's consistent. He was a curmudgeon then and he's a curmudgeon now."

Ellen nodded. "I won't argue with that. But he's a loveable curmudgeon," she added with a grin.

That sounded like an oxymoron to Joe, but he made no comment.

When the number of guests started to thin out, Joe and Karen gave a hand with the clean-up detail in the kitchen. Joe was pleased she felt comfortable enough to lend a hand, but was a little concerned when Kelly kicked him out of the room declaring, "Give us girls a chance to get to know one another better." He didn't want Kelly to assume a relationship that wasn't there and then bring the topic up with Karen. He would have to trust in his daughter's better judgment. He ended up sitting on the deck talking with some of the stragglers, Jack Priestly and the Steeles among them. The proposed QuickMart on its way to town was again the hot topic of discussion.

Jack was ever the doomsayer. "Remember a few years back when they put up that convenience store in River Mills? It wasn't but six months before Robie's General Store was out of business."

"So what are your plans, Joe, when the QuickMart comes to town?" Ellen asked the question presumably on everyone's mind. Especially Joe's.

"To tell you the truth, I haven't quite decided what I'll do. The way I see it I have three options: I can retire and start shopping at QuickMart." The comment brought a few chuckles from the group. "I can close my eyes, put my fingers in my ears and hope for the best, or I can change with the times and modernize." The thought of altering the store was Joe's least preferred choice. The store was what it was for over 120 years; it almost seemed sacrilegious to think about making it over. But, he supposed, small changes they'd made in the past were beneficial, aiding in its longevity. After all, great-grandpa Whitmire never sold a slice of pizza in his life.

John Herman, from next door, wanted to add his opinion. "If you ask me, I don't think progress designed to keep up with the break-neck pace we force upon ourselves is good for us in the long run. I, for one, like coming home to a small town way of life when I leave the rat race at 5PM. I don't want a QuickMart and a superhighway taking over Main Street." John had a reputation for fighting growth in town, being especially outspoken against development projects that would change Wheatfield Bridge's small town feel. He was the poster child for stagnation and those gathered around didn't hesitate to tell him so with a little friendly teasing.

"So John, are you ever going to run electricity out to your place?"

"How's that outhouse working for you?"

"You should try indoor plumbing, it's great."

"I know," he said with good humor. "I've got the well hand pump right over the kitchen sink now.

Don't have to go outside for water anymore." They all laughed. Still John wanted to make his point. "But don't come crying to me when 'progress,'" he put his fingers in air quotes, "starts to build a high rise right there on the town green. I'll just say I told you so."

Brad shook his head. "Hey Joe, if you decide to modernize the store, you might try updating John as well."

"I'll take that under advisement, Brad. I'll take that under advisement."

When Joe caught up with Karen later on, he found her and Kelly drying the clean dishes and stacking them in the cabinet. The two seemed to be pleasantly engaged in conversation, which made him happy. It was important to him they got along. Not that he needed approval from Kelly for how he lived his life, but it was nice just the same. Plus, Karen was also an employee. She needed to be on good terms with the staff. He moved across the kitchen to stand behind his daughter and gave her a hug. "How's my girl?"

He looked at Karen across the room. Her head tilted to one side as she watched them embrace and she smiled at his show of affection.

Kelly turned and released the embrace. "Dad, Karen was just telling me she took some business classes in college. Maybe she could help you with a new marketing plan to grow the business in preparation for when that store opens up."

Joe thought he heard a bit of contempt in the

way she referred to that store.

Kelly's notion of Karen's abilities caught her off guard and she was quick to clarify. "Oh! I never did graduate; I don't want you to have the wrong impression. My knowledge of such things is pretty limited."

Joe was tired of dealing with the QuickMart issue. He wished he could just make it go away and be done with it. However, putting his fingers in his ears and going la, la, la, la, la was as impractical as it was stupid. "You know, that silly convenience store seems to be the only thing anyone wants to talk about. Even John Herman was on one of his anti-progress soapboxes about it. But, it got me thinking. I don't want the general store to fade away to more modern conveniences like some old dinosaur. It wouldn't be right. That store has served this community for over a hundred years. And I'm sure not ready to retire. Which leaves only one viable option – I have to change with the times." He put forward his next sentence directly to Karen. "So, maybe we can put that education you're so modest about to good use. Eh?"

"I'll be glad to help in whatever way I can."

"Good. But I tell you, today is my day off. I want to forget about business and just enjoy my family and my friends." He looked from Kelly to Karen. "So you know what I'm going to do?" He moved away from Kelly and reached out to take Karen's hand. It was the first time he'd reached for another woman in decades. It was a spur of the moment action and he wasn't entirely sure it was a wise move. What if it's too soon? What if she doesn't want to hold my hand? What if... What if... It didn't matter at this point. His hand was out there awaiting acceptance or rejection. He hoped for the latter and pressed on with gusto. "I'm going to show you where I used to take all the girls down to the river to make out in my younger days."

"Daddy!" "Joe!" The women exclaimed in unison.

Joe tried to look innocent, realizing his attempt at humor went over like a lead balloon. "What? I'll have you know it's lovely sitting on the dark beach this time of night looking for shooting stars. It's one of the nicest places in all of Wheatfield Bridge, water views from a patch of sand surrounded by woods. Shame on you; your minds are in the gutter." He wagged a finger at them and then extended his hand again. "Shall we?" Karen looked at the outstretched hand. The pause as she considered the option seemed like an eternity and he began to get weak in the knees.

Karen narrowed her eyes and verbally played with him. "What if it's a cloud-covered sky?"

"Then we'll listen to the water lap on shore."

"And what if the waters are calm?"

"We'll skip stones on the surface."

"And if we get tired of that?"

"We can marvel at God's wonderful creation."

Karen reached out and took his hand. Joe

breathed a sigh of relief and led them out the door.

*   *   *

"Have fun," Kelly called out as she closed the door behind him and Karen. But not too much fun. She was conflicted as she watched them walking down the steps off the deck, he in front, though still hand in hand. It was the first time she'd ever seen him hold a woman's hand who was not a family member, specifically her mother. Despite the gnawing discomfort in the pit of her stomach, she couldn't remember the last time he'd looked so happy. Still, this was all going way too fast; they barely knew each other.

"Was that your father leaving without saying goodbye?" Bill had snuck up behind her and rested his hands on her shoulders.

She turned to face her husband and he comfortably slipped his arms down around her waist. "Yes, I mean, no. He and Karen are going down to the river to stargaze." The roll of her eyes on that last word left nothing to the imagination about her feelings.

"Do I detect a hint of, what, jealousy? Or maybe disapproval?"

"Really, Bill? He's a grown man, he can live his life however he wants." She pulled away from his embrace to put the last dish away in the closet. "...within reason."

Bill laughed. "Aha! That's what I thought."

"No, you don't understand." She laughed in spite

of herself. "They just met and already they're out on a date." And what was that little game they were playing there, with the questions and answers? Oh my gosh, they were flirting. "And they were flirting, Bill, right in front of me."

"Seems to me as if your dad is finally ready to move on. You knew that was always a possibility, right? After all, it's been a long time."

She took one last swipe of the counter with the sponge and then threw it onto the small dish beside the sink so that there was an audible clink when it landed. "No. I mean, yes. No. Oh, I don't know. Well, maybe he's ready, but I'm not."

It wasn't only about seeing him with another woman, which was hard enough, but their relationship had become a vital part of who she was. She wasn't just Kelly Loggins, wife, mother and teacher. She was also the person who took care of Joe Whitmire, and she wasn't sure she was ready to cede the care and maintenance of her father back to him and lose that aspect of herself. However, that thought did give her pause to wonder if perhaps the things she did for her father might be doing more harm than good. Doing his paperwork and laundry is helpful but not at the expense of his independence. The laundry and dishes pile up on those occasions when she's unable to get there on her regular schedule, and the store invoices would never get paid if she didn't take care of them. At least, that's what she thought. In truth, she never really did give him a chance to do it on his own, never even tested the waters. After three years it was just how things were done. And the added benefit was that it allowed her to keep an eye on him and make sure he was doing well. There were any number of reasons why things were fine the way they were: she being the responsible daughter and him being the faithful widower. Karen would add a new dimension to a symbiotic relationship that had been working well for three years, a dimension she wasn't ready for.

Bill wrapped his arms around her again. "Kelly, he's only human, and humans need companionship." She was about to say that he had them, but Bill beat her to it. "Sure, he's got us and Tara, but he obviously needs something more. Look there's no doubt your mom was his soulmate. And no relationship he develops with Karen, or anyone else for that matter, will ever erase that." He lifted her chin so that she looked up into his eyes. "And he will always be your dad. Nothing and no one will come between you two."

"What if he falls in love, really in love?"

"Then be happy for him. Remember, love isn't just about what you get, it's about what you give." He kissed her on the forehead to solidify the point.

Despite her misgivings over the apparent relationship, she said to Bill in all honesty, "I'll try."

*   *   *

Joe and Karen took the River Road Annex by foot,

following along as it swung behind the houses toward the river, where a rutty, well-worn dirt access road eventually replaced the pavement. That road then came to an end as it spilled into a makeshift parking lot.

Although Hunter's Lake at Emmaus State Park was not far away, the townspeople of Wheatfield Bridge preferred to swim off the river banks. The town fathers generously maintained a small, private beach for residents only, allowing them to avoid the summer crowds at the park.

White Sands was the kind of place with an old rope tied to an even older branch that hung out over the river. Kids would swing on it and let go to land in the cool running water. It was a place that generated smiles and memories. It was here where Joe and Karen removed their shoes to stroll along the sand, catching silver flashes of moonlight as it danced on the water. They walked along the river's edge, daring the lapping ripples to try to catch them. Joe was happy to let Karen lead the conversation, which she did admirably like an investigative journalist, asking probing questions in an effort to learn more about him.

"What happened to your wife? I mean, if you don't mind me asking?"

The candid question caught him off guard. He thought he must have had this discussion a million times by now, hoping each time that it would be a little easier than the last. It never was. He hesitated a moment then spoke but one word: "Cancer." The pain and heartbreak of those six letters was universally understood. It always amazed him how just that one word could stir up the same dread in all who hear it. He supposed it was because in one fashion or another it has touched its miserable hand upon so many, that no one feels truly out of its gnarly reach.

"I'm sorry. It must have been very hard on you."

He gave no immediate response, remaining quiet as they walked on. How could he encapsulate a lifetime of love into a one or two sentence reply that could possibly do justice to the relationship he had with LaRue. It was not possible. Karen didn't pursue the topic any further. It was Joe who brought it up again thinking that he at least owed Karen a response. "It was quick, thank God. Three months and she was gone. Thirty-two years we were together. That was three years ago. I still think of her most days, especially at the store. We were always there. Sometimes I'll see a customer, maybe it's just the hairstyle or the way she walks and just for a moment I'm fooled into thinking it's LaRue. I like those moments." He thought about that and was quiet again. He was glad when Karen gave his revelation its own moment of respect before she spoke again. He was ready to hear her then.

"Marriages of such duration are hard to find these days. My own marriage failed almost as quickly as it began. It doesn't seem fair that one grounded in such love should die before its time."

"Oh, the marriage may be no more, but the love survives."

She gave his hand a firm squeeze. "You were lucky to have known love like that. I'm sure she was a wonderful woman."

"Yes, she was a blessing I didn't deserve.

"That's the funny thing about our existence, though. Everything in life is a gift and we want to hold on to it as if it will last forever. But it is all fleeting, that's the nature of this world. I think sometimes we'd all be a lot happier if we would just learn that one lesson, and hold on to the eternal instead." Joe's wisdom, born of experience, was that which sustained him each new day, giving him faith for all of his tomorrows. It felt right to share it with Karen at this time; however, he was beginning to feel the need to change the conversation, as he was still only able to talk about the past in small doses. "So, tell me about you."

"A gloomy tale, I'm afraid - a marriage built on an unexpected and unwanted pregnancy. We tried to make it work at first, but couldn't keep up the façade. So he drowned his unhappiness with a bottle. It brought out a side of him I never knew existed. I lost the baby in one of his violent rages and that was the end of that."

She spoke so matter-of-factly. He couldn't understand how she could relate the story without showing even an inkling of the revulsion she must feel for her ex. Joe thought it was probably a self-preservation thing; as if she erected a wall of safety around her where she couldn't be hurt anymore. It made him want to protect her.

Without a word, he walked her back from the water to a grassy area above the beach. He sat down and drew her close, putting his arm around her shoulders. She didn't hesitate to lean into and take comfort from him. They remained there watching the sun go down behind the trees on the opposite shore. As he held her and felt her nearness he wished he could take away the pain of her past and promise her a future of only good things, much like he used to bandage Kelly's woes as a child.

It was then he realized the truth.

The woman he held, whether consciously or not, was in search of a man whose love would not hurt her - someone with whom she could deconstruct that wall of protection and feel secure. And he himself, what was he looking for? It wasn't someone to replace LaRue. He wanted someone to share his remaining days with, someone closer to his own age, who like himself, was winding down this thing called life, not just stepping out into it.

He pulled Karen closer and encircled her with his arms; he felt her relax into his chest and knew this was a good thing, though it wouldn't be forever, not even by this world's transient standards. In his heart he knew Karen would eventually feel the same way - that for one brief moment in time they were able to offer each other someone safe with whom to take a chance again. And because of it, they would yet again.

14
CONNIE ANDERSEN

The weight on my chest was more determined than ever to pin me down and each shallow breath I took was never enough; my greedy body always wanted more. My heart. I couldn't tell if my heart was racing or on hiatus. My life's rhythm had changed and I didn't recognize it. I was pinned to the bed, tasered into place by my own misfiring heart and the weight of edema. Air. I needed more air. I couldn't breathe. I had to run from there. I had to find air. Oh, God help me. I tried to lift my shoulder to get momentum to roll onto my side and get out of bed. My shoulder barely budged and used all the energy I had to give to the cause. Oh God, please. I slumped back upon the bed, drained from the effort. What time was it? When would this end? How long had it been? I needed an end to this. Shadows softened the edges of my vision, my periphery nothing but darkness. I closed my eyes and became one with the shadows.

I heard voices, pleasant, female voices. I opened my eyes. Outside my window, the far wing of the hospital stood black against a swirling cloud of misty purple haze in the distance that rose up into a brighter hint of blue and the day to come. Tomorrow. It was already tomorrow. What had Jack said about that? It was God's way of saying there was always hope? Yes, that was it. The dawn never looked so beautiful, so real. Full of promise.

I was lying on my right side so that the chatting women were behind me. I rolled over onto my back. That's when I realized I could rollover, not like before when the slightest movement took all my strength, and then some. It was easy this time. The weight was off my chest and my lungs were no longer angry. Cool, forced oxygen flowed through the cannula, which I was quite certain was superfluous at that moment. Still, I savored every breath.

"Well there you are sleepy head. We've been waiting for you to wake up."

Two women sat on the vinyl chairs, one with a Starbucks cup her hand. She was the one who spoke. A pair of sunglasses pushed her chestnut hair back from her face like a hairband and let the tresses fall gracefully to the back, below her shoulders. She looked to be in her early thirties and carried a little extra weight around her middle as if she had a hard time saying no to desserts. I was taken with her eyes. Even under the dull fluorescent light I could see them sparkle. They were eyes that held no secrets, eyes filled with nothing but goodness. It felt calm being in her presence. The second woman wore her blonde hair short, austere. Her slacks were neatly pressed and her flowery top was modest, buttoned high. She looked healthy, fit, yet without a hint of a workout-defined physique. She looked at me with her head tilted to the side, taking me in, analyzing or assessing me, as if concerned. The long-haired woman placed her coffee on the dresser and stood. "So, what do you think, are you ready to blow this joint?" To my surprise, again, I felt that I could. It was happening again.

I looked at her and I looked at her friend. "I know you." I pointed to the woman who spoke. "And you." I wagged my finger back and forth, scrutinizing them.

"I should hope so," said the blonde, who then also stood. "We wouldn't be here if it wasn't for you."

I poked my finger like a dagger at the blonde. "Ellen,

Ellen Steele." She nodded. "And Kelly Loggins." The dark-haired woman confirmed.

"Now that we have that out of the way, what do you say?" Kelly put her hand out for me to take. "Ready?"

I suppose I should not have been surprised. It seemed this was getting to be old hat. I took her hand and the three of us walked through the door, down the elevator and right out of the hospital.

The sun had risen in the time it took to get from my room to the front door and it felt warm and comforting on my skin. Not long ago I wondered if I would ever feel it again. Now here I was being enveloped in its warmth. I stopped and raised my face up to the light, glad for one more opportunity to bask in the rays of a pleasant Indian summer day. A slight breeze kicked up and blew open the back door of my hospital gown giving me a slight chill where I least expected it. "Whoa!" I took my free hand, the one that was not pulling along the IV pole—yes, I still had to tag that along with me— and pulled the flaps together. The ladies laughed when they saw what happened. Ellen, ever practical, planned for what she thought would be inclement weather and pulled a raincoat out of her bag, which she draped around my shoulders to cover my impropriety.

"Sorry, I should have thought of that sooner."

We followed the wide concrete path from the front doors down the hill to the sidewalk that wound its way through the hospital campus. It was a small community to itself. The main building acted as a central hub with two radiating wings spreading out from it. A third one was under construction. An expansive lawn, dotted with benches, surrounded the place. Outbuildings housing physician practices, cafes and a medical supply store kept the landscape interesting. Visitors and doctors milled about. We looked suspect to no one. Just three ladies out for a walk. We ran into the occasional patient, like me, who was mobile and out for fresh air. I could have walked like that all day.

We talked about their lives—lives I created— their husbands, children, fathers. They both loved their families and struggled with their fathers. It was the basis for a good friendship even if they hadn't grown up together, which they had. They thanked me that I had given them each other.

The winding circular sidewalk eventually brought us back to where we started and I wondered what would happen next. I dreaded the idea that I'd have to go back upstairs to that other existence. I was just about to say as much when a deep grumbling sounded from my gut loud enough for the others to hear.

Ellen looked both shocked and amused. "What was that?"

"I think it was my stomach," I said touching it, amazed that it could be so loud. I'd had no appetite as of late, but at that moment I found that I really wouldn't have minded a thick juicy cheeseburger.

Kelly placed her hand on her stomach as well. "Thank goodness it's not just me; I'm starved. Let's go get something to eat." She looped her arm in mine and Ellen followed suit. Together they dragged me off, arm in arm, to a coffee shop with a sandwich board out front listing the egg and coffee specialties of the day. "Caramel toffee crunch. Oh yeah, now we're talking!" Kelly exclaimed. We opted for a sidewalk table so we could enjoy the fresh air. Just the girls going out for a bite, chatting like old friends. Kelly had bacon and eggs with her house special coffee and Ellen got a fruit cup and tea. Even though it was still early in the morning, I gave into my urge for a burger. It lived up to my expectations. About halfway through the meal Ellen and Kelly shared a look. Ellen patted her lips with her napkin, laid it on the table and cleared her throat.

"So, I understand Jack came by to visit you."

I stopped mid-chew. It never occurred to me that my characters would know each other's whereabouts and endeavors outside of my own imagination. This threw me off guard. They were conspiring behind my back. I was hesitant to respond and only offered a vague, "Maybe."

"Don't be coy. He told me all about it. That's why we're here."

"Seriously?"

I was dying, literally. I needed a heart and the previous night it felt like it had exploded in my chest. I had no energy to even talk, let alone move, and satisfactory breathing was a thing of the past. Yet, here I was out with the girls eating lunch for breakfast and wondering how it is that my characters were plotting their own story. My life and death were amiss. For whatever reason, one that defied explanation, I was here, in the midst of an unfamiliar scene self-derived by fictional characters. My options at that moment were limited as they knew the script, and I did not. I chose to play my part as if I had written it. "OK, so he was here. We went for a stroll around the ward. And to be honest, I think I am healthier than him. What's that all about?"

Kelly picked up a slice of bacon with her fingers, said, "You'll figure it out," and took a crunchy bite. That was all either of them offered on the subject of Jack.

Ellen got that psychotherapist look on her face. "Look, Connie, we know you're having a hard time forgiving yourself. Letting go of the past and moving forward is hard. It's much easier to forgive someone else than it is your own faults. I get that." She rubbed my shoulder. "But without it you'll never find peace."

She hit a nerve, a deep-centered raw nerve and I lost it. "Peace? Move forward? What part of 'I'm dying' don't you get? I neglected my family in the name of serving God, doing a disservice to both in the process, and causing pain to the ones I love most in life. So, what am I supposed to do, make a formal apology to a husband who isn't here anymore, a son who has already moved on, and a God I profess to love but used to make a living off Him anyway? I don't deserve forgiveness."

"No, you don't." Ellen was blunt about it. "According to the world, that is. But God thinks otherwise. You know that. Why do I have to explain it? You've written about that very thing numerous times. Don't you believe your own words?"

"Yes, I do. But not in this case."

"Why?" Now it was her turn to be angry. She raised her voice and her neck turned a pinkish red. "What makes you so special that you are not worthy of forgiveness from the God who convicted you in the first place?"

I stared at her dumbfounded. I had no answer. My new girlfriend saw right through me, just as Jack had. Forgiveness was for others but not for me. What a stupid, arrogant premise. My heart began to hurt in ways it hadn't before.

"He wants you back, Connie. He wants to mend your broken heart."

I woke up feeling like I'd been hit by a MAC truck and left to die at the side of the road. Whatever happened the night before took its toll on me; that was clear. I looked around and noticed the girls were gone and I was once again hooked up to monitors and machines.

I started to think about the DNR, do not resuscitate, order the doctor mentioned months ago when it became obvious there was little left he could do for me, short of a new heart, which at my age was unlikely to materialize. There was always someone younger and healthier ahead on the list. I had always felt life and death were God's jurisdiction and I had no right forcing my own hand in the situation with a DNR. If medicine would heal me, it would; if medicine would fail me, it would. God took care of that, not me.

Dawn was awakening outside my window again, and I wondered if it was the same dawn I met with Kelly and Ellen or if it was another day. My perception of time and reality were skewed. Nothing made sense anymore. A nurse came in and wrote her name on the whiteboard on the far wall where a name was erased and a new one written every twelve hours. At lease that was dependable even if nothing else was. Martha. It was a lovely name, very Biblical. I didn't recall seeing her before. She recapped the sharpie and placed it on the sill.

"Hello Connie, my name is Martha and I will be…" She stopped what she was about to say and reached her hand up to my head, where she pulled a rust colored leaf out of my hair. "What on earth?" Martha gave me a quizzical look, as if I must have known where it came from. I had no logical answer to offer. I couldn't very well tell her it must have blown in my hair when I was outside walking with my imaginary girlfriends, Kelly and Ellen. As I frequently do when all else fails me, I resorted to humor and whispered, "I guess I'm sprouting."

She shook her head, not at all convinced and said, "Well, if you start sprouting leaves made of gold, you let me know. In the meantime if you need me just hit the button." And with that, she left, still shaking her head and mumbling, "Mm, mm, mm."

JONI VANNEST

15
MUCH WILL BE REQUIRED

They sat on the floor in the parish hall, each with an envelope they had received from Reverend Paul Hemphill. Pastor Paul, as he was known, was glad for the turnout at that night's youth group meeting. He was not the charismatic type who drew in large numbers. He even wondered if he was on the verge of being too old to do youth work anymore. His sandy hair was streaked with a lot of silver strands these days, and even though he stayed in shape, he still found it harder and harder to recoup physically after particularly active meetings. His aging body aside, it was a ministry in need of a leader and for now, he was it.

He looked around the circle of kids. They were a small group, but a devoted one. Jim, Sean, Tyler, Denny, Jodi, Beth and Andrew—a visitor tonight—all of high school age, sought to answer the age-old question, which to them in their tender years was brand-spanking new: What's life all about? Some were looking for spiritual answers while others took a more humanistic approach to the question.

However they chose to look at it, he saw it as his responsibility to expound on a foundation that hopefully their parents and Sunday School had already laid for them. He knew finding meaning in existence was something most people spend the better part of their lives trying to define. It was his goal, with God's help, to cut a few years off the process. And if he learned one thing at all in his years as a pastor, it was that most people never find that meaning until they first take the step to look beyond themselves.

"In your hands," he began, "is the means to be a blessing to someone in this community."

Paul could see curiosity was getting the better of his son, Jim. The boy held his envelope up to the light and nudged Denny to take a look. Both boys' faces grew animated at what they saw through the sealed envelope.

"Dude, he's giving us money!" Denny shouted.

The other kids then held their envelopes up to the light to confirm if theirs held the same thing. Paul didn't think to wrap the money in paper so it wouldn't be obvious. There were exclamations of, "Oh, cool!", "Wow!", and the like from the others in the circle.

Oh well, so much for the big build up to opening the envelopes. Paul went with the flow.

"Yes, you are each the beneficiary of a monetary gift. The envelopes have varying amounts, some more generous than others. The catch is, I would like you not to keep it, but rather to give it away." The room filled with sounds of disappointment.

"Man, I was gonna buy a new video game."

"I could have downloaded some tunes."

Paul was amazed how fast they were able to find ways to spend the money on themselves. He wondered if they would be able to rise to his challenge just as quickly.

"We may not realize it as often as we should," he continued, "but God gives us great gifts out of His generosity. For some that may mean financial blessings." He pointed to the envelopes in their hands. "Others are given artistic or musical talent. Still others are blessed with peace in their lives or a heart for service. The ways in which God blesses us are infinite. The question to us is, what do we do with those blessings? Well, what if I told you that God blesses us so we can be a blessing to others?"

As expected, Tyler could not let that statement go by without a fight. He never hesitated to challenge anyone with a differing opinion from his own.

"You're saying God never gives us things just for ourselves? Then what about all my stuff – my car, my video games, or even my family's house? We're just supposed to give it away? So what, God wants us all to become communists?"

Paul knew it would be a hard concept for some of them. After all, they were their parent's children and many of the adults in the church thought much the same way as Tyler.

"No, I'm not saying you need to give away all your things and go live on the streets of Calcutta or anything like that. Although my guess is that God surely rewards those who do. Tyler, what I'm saying is that God blesses us every day of our lives and then gives us choices as to how we will use those blessings. For instance, will you use your car to help someone who is in need of a ride? Or let someone borrow your video game who can't afford one of his own?" He then spoke to everyone in the circle. "Will you share from your abundance or even out of your limited means with someone else?" The kids were quiet. His lessons weren't usually this intense. He was more likely to scoop out Neapolitan ice cream and talk about the Holy Trinity than to dish out money.

"Look, here's how this works. I gave you all money to do with what you will, no rules attached. But my challenge to you is to give it away. Now, no one here will know either way; that's between you and God. If you choose to keep it, then by all means spend it on yourself however you see fit. However, if you take the gift you were given and choose to be a blessing to someone else with it, then here's what I'd like you to do. Let the recipient know it. Go out on a limb, and in the name of God's love personally reach out to that person with your gift."

The kids looked stunned, the challenge weighing heavy on their minds. This wasn't like the time they raked leaves for Ms. Helen or visited the aged parishioners at the nursing home. It wasn't even like the time they went to the work camp in Appalachia. He, their pastor, was asking them to go outside of their comfort zone to be a personal witness to someone, and no one looked pleased.

"So we can just keep it? For ourselves?" asked Sean with raised eyebrows. He was having a hard time understanding the concept.

"Or give it to someone else who needs it?" Jodi also needed clarification.

"Yes, and yes," Paul replied. "But again, my challenge to you is to be the blessing."

"That's some challenge you issued tonight." Ellen Steele had been nearby in the choir room sorting sheet music and overheard most of the youth group's conversation. She poked her head out after the meeting and commented to Paul about his challenge.

"Thank you, Ellen. Unfortunately, we may never know if the seeds we plant ever blossom. That's one of the downfalls of ministry, and yet, also one of the great opportunities in our Christian walk - to have faith God will do His part."

"Well, I just wanted to let you know I thought it was a wonderful idea."

As the kids were still milling about, Paul took the opportunity to thank Andrew Steiff for visiting with them. In a moment of evangelical outreach, Jodi

Steele, one of the core group, had invited him. Jodi mentioned to Paul that Andrew had been through some rough times recently with the death of a close friend. He was proud of Jodi for connecting with him as she did.

"Well Andrew, I hope you enjoyed being with us as much as we enjoyed having you here." Paul slipped his arm around the young man's shoulder as he spoke to him. He felt the boy tense beneath his arm. It was an action that usually caught the kids off guard, but it got their attention. Current thought had lawyers warning adults in big red letters not to have physical contact of any kind with a kid for fear of misinterpreted meaning or false accusations. Paul had no ill intentions. He believed in hugs, they played a vital role in all of his ministries, especially where a hurting person was concerned.

"Yeah, about that," Andrew said. "I think I should give you this money back since I'm not really one of you." He held the envelope out for Paul to take.

Paul thought it was an interesting choice of words – 'not one of you.' Andrew was one of those kids who did his best to make sure he didn't fit in to anything mainstream. His hair was dyed jet black and he wore all black clothes. A necklace of safety pins dangled from the collar of his tee shirt and a hollow tube piercing in his earlobe stretched it to so wide Paul thought he could probably fit a dime through it. Jodi mentioned that he had reached out to God in his recent grief. Paul knew it was important to let the boy know he was as welcome as anyone else there. "No, please," he said, holding both hands up to stop him from returning the envelope. "It's like I said, that money is a gift. But now you have to choose how to use that gift. Bless yourself or bless others. Think about that. If you want to talk about it, I'm usually here most days. Stop in and maybe we can chat – the in-person kind," he said with a wink.

From the look on his face, Paul was pretty sure Andrew still didn't get it, but seemed satisfied enough that he was walking out with more money in his pocket than he had when he came in.

Paul was sitting in his office a few days later when Jodi knocked on his door. He had just hung up with another parishioner telling him what a good job he was doing with the youth of the church. It seemed word about the challenge was making the rounds through the congregation and many of them felt the need to show their support.

"Hey Pastor Paul."

"Jodi. Come on in." Paul was accustomed to having people stop by unexpectedly during his office hours, but it brought a special joy to his heart when one of his youth group kids felt comfortable enough to talk with him and share private thoughts or concerns. "I was just about to take a walk and stretch my legs. Care to join me?" His experience taught him it was easier to connect with kids outside the formality of the office.

"Sure."

He headed down a side road that led away from church rather than on Bridge Street, feeling that she would be more comfortable talking to him further away from public view on such a main thoroughfare.

"So what's up?" he asked.

"It's about the challenge you gave us the other night."

Paul believed the important thing about his challenge was that the decision of how to respond was going to be between each person and his or her maker. He didn't know if he'd ever hear the results of their choices and was thrilled Jodi wanted to share hers.

"Well, I think I figured out what to do with the money. I just don't think I can do it in person..."

They walked on together with Paul listening intently, occasionally nodding his head in agreement, offering suggestions when necessary. It didn't take long for them to work out the small doubts she had about her idea and soon the conversation turned to other things.

"It was really great that Andrew joined us for youth group. Do you think he'll be coming back?"

"I don't know. We're not really friends. We got paired up in a class project and our lives have kind of crossed a couple of times since then. He and his friends are not exactly the kind of people I hang out with. I was actually kind of surprised he agreed to come the other night."

Paul understood. Most people in town were familiar with kids like him, and not in a good way. By their actions, the dark clothes they wore, their piercings and tattoos they did little to dispel any possible false impressions.

"I can appreciate that. But God has put him in your path, Jodi. As a Christian, even if not as a friend, it's important to know how He wants you to respond to him. So far, I think you're on the right track." They discussed it further as they ambled down the road and decided a visit from Pastor Paul might go a long way. After all, God had placed the boy in his path as well.

The air stirred gently as Paul and his wife, Hannah, with their young son, Bobby, between them walked from the parsonage up Bridge Street to Whitmire's General Store. The sun was low in the sky, casting long shadows on the sidewalk in front of them, signaling the end of a full day of ministerial and hospital visits. It was a good night for fast food, Wheatfield Bridge style. It was still a little uncomfortable going to the store since Joe Whitmire fired Jim for upsetting a customer, but it was getting easier with each visit.

"What kind of pizza is tempting your taste buds tonight?" Hannah asked.

Bobby yelled, "Cheese, lots of cheese."

Paul smiled. "That sounds good. How about an extra-large with extra cheese?"

"Yes!" Bobby was on board with it.

"Sounds good, but you may be overestimating your ability to pack it away. It's just the three of us, remember? Jim isn't around to help finish it off; he's staying at Sean's house tonight."

As they got to the store, Jim's friend Denny was just leaving. "Hi Pastor Paul, Mrs. Hemphill."

They both greeted the boy and meant to go through the still open door when Denny stopped them. "Hey Pastor Paul, you know that money you gave us Sunday night?" Paul's heart grew light. It seemed he was about to find out again how the seed had grown. "Well, we had to twist it out of Tyler's hand, but the four of us – me, Tyler, Sean, and Jim all pooled our money and bought groceries for the Hanks family. We figured since Mr. Hanks was out of work they probably could use the help."

Inside, Paul was dancing on air. The boys, his troublesome Jim included, had done the right thing.

"The hard part was bringing the food to them. Sean thought we should just sneak in and leave it on their porch or something like that. Jim and I thought it would be better if we delivered it to them personally, you know, like you told us to do. So after a lot of stalling we finally got the nerve to go ring their doorbell. When we told them what we were doing and about your challenge, Mrs. Hanks started to cry. It was pretty awkward but it was cool too. They were so appreciative. They kept thanking us. They even said to tell you if that's the kind of thing you're preaching at church they might stop in one Sunday. Pretty cool, huh?"

"Yes, Denny, very cool."

That night, he didn't know whether it was the quality of the food or his good mood or both, but Paul thoroughly enjoyed his pizza.

He stood on a patch of dry dirt in front of the aged trailer where presumably grass had grown at some time in the distant past. Now there was just an indentation in the ground where others had stood before him. These initial calls were unpredictable. Sometimes the people were glad Paul stopped by. Others clearly felt pressured to allow him in, even if he'd called ahead. Those were the most awkward appointments and usually didn't last very long. This was the first time he got the chance to make a call on a visitor to youth group so he didn't know what to expect. It had the potential to go really bad or really good. He searched for a doorbell and finding none, he knocked. There was some rustling around inside and then the door opened with a rusty squeak revealing a stunned Andrew. He wore the familiar black tee shirt and jeans, no socks or shoes. Paul could see another young man standing beside him.

"Hi Andrew. Jodi Steele told me where you live. I hope you don't mind my stopping by? I would have called first but I don't have your number." Andrew shrugged his shoulders. "I just wanted to tell you again how glad we were that you joined us for youth group on Sunday."

The other boy's eyes went wide. His mouth hung open in disbelief as Andrew turned and backhanded him in the chest to get him to close it.

Paul broke the awkward silence. "May I come in? Or have I come at a bad time?"

Still in shock over the surprise visit, Andrew hesitated a bit and then said, "Sure, I guess," and let him through the door.

Paul took in the state of the living room without passing judgment. A sofa with tears and burn marks occupied one length of the room while dirty dishes lay scattered on the floor and atop a coffee table that had long since lost its luster. A tired looking easy chair sat angled toward an equally tired looking TV. A fist-sized hole in the paneling at about shoulder height could only be interpreted as a byproduct of someone's temper. This was Andrew's home, this was his life. Paul hoped he didn't feel too exposed by his visit.

Paul signaled to the couch, asking permission to sit, to which Andrew consented. He was much more comfortable in this kind of situation than the boys could ever be. He did his best to put them at ease, to try to break the ice. He offered his hand to the unfamiliar young man, a grip firm and confident. "Hi, I'm Pastor Paul. And you are?" The boy did not respond in kind. His hand hung limp in Paul's grasp.

"Eddie."

"Well Eddie, I'm real happy to meet you. Perhaps

Andrew told you we met at our church's youth group the other night?"

Eddie barely moved his head, but gave clear indication this was news to him.

"No? Well, ask him about it. Maybe you could join us as well this Sunday."

Despite Paul's best efforts, ten minutes after his arrival the boys did not appear any more at ease than when he first showed up at the door. Then he got an idea. "You know, we have a dusty old pool table in a back room at the church. What do you say we go rack up some balls?"

Andrew looked as if he had his doubts. He turned to Eddie and communicated in silence with only facial expressions after which they both shrugged their shoulders. Paul thought perhaps he'd piqued their interest, though neither one wanted to admit it. He decided to gamble. "That is, unless you've got something better to do." The boys sniggered confirming Paul's hunch. The 10 to 1 shot paid off.

On the way to the church, Pastor Paul explained the pool table had been rescued from a yard sale by a well-meaning parishioner and was holed up in a rarely used storage room off the parish hall. "I'm hesitant to bring it out into public view, lest someone get the idea I'm converting the church into a pool hall." The boys helped Paul move aside boxes and rows of chairs to access the table and found it wasn't in bad shape.

"Eight ball," Eddie said to Andrew. The boys

racked up the balls, found a couple of cues and chalked the ends, ignoring Paul's presence. Andrew broke the formation, sinking two balls in the process. His second shot sunk another but his third failed to pocket anything. Eddie sunk one ball then missed on the next shot. As Andrew took aim again, he noticed Paul beyond the tip of his cue leaning on the wall wearing a big grin. "What are you smiling about?"

"Oh, I was just wondering what some of the folks from the congregation would think if they saw you guys shooting pool in their church. That's all."

"Isn't that what it's here for?"

"Actually, it's here because no one had the heart to tell Eustace Caldwell they believed his gift to the church was inappropriate. Some of the more prim and proper folks are a little cautious when it comes to pool tables. You see, back in the day, they got a very bad reputation from a very good movie. And I'm afraid the stereotype has stuck."

"Can you shoot?"

Paul chuckled. "Uh, no. I'm more of an intellectual than a pool shark. You may not think so at first glance, but I am dynamite at Bible Bingo."

The boys laughed. They tried to teach him to play pool but without much success. He was as bad as he said, and the boys had a good time teasing him about it. Paul found he enjoyed being with the kids, and they didn't seem to mind him too much either.

At Paul's invitation, Andrew and Eddie returned

the following afternoon. The day after that they stopped in with a couple of other friends. The games were getting to be a regular thing.

The following Sunday Andrew did not return for a second youth group meeting. When Paul asked him about it, he indicated he wasn't comfortable with the core group.

"No offense, Pastor Paul, but they're not my type."

Just as with Jodi, he understood. Andrew and his friends believed they were worlds apart from the youth group regulars. Paul wished they understood how similar they actually were. Despite their outward differences – gothic black non-conformists vs. designer jean churchgoers – under all that keeps them separate, they shared the same fears and doubts. Paul felt the Spirit moving him to reach out to both groups.

"I have a church commitment that will soon be taking up my afternoons and we won't be able to play as much. So how about this: why don't you and your friends come by on say Thursday nights? We can still shoot pool and maybe we can even have some chat time." As before, the guys had nothing better to do, so they agreed and the Thursday night get-togethers became a weekly thing. Paul was pleased and thought God was probably smiling too.

The time Paul spent befriending Andrew and his buddies did not go unnoticed by Ellen Steele who always seemed to find one reason or another to be in and out of the church. Volunteers such as her were a blessing to the ministry, but the potential for gossip because of it was also great. So he wasn't surprised when he received that first phone call. What did shock him was the number of calls and visits that followed.

Some were passive in nature. "They certainly are a rough looking bunch of kids, but if you think it's the right thing to do..." Others more passive aggressive, "Do you really think we should be letting 'those kinds of boys' into our church?" Still others were just outright aggressive. "If you let those hoodlums run amuck in our church we're going to have to bring it up at the next Pastoral Relations Committee meeting – and it won't be a pleasant discussion." Paul grew tired of defending what he knew to be his responsibility - to evangelize to "all God's children," stressing the all. He was reaching them. Maybe they looked a little different and maybe they weren't the cream of the crop, but thanks to this new open door, those kids knew they were welcome in God's house. Above all else, for some it was the first time they'd ever heard that God loves them. Truly, He was blessing this ministry.

He had been invited to an emergency meeting of the Building and Decorations Committee. It felt more like an ambush, he on one side of the crowded room and a mob on the other.

"There's only one of you. How will you be able to

keep an eye out on every one of them? I mean, what if they bring drugs into the church?" Frannie asked.

"Or what if they break something," Betty said. "Many of the items in this church were donated out of the generosity of its members, people who appreciate and know how to take care of things. We have to protect our building and its contents."

"Betty's right, you can't be everywhere at once. Some kids might slip away and get into trouble in other parts of the building."

"No one is going to desecrate the Sanctuary, Ellen!" Paul couldn't read Ellen Steele's mind but he had a good idea of what lay behind her statement. Her conservatism and homage to all things prim and proper were familiar to all who knew her. He did his best to refrain from anger.

"Please. Look beyond the clothes. Look beyond the spikes and piercings. What you have is a bunch of kids with nowhere else to go. No one wants them. They're not athletes, they have no organized activities. They don't belong to academic clubs or the scouts. These are the kids society has given up on, the ones even our own children refer to as 'losers.' We can't turn them away and at the same time call ourselves Christian. How can you sit there and pass judgment on someone you've never taken the time or made the effort to know?" Paul knew he had crossed a line on that last statement. "I'm sorry. Please excuse me I need some fresh air." He walked into the night and prayed, "Father, help them to see."

The following Sunday Pastor Paul Hemphill stood in the pulpit to face his congregation, some of whom were not very pleased with him at that moment. He held a hand-written letter on lined paper produced in a child-like scrawl. He wasn't trying to prove anything or even to use its content to support his cause. The Spirit worked hard convincing him to read it as part of the Worship Service, ultimately breaking through Paul's stubbornness. He began. "I have a letter here that I have been moved to share with you. I ask for your time and indulgence. It reads:

Dear Pastor Paul,

This week I got a present in the mail. It was a book called the Extreme Teen Bible. I'm pretty sure it was from some one in your church. No one else I know would ever think of giving me a present, let a lone a bible. I want you to know I sat write down and started reading it even though some of the words are kind of tuff. It says the same thing you say. God loves me. I like that.

I started to think about that envelope you gave me the time I came to youth group. How you gave us all money and said we should be a blessing to other's with the gifts God gives us. I still have mine. I didn't no what to do with it. Now I do. I'm

giving it to you for your church. It's not to
payback for the bible. Your church is being
nice to me and my friends so I want to be
nice back to them so they can keep doing
things for God because it really maters.
Anyway, thanks for listening.
Andrew

Paul looked up and saw that Jodi was wiping her eyes with a tissue. Her seed had taken root. He cleared his throat. "Thirty dollars was enclosed in the letter. The same amount he received when I challenged the youth to either keep the money or use it to be a blessing to someone else.

"My friends, God is at work here."

That Thursday night, Andrew and his friends and even some others who'd heard about the church that invites kids to hang out there, gathered in the back room with the pool table. Pastor Paul Hemphill smiled a broad grin as he walked around introducing everyone to the person who showed up to volunteer and help keep the doors open for their Thursday Fun Night, as they had started to call it.

"Andrew," he said. "I'd like you to meet my good friend, Ellen Steele."

JONI VANNEST

16
INTO DARK CORNERS

"Mrs. Boudreau, you're going to have to trim back some of these vines if you want me to continue delivering mail to you." Lindy Robertson sighed. She didn't want to be short tempered with her customer, but she also didn't want to dig through flowers to deliver mail. On two other occasions she had spoken to Helen Boudreau about the vines covering the mailbox that made it hard for her to do her job efficiently. She really wasn't in the mood to deal with this, not today. Of course, in the greater scheme of things Helen's vines were only a small nuisance. But when all those little inconveniences of life got together they added up, piling onto the mood she found herself in already, a mood that for no other reason than "because" was affecting her relationship with those whom she came into contact.

Helen ran her open palm alongside one of the flowers like a geriatric Vanna White. "Oh, but the morning glories are so beautiful; they're like colorful smiles to welcome guests."

"Well, if you don't cut them back soon they won't be welcoming any more mail. The Post Office has its rules, including clear access for delivery. Sorry." Lindy handed the letters and circulars to Helen who had been standing near the curb when she pulled up.

"You young people just don't take time to appreciate the little things in life."

"Actually Helen, right now it's the little things that are causing me more grief than I care to think about."

"Aw honey, boy trouble again?"

"Nah, just life."

"Well, come by one day after work. We can have some girl time and see if we can't fix what's ailing you."

It was the same offer every time they spoke. Helen was a lonely woman who seemed to relish when Lindy stopped to chat. She suspected it was because it wasn't just a one sided conversation, such as those the woman had with her cat or dead husband. At least a couple of times a week in good weather she met Lindy at the curb just for the company. Lindy would linger to talk for a moment or two then be on her way again, but even that seemed to be enough for Helen. "Who knows, maybe I will come by one of these days Helen, maybe I will." She gave a brief wave and started to pull slowly away toward the next mailbox knowing she never would. Somewhere behind the mail truck a song bird sang a sweet tune. In her rearview mirror Lindy saw the elderly woman look up to answer the bird. Helen found friends wherever she could.

Continuing on her route, Lindy thought about her attitude and wished it could simply be fixed with a little girl time. Here she was 25, with her whole life ahead of her and she couldn't see past the dreariness of today. It was the same thing day in and day out: get up, go to work, go home and get up the next day to do it all over again. Now and again she'd toss in some social activity to break up the monotony, but for the most part her life was predictable and boring. The bright future she'd been promised through her school years never quite materialized, at least not for her. She watched as many of her classmates went off to college or married and had children. Others moved away. Some joined the military. She, on the other hand, found herself in the sad position of spinning her wheels in a sleepy town about the size of a postage stamp. Her inner self screamed for something different; yet here she remained. "Ugh!" she exclaimed, while slamming the door on the Hemphill's mailbox and driving on.

Her foul mood stuck with her as she finished the route, looping through the town's side streets and country roads, eventually winding her way back to the point of origin at the Post Office. Her father, who also happened to be her boss, was standing on the loading dock as she pulled up. Although she had been working at the post office for over a year now, her father still enjoyed meeting her on the dock each day. He was thrilled to have his daughter working with him and he let her know it. A few heads turned upon her being hired; some believed nepotism didn't belong in civil service. But she scored well on the exam and had since worked hard to prove herself a good and reliable worker. The other employees noticed and came around.

"There she is, a sight for sore eyes."

"Hey Dad." Her voice was dull and lifeless, like her mood.

Lindy and her father unloaded the empty mail trays from the vehicle, dropping them with a loud crash as they fell in and nestled with the others already stacked on the deck.

"So, how'd it go today?"

She could sense him trying to find the source of her sour disposition.

"Did the McKenna's dog chase you again?"

"No, but if he did I probably would have run over him." Sarcasm was Lindy's trademark when we she was feeling down, which lately was more common than not.

Her father tapped her shoulder to get her attention and stand still. "Hey, what did the angry lobsterman say to the loud lobsterman?"

She saw it coming like a steamroller - he always used stupid jokes to try to cheer her up when she was down. She went along with him anyway. "I don't know, Dad, what did the angry lobsterman say to the loud lobsterman?"

"Shut your trap. Get it? Huh?"

She rolled her eyes and tried to suppress a smile. She wasn't ready to be cheerful. "Your jokes get worse as you get older, you know."

"Really? I'm finally getting it right!"

Lindy spent the last hour of the workday slipping sales flyers into circular packets being prepared for the next day's deliveries. It always helped when they could get a jump on the work. The advertisement on the stack in front of her showed a white sandy beach with palm trees and a woman sunbathing alone near the surf. The tag line read: Tropical paradise can be yours! Sure, thought Lindy. For a hefty sum. Then she stopped and really looked at the flyer. In that moment she realized it wasn't the cost of the trip or the beautiful model bronzing herself in the sun that disturbed her so. It was the very fact that this woman was able to go, able to leave wherever it was she came from to do what made her happy. The woman in the ad had her freedom. Lindy wanted it too.

"Lindy, will you stir the sauce for me, please?" Her mother looked harried as she slathered garlic butter on a loaf of Italian bread. "I'm going to need a little help here in the kitchen if I'm going to make it to my meeting on time tonight."

"So of course that means I have to help. Well, what if I had plans for this evening? I'm allowed to have a life too, you know. Why can't Dad help?"

"Lindy Robertson, what has gotten into you?" Her mother stopped what she was doing to face her daughter. An outburst like that was unusual. Lindy wasn't surprised her mother gave it her full attention.

"This... all of it!" Lindy said, waving the sauce ladle like a wand in front of her, indicating the entire room and beyond. "Is this all there is – work, eat, sleep and pay bills?"

"It's life, Lindy, and it suited us well all these years - kept food on the table and a roof over our heads."

"Maybe it was ok for you, but I'm tired of it. I want more out of life than the daily grind – more than slaving away for 51 weeks a year just to make it to that one week the Post Office has generously set aside for me."

"You know your Dad put a lot on the line hiring you. You should be grateful for such a good job, and one with benefits. Not everyone your age is lucky enough to have that."

Lindy didn't think her mother went out of her way to inflict guilt on her only child, it just seemed to come naturally. "I know and I appreciate it, but it's not enough, not for me."

Guilt didn't work, so her mother moved on to logic. "Society has been running just fine for some time now thanks to the work ethic. Those who disagree are sleeping under bridges. Besides, if you wanted something more you should have gone off to college when you had the opportunity."

"That's just the thing, there has to be something more than this. Even if I did go to college it only would have delayed the inevitable, 9 to 5 would have caught up eventually. Look at me, I'm stuck in a rut at the ripe old age of 25. I can't do this for another 50 years. I want control of my own life, I want my freedom."

Her mother paused for a moment leaving the air between them full of potential responses until in a less confrontational tone she said, "Even freedom isn't free."

Lindy didn't stay in the kitchen long enough to allow that thought settle in. Instead, she walked out the door letting it slam behind her.

The truck jerked forward as Lindy put the vehicle into gear. She decided that driving a standard transmission was an art form she had yet to master. Her inefficiencies caused the tires to spin out pebbles on the road as she drove on to the next mailbox in Bay Cove, a labyrinth-like development of questionable mobile homes. Up ahead she saw the Steiff boy. They occasionally reached his family's mailbox at the same time, she on her route and he walking home from summer school, reminding her again of how routine and mundane her life was – predictable as the weather.

Observing the boy as she did, it always seemed to her as if his gait propelled him forward without purpose, as one who was being moved along by life and not of his own doing. She could relate. However, in recent weeks she saw a change in him - a small, yet noticeable change - an attitude adjustment more or less. Most evident, was his traditional black attire having given way to browns and blues. "Hi," she said handing mail off to him.

A disappointing, "Hey," was all she got in return.

Well, I could be wrong about that change, she thought as she put the car back in gear. Then she heard a loud, "Thanks!" She looked in her rearview mirror and saw he had raised his hand in appreciation and goodbye. Or I could be right.

Lindy continued to wind her way through the trailer park. The homes in varying states of disrepair intensified her depression, although it didn't take much to do that. Small rusted buildings, many surrounded by rusting metal fences looked to her like prisons. Her own desire for freedom led her to wonder if the people who lived here felt much the same as she did – trapped with no way out. She turned the radio on to drown out her thoughts and tried to move her eyes only from one mailbox to the next without taking in the scenery.

It was summer and the air was dry and pleasant with a soft breeze. It was days like this when being a letter carrier had its perks. As she approached the center of town, her negative thoughts began to fade as she anticipated an enjoyable stroll around the green delivering mail on the walking portion of her route. She parked the vehicle in her usual spot, got out and stretched the idleness out of her legs before hitting the pavement. A faint hint of roses from the flower garden surrounding a war memorial drifted on the air. The heartbeat of Wheatfield Bridge pulsed on the green. Small specialty shops and the town administrative building wrapped around the grassy center, drawing foot traffic to the area. A white gazebo in the center sported a semi-circle of flags around its perimeter. Americana on display.

It was almost a sure thing Lindy would run into someone she knew along the way, other than her customers. Wheatfield Bridge was just that sort of place – small enough to know most everyone and small enough that just about everyone knew you as well. It wasn't long before she heard her name.

"Lindy, Lindy!"

Kenny Roberts was crossing the street. He and Lindy had a history almost two decades long, beginning in Miss Thomas' kindergarten class where the first thing they learned was that students were grouped alphabetically. So it was that Kenny Roberts and Lindy Robertson remained in close proximity throughout their elementary school education. In high school, Dianne Rock joined the alpha-social club when she moved to town in their sophomore year. It wasn't long before Dianne and Kenny were an item and, as it sometimes happens, love eventually grew from high school sweethearts to man and wife. The three were friends to this day.

"Hey Kenny. I don't often see you in the middle of

a workday. Did they let you out of your cubicle for good behavior?"

"I had to run an errand, but I'm glad I bumped into you. I was thinking about our discussion the other night."

After the sauce incident with her mother, Lindy walked out of the house and drove around aimlessly for about an hour, finally ending up at Kenny and Dianne's apartment where she unloaded her frustrations on the two unsuspecting souls. Being loyal friends they listened carefully, bobbing and nodding in all the appropriate places, although Lindy didn't think they really understood the depth of her angst.

"Yeah, about that... I really appreciate you guys hearing me out and letting me go on like that. I must have sounded like some spoiled brat or something."

"Well, the thought did cross my mind. But hey, that's what friends are for, right?"

Lindy chuckled, mildly embarrassed, and shoved his shoulder. "That's one of the things I love about you Kenny – honest to a fault."

"Anyway, like I said, Dianne and I were thinking about your, uh, 'unrest' shall we say, and while we were talking about it a thought came to mind. Actually, it was a scripture. I kind of thought it was worth mentioning to you."

"Really?" Lindy fought the urge to roll her eyes at the mention of scripture. She was a regular churchgoer, had been for years. She believed in God, even answered an alter call back in her youth group days, but she didn't take her faith to the extremes they did. In the Roberts' home God took part in all aspects of their lives. They prayed together, did Bible studies, looked for God's will in everything they undertook, as well as being very active in the church. The trio's friendship continued not because of their religious similarities but in spite of their differences.

"Yes. It's from Matthew 6, verses 33 and 34: 'But seek first His kingdom and His righteousness; and all these things shall be added to you. Therefore do not be anxious for tomorrow; for tomorrow will care for itself. Each day has enough trouble of its own.' Here, I even wrote it down on a piece of paper for you and stuck it in my wallet. I figured I'd run into you at some point and give it to you." His outstretched hand looked strong and firm, not unlike the rest of his countenance. Even these few years out of high school and the corporate takeover of his life had not erased his athlete's build.

"Aw, that's really sweet of you." She half choked on the words while taking the paper, looking at the writing on it. Then looking up she was moved by the sincerity she saw in his eyes. Kenny and Dianne may be on the fanatical side, but they were her closest and dearest friends. "Thank you," she said and really meant it.

"Well listen I, uh..."

"Yeah, me too. You know what they say, 'The mail

must go through.'"

Lindy gave him a quick hug and for the first time was conscious, as a woman, of the masculine feel of his body against hers. It felt nice, sturdy, secure. The smell of his cologne filled her nostrils making her dizzy with sudden desire. She wanted to linger in his arms, escape to a place where passion ruled, not reality. In the end reality won. She pulled apart from him, confused. After all she'd hugged Kenny a thousand times before and never experienced anything like this. What is wrong with me? Did he even notice? Ugh, I'm such a loser. She quickly regained her composure and offered a hesitant smile. "Uh, say hi to Dianne for me."

"Will do."

She watched Kenny head off down the sidewalk, hopefully blissfully unaware of her inappropriate thoughts.

Lindy took a couple of deep breaths in an effort to decompress after the awkward moment. I think I'm losing my mind. In the midst of the anguish that had been taking over her life, that particular issue had never been part of it. Things were confusing enough right now without adding the stress of a relationship to the unsettled mixture, especially an inappropriate one.

She vaguely became conscious again of the paper in her hand. She read the scripture then folded and tucked it in her uniform pocket. Seek You first, eh? The thought never crossed her mind. Even after hearing and then reading it, the idea was still not something she felt compelled to put into practice. God was not first in her life, never was and there were no plans for that to change. Although somewhere in the back of her mind, especially after what just happened with Kenny, she knew something had to give.

"Good afternoon, Caroline." Lindy had entered The Village Toy Shoppe and handed the proprietor her mail.

"Right on time."

Caroline was a middle-aged woman who held no claim on vanity. Her hair was graying without the mask of artificial color and she wore half-glasses to read and mark price tags. A flowery cotton dress topped with a white apron adorned her somewhat plump figure, while a generous smile rounded out her appearance, which to Lindy greatly resembled none other than the immortal Mother Goose. Caroline Neddick was well suited to her profession.

"So how are things in Toyland?" Lindy teased, trying to raise her own spirits.

"Oh, a little slow this time of year. Things will pick up again in the fall, that's the way this business goes. Other than the occasional birthday present, parents don't think too much about buying toys until the holidays are just around the corner.

"Say, do you have a moment? I need help with something."

Lindy knew she shouldn't stop, she had a

schedule to keep. Caroline must have seen her hesitation.

"It won't take but a minute."

Lindy gave a quick peak at her watch and decided she could spare some time, but not much. "Sure, as long as it's brief."

The shopkeeper motioned for Lindy to walk to the storeroom with her. "I was thinking of having a Christmas in July sale to help get rid of some of the slower moving items. Thought I'd put up a tree to advertise. But wouldn't you know it the young boy I had helping me last year put it up where I can't reach. If you could help me get it down, I'd really appreciate it."

Lindy saw the elongated box high on the top shelf in the back room. What was that kid thinking? "Guess he wanted to have a little job security for when the season rolled around again, huh?"

"I suppose that must be it," Caroline agreed.

The two women stood on separate stepladders and grasped firmly on either side of the box. A cloud of dust burst into the air as they took it down from the shelf and laid it on the floor, causing Lindy to cough. She waved her hand in front of her face to clear the immediate area of the dirty fog.

"Thank you so much Lindy. I couldn't have done it without your help."

"Glad to be of service. Listen, you take care and I'll see you tomorrow." Lindy blinked as she walked into the bright sunlight, a smile on her face where there wasn't one before.

Lindy was slow to awaken. The smell of coffee wafting from the kitchen earlier hadn't been enough inspiration to get up. The clock on the nightstand flashed 10:34 in bold white numbers. By this time her parents would be at church. She opted out this week. At least that was one ride on the merry-go-round she didn't have to oblige. The window was open but the room was steamy, the cool night air having already moved on. The forecasted heat wave had arrived.

Lindy slid out of bed and dragged herself to the bathroom. She was afraid to look in the mirror, afraid she wouldn't recognize the reflection. Somehow she'd changed; life changed, it had no purpose. Its undelivered promises taunted her, turning her into someone she didn't like anymore. She tried to put her finger on what was missing, what had gone wrong, but nothing stood out. She only knew the facts: she was tired of living by the rules and was tired of responsibility. No one warned her life was simply jumping from one hamster wheel to another. She needed challenge, needed to feel alive. It was time to be in charge of her own destiny and break away before she lost herself forever. She raised her eyes, looking hard in the mirror. It was time to let the world know Lindy Robertson was here.

It was time to do the laundry. Reality bit her in

the leg. Again.

Lindy shuffled back into her bedroom and grabbed some clothes out of her hamper. She heard a jingle of coins and reached into a pocket she forgot to empty, dumping the contents, money and a folded piece of paper, on her dresser. She remembered Kenny's note. She opened the paper and once again looked at the scripture he wrote out for her, "But seek first His kingdom and His righteousness; and all these things shall be added to you." She stood there and thought about it for a minute, her mind racing with random thoughts. Yeah, as if I need one more person telling me what to do. Besides, what does it mean anyway? Seek Him first and I'll get everything I want? Like that's gonna happen! She let her mind dwell on that idea for a second. Actually... that... kind of has potential... Yeah, whatever. She picked up the laundry and left the room.

She could hear the water running into the washing machine as she poured herself a cup of coffee. Lindy picked up the remote and clicked on the TV, drowning out the sound of responsibility. She plopped down in a chair and raised the mug to her lips. The bitter-smooth flavor rolled over her tongue, slightly burning her throat. A thin, "Ahh" escaped from her lips as the drink worked its magic.

A Sunday morning preacher standing on the stage of a large auditorium filled the television screen. The faces of his captivated audience displayed a mixture of awe and guilt.

"Dear Ones," he said in a sincere voice mustered for the occasion. His southern drawl seemed almost cliché to her. "Has darkness crept into your life? Does it all seem for naught? I'm here to tell you God doesn't want you to live that way. God wants you to prosper in this life; He wants you to be happy and fulfilled. And, Dear Ones, if you are not reaching your greatest potential then you need to move over and let God shower you with his many blessings.

"Do you say to yourself, 'Why can't I do this, or why don't I have that?' Well, my friends, I can tell you why your lives are not filled with the joys and blessings of your maker. You need to turn these things over to God. Give it to Him and He will bless you tenfold. And right here in my hand is the means by which He will show you how to do just that."

Lindy looked closely; she wanted to believe his words offered hope. She expected to see the man who was dressed in a tailored suit and blow-dried hair with just a touch of gel hold out a Bible as the way to his Truth. Instead, he held up a thick hardcover book entitled, A Generous God, with his own picture on the book jacket. "For just a small love offering of $29.99 you can learn the secrets to living the blessed life God intends you to have."

The show was no better than a three-ring circus. She could just about hear the ringmaster. "That's right folks. Step right this way and get all the desires of your heart."

"Ugh! You disgust me!" She tossed a balled up napkin at the TV. It dawned on her then that her earlier thoughts on the scripture from Kenny were childish. God didn't offer cheap magic tricks. Seeing that very idea espoused by a swindling preacher, enlightened her as to how wrong she had been. Ok, so I guess that's not what it meant. But I don't care anyway. It's just Kenny and Dianne's fundamental fanaticism at work on me... "I need to get a life." She clicked off the preacher, leaving his concocted enriching gospel behind.

Monday morning arrived like every other. The sun arose, the coffee brewed, commuters spun their tires anew on the never-ending hamster wheel. Lindy sat in her truck at the intersection of Brewster Street and High Lane Road. The people who lived on Brewster Street would be expecting their bills and junk mail right about this time, just as they do every weekday. And every other Monday at this time she would put the car in first gear, release the clutch while pressing on the gas pedal and drive over High Lane Road to continue her route on Brewster. But this wasn't every other Monday. In the quiet of the truck, High Lane Road called her name, called her over the hill and out of town, away from the drudgery of her life. It spoke quietly with a lusty voice, begging, "Come this way." She put the truck in first and moved into the intersection, focusing her eyes on the hill and road beyond, longing to answer the call.

She didn't hear the car. It came around the bend on the lower stretch of High Lane Road, showing up in the periphery of her vision as she sat in the intersection. Lindy turned to see a rusted black sedan speeding toward her. Her mind froze, paralyzed in the moment, her actions purely instinct, not decisive. She engaged the clutch, thrust the shift into third gear bypassing second, and floored the accelerator. And prayed. The engine both roared and hesitated then gained momentum, propelling the car through the intersection and across High Lane Road to safety. Once out of danger, instinct released its command of the situation, turning authority back over to Lindy who, in a state of panic, immediately pulled her foot off the gas. The truck lost speed and sputtered to an abrupt stop. She was vaguely aware of the car's horn blaring as it drove up over the hill. Lindy's chest rose and fell in great waves as her body sought to calm itself. Her heart raced, she trembled uncontrollably and ultimately succumbed to the tears that overtook her - tears of trepidation, tears of indecision. The lack of traffic on secondary streets such as Brewster allowed the mail truck to remain there in the road where it stopped until Lindy was able to compose herself and drive on to continue her deliveries. Thus it was, later that day, she entered Whitmire's General Store in a somber mood.

Joe, the proprietor, was behind the counter. He was standing with his head tilted up toward a radio placed on a shelf and appeared to be listening to something with great interest.

"Hey, Joe," she said in a noncommittal voice. He waved his hand downward as if to quiet her.

"O-kay," she whispered to herself, taken aback by the normally affable Joe's strange greeting. Lindy laid the mail on the counter and started to leave, then changed her mind, intrigued to know what had captured his attention so. She placed her mail pouch on the counter and leaned across so she could hear as well.

"...8.9 on the Richter scale. According to the US Geological Survey, the quake's epicenter was below the Indian Ocean about 220 miles east of Sri Lanka. Fears of a tsunami such as occurred in the aftermath of a similar strength earthquake off the coast of Sumatra in 2004 are prompting mass evacuations in areas still struggling to rebuild after the devastation of that disaster almost 3½ years ago. Government officials have ordered..."

Lindy thought back to that horrible day. She remembered the images broadcast on CNN and other stations of the terrible destruction wrought by those merciless waves. She recalled sitting on the couch watching scenes of carnage while being dry and safe under the warmth of her grandmother's quilt. Her own comfort and the illuminated Christmas tree in the corner of the room made a mockery of the unfolding tragedy half a planet away with its unthinkable stories of death and survival.

"Oh no, not again," she said. "Not again." Joe looked at her through moist eyes. Her appointed rounds would have to wait; Lindy stayed to hear the broadcast. It brought back memories of the news reports after the events of 2004 in Southeast Asia. The death toll was incomprehensibly staggering, so many lives lost, so many lives shattered. She was most touched by those selfless individuals who left the safety and security of their homes to tend to those who could not do for themselves. They brought clean water, medical supplies, food and clothing, nursed the sick and wounded, rescued orphans and the displaced and homeless - angels without wings doing the work of God.

It was then she understood the meaning of the scripture.

*   *   *

"What can I get you to drink?" the flight attendant inquired of Lindy.

"Nothing, thank you." She looked out the tiny window beside her seat on the 737. It was a strange sensation to be looking at the wrong side of the clouds. The sun caressing them from above cast a dazzling aura across the billowy horizon like a haze, an image that would be forever burned in her memory. Lindy suddenly felt the urge to make sure she hadn't lost her passport and rummaged through her bag until she found it, still waiting to be stamped when she landed on foreign soil.

She smiled.

It was so hard to sympathize with her parents earlier when they saw her off at the airport. The tears in their eyes sprung from a mixture of concern and pride. She was sure her own face could only express wonder and excitement at what she was about to do. Of course she would miss them and the comforts of home, but that's what it was all about. She smiled again, finally glad for what tomorrow would bring.

She closed her eyes and tried to picture her parents finding the letter she left, perhaps that very evening after they got home from the airport. They might have found themselves drawn to her empty room. Leaning on the pillow where her teddy bear had always waited each day for her return would have been an envelope simply addressed, For You. Her father would have opened the letter and read it aloud to his mother.

> *Dear Mom and Dad:*
> *Some things are just easier said in a letter, so here goes...*
> *First of all, thank you. Thank you for all the love and patience you've shown me over the years, especially in the months leading up to my decision to be a disaster relief volunteer. I know there have been times when my attitude must have been very trying. For those occasions I apologize and ask your forgiveness.*

I feel like I've grown up quite a bit in the last few months, ever since Kenny shared that verse with me, Matthew 6:33. "Seek ye first the kingdom of God and His righteousness, then all these things shall be added unto you." Whoever thought I'd ever be so affected by scripture? Certainly not me. I think I've spent the better part of my life seeking my own way, a way that was selfish and self-satisfying, putting my happiness above all else and, even then, I never found it. I saw this preacher guy on TV one day and he basically said I needed to seek God first and He'd give me everything I wanted. That wasn't right either. God isn't big on material rewards, He's more into the eternal, if you know what I mean.

I bless the day I finally listened to what God was saying in that verse - be about the business of God's work and He'll take care of the rest. I had been about my own business, not His, seeking material rewards not spiritual ones, the ones that really matter. At that point I was reminded of missionaries and others who put their own needs aside and go out into the poorest parts of the world to do good things. They have hard lives, but gratifying ones. Sure, I was a good person, I did good things, but that wasn't enough. There was no satisfaction in my life because it had no purpose. Until then I was convinced the only way I'd be content was when I was free from responsibility, but now I understand it is only when we are responsible to something that our lives really have purpose. I'm finally glad for what tomorrow will bring.

So Mom and Dad, by the grace of God this selfish life has been turned around. Please pray for me in this time we are apart, and I will for you.

With All My Love,
Lindy

Centered on the bottom of the page she had scrawled a message, as if it was a footer on letterhead, to be shared over and over again with each new correspondence.

I will bear witness to God like a mirror, reflecting Light into dark corners.

Lindy opened her eyes and peered out the window. She must have been asleep for some time, for through the glass of the airplane window the sun was rising. Tomorrow had arrived.

17
PATRIOT WOODS

As far as summers go, this one had been long and hot, quite out of the ordinary for New England whose pleasant summer days and cool summer nights are things of legend and great envy. This year was different. It was August and the dog days were howling with no sign of letting up.

"Whose idea was it to do this in the park anyway?" Hannah asked, fanning herself with a paper plate. "At least if we'd gone to the restaurant for Lunch Club like we've always done it would have been air conditioned." The women had a standing date at the Country Porch Restaurant the first Sunday of every month for a little down time and grown-up conversation.

"Ellen, I think you're to blame for this one." Kelly flapped her blouse in and out a couple of times trying to get a breeze of her own. She had pulled her hair up in a ponytail earlier in an attempt to stay cool but it didn't provide any relief from the unrelenting heat.

"Hey, I only made the suggestion, we all voted on it. Besides," Ellen said, spreading her arms and waving them to indicate the vastness of the great outdoors, "This is what summer is about - communing with nature, enjoying fresh air." She added an ironic, "Even if it is 90 degrees in the shade."

"Hmmm," Kelly groaned. "A picnic in the woods sounded great in theory. I just wasn't expecting a steam bath along with my potato salad." She fluffed her blouse a few more times. "Karen, you'll have to forgive us, we're normally a much livelier group, and a lot less whiney." This was the first time Karen Tanner had joined the women for their monthly lunch date, joining them at Kelly's invitation. Karen was currently that special someone in her father's life, so Kelly thought it would be a great opportunity to get to know her better, outside of her father's eye and earshot. Karen was considerably younger than her father, which added a layer of tension to the already uncomfortable situation of watching someone take her mother's place in her father's heart. She hoped that by getting to know Karen better she would feel more at ease with their relationship, but the heat was putting a damper on her plan for a fun time together.

Karen lifted her hair off her neck and let it drop back down. "I really appreciate you asking me to come along, considering." She raised her eyebrows and shrugged her shoulders, apparently understanding Kelly's feelings. "Besides, being pretty new in town, I take all the opportunities I can to get to know people. Even sweaty ones." She smiled at the women. Kelly was glad she was so agreeable.

A tiny stream of water dripped from an ice cube in Kelly's cup, reducing its size just enough to cause it to slip and hit another cube below. The clink of the transaction prompted her to lift the cup and move it across her forehead several times, giving her a moment's reprieve from the heat.

They were gathered around a picnic table at Patriot Woods on a grassy spot not far from the parking lot, their stomachs full from cold fried chicken, salads and fruit. They had kicked back to relax, waiting for motivation to do something more than sweat.

Kelly took a big breath and sighed. "So, are we going to do this thing or not?" She stood, wiped some crumbs from her lap and pulled the legs of her shorts out from where they had stuck to her thighs while sitting. She didn't really want to go for the hike but she also didn't want to make it seem as if she'd invited Karen on false pretenses. She promised her a picnic and a hike, so that's what she was going to get. Even if it kills me.

"I'm game." Hannah Hemphill was always up for doing things with her friends, even on the spur of the moment. She was a volunteer, the type of person whose spring-loaded arm raised along with a shout of, "I'll help," at the first inkling of someone in need. Committee work was in her blood; and because her husband was pastor of the Wheatfield Bridge Congregational Church, she got to volunteer to her heart's content. So it was no surprise that she was the first to follow in line behind Kelly in tackling the hike they had planned. "I can't believe I'm going to be dragged on a death march through the woods, but I'm game." Hannah sometimes allowed her flair for the dramatic to show. It was promptly countered by Ellen Steele's practicality.

"If you're complaining before we've even started, it's going to be a long afternoon. Perhaps we should rethink this."

Karen stood. "I'm with them. If we're going to go, let's just do it." Ellen, outnumbered, reluctantly agreed and together they headed off to find the trailhead to Beaver Falls.

"It's the blue arrow trail," Ellen said, though they were all capable of seeing for themselves on the map of the park before them. The map itself, carved in wood and situated on posts, outlined and color-coded each trail individually. Kelly wondered how she got herself roped into this. Her idea of communing with nature was more akin to laying on a sandy beach under a sun umbrella reading a good book and tossing back a cold drink with a little paper parasol. Woods, bugs and critters were not part of that fantasy.

"Five miles, round trip. That shouldn't be too bad," said Karen.

Hannah placed her hand on Karen's shoulder and spoke as one with wisdom of the ages. "You may regret those words before the day is out."

The first ten minutes of the hike were comfortable going in spite of the heat. The leafy canopy of maples and oaks shielded them from the burning sun, making the going easier than it would have been without it. The trail led them past ancient stone fences deteriorated with age that had once delineated the beginning and ending of men's lands. Heavy forest now stood in those formerly plowed fields. An old cemetery hidden deep in the woods looked out of place. No church, not even a road was its companion. Headstones tilted by the seasons bore the names of those long gone. Kelly passed it with reverence and a touch of fear.

"Now this is better," Karen announced as they headed up an incline, "sweating for a good cause."

Ellen took a bandana from her pocket, doused it with water from a Nalgene bottle then wiped her face and neck with it. In similar fashion, Kelly poured some of her drinking water over her head and felt its cool refreshing flow run down her hair causing it to cling in wet strands against her neck. Wasting her drinking water like that failed to register as a mistake before it was too late. And so it was they all diminished their drinking water supplies quicker than expected.

The trail gradually changed from a small incline to a much steeper hill filled with unsteady rocks and islands of smooth dirt created by runoff in heavy rains.

"So Karen," Hannah said with enthusiasm Kelly couldn't fathom could be found in this heat. "Kelly tells us that Joe wants you to bring the old general store into the 21st century. That's quite a task."

Karen looked at Kelly with questioning eyes, to which Kelly replied, "Well, it's not exactly a tale out of school."

"Actually," Karen said, "I'm only helping him. I give him ideas and if he likes them we try to implement them."

"She's being modest. Dad has really come to rely on Karen's fine-tuned business sense. And everyone can see the difference it makes in the store." Karen blushed, making her face redder than it already was from exertion, but Kelly believed in giving credit where credit was due. The store had seen a small, yet perceptible increase in sales since they began working together.

By this time, Kelly, who was leading the expedition, became aware the blue arrows were fewer in number and further apart and she did not like it. Patriot Woods was a rustic park, a dense forest with a handful of hiking paths for the sturdy in nature. She believed the limited number of arrows was a result of poor planning on the part of the state's Department of Forests. Nearby Emmaus State Park got most of the glory in these parts for its well-tended, family-oriented facilities. Patriot Woods was given over to Mother Nature and her wild ways. She did not want to get lost there, as she did not know who or what they might come across. She slowed her steps and panned the trees looking for a blue arrow. It gave Karen the opportunity to pull up beside her and have a quiet word with her. "Thank you for inviting me today. It means a lot that you'd introduce me to your friends like this."

Kelly looked straight at Karen, forgetting about her search for the blue arrow. There were so many things she wanted to say in return. Thank you for bringing Dad out of hiding since mom died. Thank you for showing me that he's ready to resume his life without me pointing the way. Thank you for helping him keep the store vital in this age of convenience store mentalities. Thank you for being a friend. "I'm glad you agreed to join us."

Karen continued. "You know, when I first moved to town a couple of months ago I was really afraid. Starting over in a new place and redefining myself after a failed marriage seemed like a monumental mission. You and Joe have made it so much easier than I could have imagined. Thanks... for everything."

Kelly wasn't entirely sure what 'for everything' meant. Was it for not being vocal about their May - December romance, in spite of her wariness, or for just being her friend? "No problem. It's nice getting to know you."

Kelly stopped and looked for but could not find

the surreptitious blue arrow. The path they were on appeared correct but one never knew in the woods. Paths that look like trails branch off all the time. They start strong and confident then gradually peter out leaving the traveler stranded in nothing more than a leaf filled gully. She wiped the sweat from her brow and continued walking, praying there would be an arrow up ahead.

The trail rose higher and steeper and everyone seemed to be having a harder time of it. Hannah, who by this time was plodding along with the aid of a walking stick, flapped her shirt collar to get a breeze as she huffed and puffed with each step. Ellen looked as if she'd had enough of the great outdoors, looking as worn and hot as Kelly felt. Even the young and vibrant Karen was fading and occasionally lost her footing and slipped on a loose stone. Still, they kept at it, neither one ready to give in and call it defeat, neither one wanting to look weaker to the other.

They walked in silence for a few minutes, which wasn't in Ellen's nature to maintain. Eventually, in an exhausted, panting voice she spoke to Kelly under her breath in a way that the others would not be invited into the conversation. "You know Kelly, I've been thinking about how you and your father get along so well. I have to admit, I'm really envious. I've tried so hard to create that kind of relationship with my dad but it's like he exists behind a brick wall and won't let anyone in, not even me."

The statement was from out of left field and Kelly saw the sadness in Ellen's eyes in her moment of confession. She knew her friend believed in being forthright; psychologists held communication in high regard. Still, her blunt honesty took Kelly by surprise. Ellen's father, Jack Priestly, was old school. He was the wage earner and head of the household. Warm and fuzzy feelings and such were the housewife's jurisdiction. To this day, he still didn't know how to relate to the ones he loved the most. Kelly couldn't imagine what life would be like without the bond she had with her father. "Yeah, I guess I am lucky. And who knows," she said to her friend, "maybe one day your dad will come around. Don't give up on that, there's always hope." She squeezed Ellen's hand and right there, on a twisted rocky trail in the midst of Patriot Woods, said a silent prayer for her friend.

The group labored on for another half hour, travel being much, much harder than before. The landscape had risen from an even walking path to a steep climb that required surefooted steps. Rocks that seemed to be firm rolled under foot on the incline of the hill. Several times Kelly had to grab at a tree branch to help pull her up over a ridge. The others did likewise. Their faces grew long and tempers grew short, and all bore her share of scraped hands and knees. At the crest of the hill, Kelly stopped to catch her breath. This was supposed to be an easy hike, appropriate for middle-aged, out of shape people and young children. The strenuous ascent they just made would not have been appropriate for either. By this time, Kelly was certain it had been way too long since she'd seen a trail marker. "Hey guys, has anyone seen a blue arrow lately?"

The women slowed en masse, looking up to the trees for guidance or at least a blue arrow. It was true; no one recalled having seen one for some time. Ellen slid to the ground, exhausted, looking like she couldn't take one more step. She pulled the bottom hem of her shirt up to dry her dirt and sweat stained face, which only made it look that much worse. They all looked like a ragged bunch, worn out and drenched in sweat. No one was prepared for this kind of hike and they had long since run out of drinking water. Kelly joined Ellen and sat down in the dirt. She felt awful for leading them the wrong way. "How could I have wandered off a marked trail? I'm sorry, it's all my fault, I led you astray."

"Now what?" Hannah asked, sitting down as well and leaning back against a tree.

Kelly thought she heard the sound of defeat in her voice. The circumstances so easily lent itself to that. She hated to fuel the situation but nonetheless felt compelled to state the obvious. "Looks like we're lost."

Those words proved to be too much for Ellen who seemed to be suffering the most from exhaustion, and threw her into a hyperventilating panic. "Oh. No! We. can't. be." Her words were punctuated with sucking breaths. She braced her hands against two trees on either side of where she sat and closed her eyes. When she opened them again she was no more composed but had drawn in enough oxygen to sputter out a few cohesive thoughts. "What will happen? We've run out of water. We can't survive long in this heat without water. Oh God. What will become of my family? My family needs me."

Hannah had little patience for Ellen's unfolding drama. "Ellen get a grip on yourself!" Ellen was stunned into silence for a moment at Hannah's outburst then resumed hyperventilating with even greater intensity.

Kelly tried to take control of the situation, setting aside her own apprehensions. "Stop it now, both of you! I think we should..."

"Wait a minute," Karen cried, interrupting her. "Listen."

They all sat motionless. Even Ellen quieted down to listen. The faint noise in the distance wasn't discernable to everyone at first, but like a chorus line of dancers moving in turn, the tension left their faces one by one as they realized it was the gurgle of rushing water teasing their ears. In a rebirth of stamina, they jumped up and headed toward the sound. It led them through brambles and thick undergrowth, over fallen trees and around huge boulders until they found its source. Beaver Falls.

The Blue Arrow Trail was to have taken them to the foot of the falls. Somewhere after they left the trail their path took them to higher ground so that they ascended above the falls and were now looking from the top as Beaver Damn River spilled into the basin far below. They half climbed, half slid down the slope at the side of the falls, being showered with refreshing mist along the way and were covered in cuts and scratches by time they reached the bottom. On the far side of the basin they saw the cutaway of a trail and a Blue Arrow. They sighed with relief anticipating an easier journey back to the picnic area.

Ellen and Hannah knelt to cup the cold, revitalizing water and splashed it over their heads and necks. Kelly and Karen stood side by side and looked into the depths of the basin and then at each other. A mischievous twinkle formed in their eyes as if they both knew what the other was thinking. Karen smiled at Kelly and questioned, "Yeah?" Kelly broadened her grin and gave an enthusiastic, "Oh, yeah." She reached out to Karen and they grasped each other's hand and together they jumped. Kelly's heart raced with exhilaration as they plummeted toward the surface, feeling like a child again, living life with abandon as she hadn't done in ages. They broke the surface into a sudden shock of cold from the spring fed river. It pressed in on her, making it difficult at first to catch her breath. A moment later she was treading water, enjoying the icy bath. A wave of their displaced water had splashed the others on shore. Hannah flapped her wet hands to dry them from the dousing. However, the cooling effect of the spritz must have felt good because she paused, shrugged her shoulders and said, "What the heck, why not?" Another great splash left Ellen alone at the edge of the basin. That kind of spontaneity was not in her personality, so she removed her shoes and sat at the water's edge with her feet dangling in.

Kelly swam a few strokes then rolled over to stretch out and float on her back. "Oh man, this is awesome. Ellen, come on in."

"I'm fine right where I am, thank you." She splashed her feet, kicking up a little water, to prove the point.

Hannah dipped her head under and brought it back up fast, which formed an arc of spraying water from her hair resembling a large aqua mohawk. "Whoohoo!" She used her hands to slick it back away from her face. "Come on, Ellen. You don't know what you're missing. Join the fun."

She wouldn't budge. "I know what I'm missing – looking and acting ridiculous, that's what. Grown women behaving like little kids."

They tried goading and taunting her into jumping in with no result, but the women refused to leave well enough alone, they'd been through too much that day. Refusing to take no for an answer, together they rushed the shore and dragged Ellen in. "Agh!!!

It's cold! Oh my gosh, it's cold. Oh my..." She complained until she realized just how refreshing the water was, and changed her tune. She threw her hands in the air and shouted, "Woohoo, this is great!"

Hannah raised her eyebrows. "Who are you and what have you done with Ellen?"

Kelly, likewise, had to tease her friend. "You mean behaving like kids can be fun?"

Ellen re-joined, "Adulthood is vastly overrated," and pushed her hand along the surface of the water splashing them both.

Their mood was much lighter after they were refreshed and back on the trail to the picnic area. Even their soaking wet sneakers that squished with each step couldn't drag them down. They laughed all the way, with Ellen's distinct cackle and snort clearly louder than the rest. Eventually the four of them emerged from the trail battered and worn, with arms linked together in a chain and still damp from their adventure. They were beyond tired and everything they said and did seemed to set them giggling like schoolchildren. Hannah's face was red from laughing hard as she recounted the highlights of the expedition, the finer details getting mixed up in the process and the laughing. "...and then the blue arrows got lost."

"And we had to go find them!" Ellen jumped in with uncharacteristic humor. A fit of riotous laughter and snorts took her off balance toppling her to the ground, dragging the rest of the linked women with her. Kelly believed if a vote were taken at that moment, it would no doubt be declared, hands down and by far, the worst and best meeting of the Lunch Club to date.

JONI VANNEST

18
CONNIE ANDERSEN

I had plenty of time to think. After all, there's not a whole lot you can do in a hospital, especially in my condition. Even the thinking got a little fuzzy at times, what with the drugs and oxygen deprivation. There weren't many visitors either. Even if I hadn't discouraged it, there aren't a whole lot of folks who like to visit the sick and dying. William and Molly were faithful, as expected, but had thought it better to start leaving the kids home with a sitter when they came by. That was disappointing, but for the best. Life, what there was of it, ticked from one moment to the next and each moment felt like an eternity to reach. I thought a lot about forgiveness during that time and how I couldn't get past myself. Why was I so stubborn that I could write about the need to forgive and to be forgiven, I had practiced it in life and, mercifully, taught my son how to forgive, yet I could not forgive myself. There was no peace in my soul when I needed it most.

When Jack came around again he didn't look so well either. He was pale and didn't want to walk far from an available restroom. The respite he provided from my illness on his visits was a godsend. He allowed me to briefly step outside of my circumstances into an alternate universe free of suffering. Actually, all my characters allowed me that blessing. I will always love them for that. So it rather disturbed me that in the alternate reality when I was feeling better Jack seemed to be getting worse. He offered no explanation. It was just how it was. My imagination went to work overtime on it.

19
39½ RIVER ROAD

This isn't fair. What right do you have to come and take over my life like this? I call the shots, not you. And, don't think I'm going to make it easy for you either, because I won't. I'm not ready to walk into the sunset. Not yet anyway. I'll deal with that when the time comes - but I'll tell you one thing, it isn't now!

"Bah! This is sissy stuff." Jack Priestly slammed his pen down in disgust. Did Ellen really think this would make a difference, that it would make him feel any better? He took a swig of coffee and stared out the kitchen window up the drive to Ellen and Brad's house. Only forty feet away according to his measuring tool - his own home not even worthy of its own address, instead numbered in relation to the main house, 39 ½, yet so far apart on so many other levels, especially this one. This was his problem and he wanted to deal with it in his own way. Ellen insisted journaling was a good method of dealing with anger and a great one to get in touch with his confused emotions. "There is nothing confused about it," he had told her. "It's a bad situation and I

241

just want it to go away." Of course, he knew it wouldn't, not on its own. But he didn't want to face it either.

Jack took another drink and the phone rang. He stared at the handset sitting on its base on the counter, so insistent, so rude, interrupting his life unbidden as it was. He'd had his years of slavery to a phone and a desk. These were supposed to be his golden years. He let it ring and continued draining his mug. The phone eventually went silent, then a moment later started to ring again. "Probably Ellen," he said aloud for no one to hear. Jack took his time getting up from the table to answer as he was in no hurry to talk with anyone, let alone his daughter. By the fifth ring of the second round he picked it up.

"Hey Dad, I'd almost given up on you. I was about to come over there and see if you were all right." Jack hated the way Ellen fussed over him like a mother hen. He was perfectly capable of taking care of himself, and if he didn't feel like answering the phone it was his prerogative. "Just a little slow today, I guess."

"So how's it going? Are you feeling okay this morning?" Her mothering had gotten worse since the diagnosis, as if monitoring the situation would somehow slow its progress. Without giving him the opportunity to answer she added in her I hear you therapist's voice, "I hope you had a chance to put some of your feelings down on paper as I suggested last night. I think you'll find it very helpful."

"I'm not so sure. Thoughts are the same poisonous things whether they're in my head or in a notebook."

"Dad, it's that kind of thinking that's got you bogged down in this angered state."

"It's the cancer that has me bogged down in this angered state," he fired back.

Ellen had no quick response to his outburst. For a few vacuous seconds she said nothing. Jack could picture her carefully weighing her options. He was pleased when she caught on that he was not in the mood for conversation and ended the call. "Look, I just wanted to check in with you before my first client gets here. Glad you're still the same irascible you."

The sarcasm was not lost on him. "You have a nice day too, dear."

Jack hung up the phone refusing to look back out the window. He knew he would see Ellen standing at her kitchen window looking into his. Sometimes forty feet seemed even closer than it was. He crumpled the paper that he'd written on and tossed it in the garbage.

*   *   *

Ellen Steele pulled the car in line behind the other parents waiting to pick up their kids. As always, she was on time: 2:35. Monday through Friday. The routine worked for her, especially now with so much going on. It was nice to know there was a small piece of stability she could count on.

Several times lately she had to juggle her clients at the last minute in order to make it to a doctor's appointment with her father. She wanted to be the second ear in the room so he would not miss any important information.

And Brad hadn't been home much these last few months, being out on the road promoting the company's new product. The family responsibilities were all falling on her, and it was all she could do to keep from being resentful toward her loved ones. Thank God for the school's dependability of 8:20 to 2:35.

The dismissal bell cut through the air. The children had been waiting behind the doors, pressing on them until they heard the sound of freedom. They poured out into the courtyard even before the clanging ended. Ellen spotted Avery first, lumbering under the weight of his backpack, jacket draped over his shoulder by one finger. This was his fourth year of elementary school, the tough year, when teacher expectations grew to new heights and kids have a hard time adjusting. Avery was no exception. The fun and games of the younger grades were over and serious learning was now underway. His previous As had turned to Bs and Cs, making his efforts feel futile, souring his attitude about school. As he got in the car she could see his demeanor this afternoon wasn't much better than her father's that morning.

"Hey sunshine."

"Hey." He was also, apparently, a boy of few words this afternoon.

"Rough day?"

"Mmm."

"Want to talk?" She offered her sympathetic ear.

"Unh unh."

"Well then, TGIF, huh? Thank goodness it's Friday. We'll have the whole weekend to make whatever it is better."

Avery perked up like a lightbulb went off in his head. "That's right! Tomorrow is Saturday. That's when Grandpa and I are going to start building my fort. Whoohoo!" He shot a hand up in the air and Ellen was quick to return the high five. The turnaround was quick, his blues forgotten.

"Listen sport, Grandpa had a rough morning. We'll see if he's up to working with you tomorrow."

After the diagnosis, she and Brad sat the kids down to explain what was happening with their grandfather. Jodi had a hard time dealing with the news. Grandparents, much like parents were still invincible even to teenagers, as they hadn't yet reconciled their parents' lack of immortality. She spent a lot of her spare time these days sitting by the river and thinking. Avery and Brielle took the news as well as children their age could. However, some questions still remained unanswered for all of them, specifically the big one: Why? There were no good answers for that one.

Ellen replayed her remark to Avery over again in

her mind. She did not mean to sound so pessimistic. Tomorrow was the big day and she knew Avery was counting on his grandpa not to let him down. In approaching her father's illness she felt it was important to be cautiously optimistic about his future, but she also believed it was important to keep grounded in reality. She looked in the rearview mirror and was glad to see Avery remained bright. Her father had been talking about building the fort for a while but never got around to it. Understandably, he now seemed to have developed a sense of urgency about constructing it, wanting to "get 'er done." This had Avery's heart soaring. She teased them both about it being their time for male bonding. Avery said he didn't care what it was called as long as he and his grandpa were building the fort together.

Children continued to spill out of the building until their numbers dwindled and the courtyard emptied. Most of the cars had pulled away. Then in her own sweet time, little Brielle pushed open the door and gently skipped her way to the car, red ringlets bouncing in unison with her steps. She held a piece of a paper displaying what appeared to be her latest art masterpiece. Unlike fourth grade, kindergarten was still fun. "Hi Mommy." She climbed into the back and leaned over the seat to give her mother a hug and kiss.

"What have you got there?"

"A picture of an apple. Miss Raduazzo is teaching

us about the seasons. This is fall and in fall we pick apples. So I drew an apple." Her logic was flawless.

*   *   *

Saturday dawned with promise. Avery woke up early finding himself too anxious to sleep in as he usually did on Saturdays. A misty vapor covered the landscape outside his window coating all within its moist reach with a layer of dew. Avery knew September mornings were like that. He also knew that some morning soon the dew would be frost and then snow. It was now or never to build his fort.

Trying to be quiet so as not to wake his parents, he slipped down to the kitchen and poured himself a bowl of cereal. He sat at the table in his pajamas and unfolded a piece of paper that he pulled from beneath his pillow before getting out of bed. On it was a pencil drawing, the sketch he and his grandfather made of the proposed fort. Avery's imagination was much keener than his or his grandfather's carpentry skills. So for the sake of actually finishing the project, they had to scale back to a simple design: four walls, a roof and an open door they planned to cover with a tarp. The window was an afterthought. It would have to be plain, cut out of the plywood wall with a circular saw.

He was putting the breakfast things away when a sleepy-eyed Brielle walked into the room with Mr. Theodore Bear held tight under her arm.

"Why are you up before Mommy and Daddy?"

"Just cuz," he said.

"Will you pour me some cereal?"

Even though he had just cleaned up, Avery took care of his little sister. He pulled out the step stool and placed it as he did before to where he could reach the cereal box on the shelf. As he was stepping down, he happened to glance out the window and saw his grandfather moving about in his kitchen, presumably making his own breakfast. Avery quickly poured the cereal and milk for Brielle then ran upstairs to get dressed. He was out the door in record time.

*   *   *

Avery didn't knock before entering the cottage, but Jack was used to it. He understood that, although the bungalow was his home, Avery believed both buildings were part of his home at large; thus, his presence needed no introduction.

"Are you ready to start Grandpa?"

The boy was oblivious to the fact that Jack was not yet dressed for the day. "Whoa, there. Can't a man have a cup of wake-me-up before he's accosted with intruders and questions? Besides, does it look like I'm ready?" Jack held up his arms exposing his pajama-clad body to his grandson.

"Sorry."

Avery slunk low into a chair at the kitchen table, his eyes cast downward. He traced his finger along the edge of the oak table, up and around, following the grain of the wood.

"Well now, there's really nothing to be sorry

about." Jack was feeling a little ashamed for coming close to snapping at Avery.

"Are you sick yet? Mom said you might not be able to build the fort with me today."

Are you sick yet? Now what kind of thing is that to ask? He tried to see it from Avery's perspective. Here was his grandpa who, for all appearances, looked as healthy as any other day of his life, yet hiding somewhere inside of him was a deadly disease of unknown status. Of course he was perplexed. Now there are the confused emotions Ellen was anticipating. They just didn't show up where she expected. "Eh, don't you worry about me." He made a fist and banged his chest. "Strong as an ox. And don't go listening to everything your mother says... But don't tell her I said so."

Avery's face registered relief and he smiled, albeit a cautious one.

"Tell you what," his grandfather said. "Why don't you go to the garage and bring around the wood we'll need, at least the pieces you can carry."

*   *   *

Avery was delighted. The project was officially underway. Since Tuesday the garage had been the storehouse of what was to become Fort Avery, the family car having been delegated to the driveway for the last four days. Avery and his grandfather visited the home center store last weekend to pick out the wood and supplies for delivery later in the week. He looked at the lumber laying in piles on the garage floor. In his mind's eye he could see the various lengths of wood being sized then taking shape, coming together as if by magic under the skill of an experienced hand. He and his grandfather, two inexperienced craftsmen, would not have it so easy. This didn't deter Avery one bit. His fort was going to be awesome! The 2x4s would be easier to carry than the plywood. He dragged them one at a time to the far end of the backyard, to a corner almost concealed by the overgrowth of forsythia bushes his mother refused to trim. "They're so full and beautiful in springtime. The yard lights up with sunshine," she would say. It was the perfect place for a secret hideout. When Avery moved all of the wood he was able to lift, he began bringing out the sawhorses and supplies. He would be ready when his grandfather was.

"So, do you have the plans?" Avery turned to see his grandfather walking toward him.

"Got 'em right here." Avery produced the folded drawing from his pocket.

His grandfather looked at the paper. "Hmm."

"Do you have your measuring tool?" Avery countered.

The old man turned and thrust his right hip toward the boy. A square metal case housing his measuring tape hung clipped to his belt. "Of course, can't build a fort without one." Avery didn't know why his grandfather called it a measuring tool instead of a tape measure like everyone else, he assumed it was one of those things that made him unique. Occasionally, after his grandfather had done something requiring the use of a measuring tape, Avery would catch him measuring this wall or that piece of furniture for no apparent reason. "Just checking," he'd say in defense of his actions. Avery was never sure what he was checking, but that was okay. His love for his grandfather had no qualifying standards.

*   *   *

Jack looked at Avery. He wasn't really sure how he got roped into doing this. The boy's father should be helping him, not a feeble old man without any woodworking experience. He stared at the pile of wood and materials before them. What have I gotten myself into? "Well, I guess we should get started. Got a lot to do."

"What's first, Grandpa?"

"The floor is as good a place to begin as any. What we'll do is hammer our support studs perpendicular to two parallel boards until we have a frame. Let's mark it out."

Jack unhooked his measuring tool and went through the motions of measuring the boards he already knew to be approximately six feet long.

"Now, these boards are six feet. How long is that in inches?"

"I don't know."

"Well do the math," Jack demanded, annoyed at the boy's lack of initiative. He never liked the way kids were allowed to use calculators in school these days. "They teach kids to press buttons instead of using their brains," he would complain. Avery flipped over the paper with the drawing and calculated six times twelve.

"Seventy-two."

"That's right. Now, if we make our first two marks at one inch on either end that leaves us with seventy inches. We have to evenly distribute the support studs in those remaining seventy inches. So, how many marks do we need to make?"

Avery gulped. His sinking grades this year were most notable in math. He stared at his grandfather, speechless.

"Look, the building standard for studs is sixteen inches on center, so the marks shouldn't be any further away than that. You with me so far?" Avery nodded and watched Jack do the math. "Seventy divided by sixteen is four and some change. Since we don't have a board that measures "some change" we'll evenly space them. We know we can't do less than four support beams, so let's try five. Here, you divide."

Avery took the paper and pencil, carefully dividing seventy by five to see what happens. "Fourteen."

"Well there you go, every fourteen inches; see that wasn't so hard. Those teachers ought to spend more time teaching logic in that school of yours. Seems all our taxes are doing is making mush out of your brains." Throughout all his calculating and instructions Jack did his best to sound like he was an expert at fort making and, right or wrong, Avery hung on his every word. Jack made the first mark and had Avery do the rest.

Attaching the perpendicular pieces to make the flooring frame was not as easy as it looked on This Old House; they made it look so effortless. They had a nail gun he reminded himself. Avery's efforts were to be commended, however. His aim had greatly improved since taking the first swing of his hammer and nearly crushing his thumb. He pulled it away just in the nick of time. His technique, however, needed work. The hammer had bounced back at Avery with each tap, tap, tap he made to drive a nail. His timid efforts saw barely any movement of the point into the wood. Jack finally suggested he try a little harder. Avery then slammed the hammer down without taking aim, hitting the nail off center and sending it in a skewed direction. This happened a couple of times until Jack decided to intervene, if just for the nail's sake.

"Here, let's try this." Jack grabbed a piece of scrap wood from the garage and laid it on the ground. Grabbing some nails and the hammer, he gently tapped one nail into the wood until it stood upright on its own. Then holding the block of wood in one hand and the hammer in the other he said, "Now, watch. Hold the hammer further up the handle away from the head to get some leverage, like this. See?" Avery was all eyes and ears. "Draw your arm back – now here's the important part – draw it back while keeping your eye on the nail head the whole time. Then in one swift motion, like you really mean it, pound that hammer down. And, BAM! You've driven the nail." Jack was almost surprised at his own success. He was banking on it working but couldn't let on as to his doubts. After all, he was the supervisor. "Now you try."

Avery's first few attempts on the piece of scrap didn't prove to be any more successful or cleaner than those on the framework. He tapped the nail upright and drew the hammer back as instructed and BAM! pounded the nail. The result was a twisted deck nail now at a 45 degree angle. He let out a loud and angry four letter expletive.

"Hey, watch that mouth. Where'd you learn to talk like that?" Jack was instantly sorry he'd asked that question, knowing the boy had heard that same word more than once form his own lips.

Avery shrugged noncommittal shoulders. "I don't know, the kids at school, I guess."

"Ignorant words for ignorant minds. Be a leader not a follower, you'll get more places."

"Yes, sir."

"Go ahead, try again."

Avery set the nail and lifted the hammer, testing for the leverage his grandfather spoke of. He held his breath. This time he swung with an intensity that was not present on any of his other tries. A newfound magnetism seemed to be pulling the hammer and nail head together with unexpected force. BAM! He drove the nail straight into the scrap of wood. His arm reflexively returned to the upright position as if to try again. Avery drew a breath and stared down at his accomplishment.

"Well, how about that. Good job," said Jack, tousling Avery's hair. "Try again."

He did, repeatedly, until the action became involuntary. Skill learned, he now knew how to drive a nail. "Grandpa, this is going to be a piece of cake."

Jack smiled for the first time that day.

The two worked diligently throughout the morning. By noon the first frame was complete and the plywood flooring had been laid on top of it. Clouds were gathering and the temperature falling as they broke for lunch. Ellen warmed them up with grilled cheese sandwiches and tomato soup.

"Can I come see the fort after lunch?" Brielle inquired in between slurps of soup. Her mother had kept her out of the way all morning so she wouldn't get hurt by a power tool or misfired nail.

"Sure, as long as you promise to stay close and not touch anything," Jack replied.

"I promise."

"Dad, do you really think that's such a good idea?" Ellen had opened her mouth ready to justify her concerns when Jack spoke first, his voice slightly raised.

"Ellen, you worry too much about these kids;

everyone, for that matter. Things are just going to happen or not happen and nothing you can do will change that." He didn't intend on the Freudian double-entendre, it just came out. He sensed himself getting red in the face and felt a queasiness in his stomach. He rose and left the table.

Avery's presence stirred the old man from a restless nap on the couch where he was still recovering from a regurgitated grilled cheese sandwich. The boy stood above him staring intently at his stomach.

"What are you looking at?" Jack wasn't accustomed to being the subject of investigation, although he had more than his fair share in the last few weeks. His tone was sharp.

"I was just wondering."

"Wondering what?" Jack sat up, groaning as he did so.

"Can you feel it?

"Feel what?"

"It. Mom said it's eating your intestines and I just wondered if you could feel it happening."

Jack knew this particular subject was bound to arise eventually; it was the proverbial elephant in the room. He hadn't yet talked to Avery about it. Heart to hearts were never his strong point. Over the years he had left all that "sentimental stuff" to his wife, especially when it came to dealing with Ellen as she was growing up. Even now, his relationship with his family was somewhat detached, both emotionally and physically. Hugs were few and far between, usually substituted with a good hair tousle, and when they did happen, they were brief and quickly released. But his wife wasn't here anymore to field the boy's inquisition.

"It's like having a question mark over your head." Avery didn't appear to understand and Jack wasn't in the mood to explain any further, his stomach still ached and he hadn't yet recouped his energy after running to the bathroom for the last half hour. He could see Avery expected additional words of explanation but he offered none. Instead, Jack said, "Give me a couple more minutes and then I'll come out there." That, Avery did understand. He shook his head in acknowledgement and walked out the door.

By the time Jack rejoined Avery, there was a third party on the construction crew. Frankie, Avery's sidekick and partner in crime, was holding a two by four steady for him to hammer into place. Jack observed with pride the confidence Avery displayed in his work. We might just get this done, he thought to himself. He walked around the frame in progress like an inspector general, nodding his head in approval.

"Tell you what," he said. "How about I play foreman on this team for the rest of the day?"

Avery keenly eyed where Jack held his side. "No prob."

They worked the rest of the afternoon framing

up the second wall, securing it and the first wall to the floor and to each other with nails and bolts, so that together the walls stood at a right angle. The sky was dark with storm clouds when they decided to call it quits for the day. The kids put the tools away before Frankie rode home on his bicycle, leaving Jack alone with Avery in the yard. "You worked real hard today. It's coming along real nice." Avery beamed. Jack wondered if he should offer a pat on the back or handshake to accompany his praise for the boy's handiwork, but just stood with his hands on his hips. "I'm going to get a little shut eye before dinner."

"Ok, gramps."

He walk back to the cottage holding his side.

The ringing phone woke Jack up from his nap. "Dad, Brad's not going to make it home for dinner, Jodi is covering a shift at the Parkside, and I don't feel like cooking so I'm taking the kids to the diner. Would you like to join us?"

Ellen's invitation couldn't have come at a better time. Although he had worked up an appetite, Jack didn't know if he would be able to muster up the energy to cook the chicken he set out for supper. Dinner with the family seemed like a good idea, if not a mercenary one. "Sure, sounds good." Even through the phone he could sense Ellen's surprise at how quickly he agreed.

"Well... great. I'll send the kids over to get you in

about a half hour."

When he hung up the phone, Jack noticed the pad of paper he wrote on the previous morning was still on the table. He sat down and picked up the pen.

> *I'm finally getting around to building that fort with Avery. I'll say one thing, you're a good motivator. I have to admit, working with him today has been enjoyable despite my misgivings about our combined abilities. It saddens me to think this could be our swan song. Bah! Scratch that. It doesn't make me sad it makes me fuming mad - mad at us both: you for the evil entity that you are, and me for opportunities lost by my own design... Hmm, I never looked at it that way before. Damn you.*

"Welcome to the Parkside Diner. My name is Jodi and I'll be your server tonight."

Jack got a kick out of seeing his granddaughter in action. This was the first time he'd come to the diner on one of her shifts. Jodi broke with the feigned formality and gave him a hug. "Hi Grandpa." She sat the family in a booth, Ellen and Brielle on one side, himself and Avery on the other. "So, what can I get for you?"

After much deliberation, everyone placed his or her order. Jack was acutely aware this would be his last regular meal before beginning the prep for surgery - one day of soft foods followed by one day of liquids only, followed by the main event. At first he wasn't sure whether to live it up tonight, especially since he wasn't particularly hungry. Ultimately, he threw caution to the wind, ordering two appetizers and fried chicken and french fries. He planned to close out the meal with the most decadent piece of cake he could find in the display case. He could feel Ellen's scolding eyes on him as he ordered. To her credit, she said nothing of her disapproval. Putting on her best I'm ignoring an unpleasant confrontation face, Ellen said, "It looks like you guys made great headway on the fort."

The plan was to complete it over the course of these two days. Jack figured any fool, himself included, could finish a kid's hideout in that timeframe. Avery confirmed his mother's observation. "Yep. And tomorrow we'll 'git 'er done!'" He smiled up at Jack who smiled back.

"Mommy, can we make curtains for the window when it's done?" Brielle inquired.

"There aren't gonna be any curtains on the window," Avery said, emphasizing the word curtains with great disdain. "This is a man's fort, not some froofroo girly thing."

"Mom, he called me a froofroo."

Jack hid the laugh that wanted to escape at that moment. Avery was more like him than he realized. Ellen quickly intervened before things escalated into a full-blown argument. "Sweetheart, I think it's best that Avery decorates his fort the way he sees fit, don't you? After all, he's the one who's building it." Brielle resigned herself to her mother's judgment and pouted her way through dinner.

Jack devoured his meal with gusto, exaggerating each bite with an expression of pure pleasure, adding the occasional "mmm, mmm" for effect. Avery started to copy him until his mother put an end to it. Over coffee and dessert—Jack opting for both a piece of chocolate cake and apple pie—Jack started feeling the consequences of his dining choices.

Then he noticed the drops on the plate glass window. He hadn't checked the weekend forecast, he just assumed pleasant weather for their outdoor task. He feared Mother Nature was about to throw a monkey wrench on their plans. Avery was apparently too involved with his ice cream to notice, so he said nothing.

Dessert seemed to lighten Brielle's former mood and she once again became her usual chatty self. Somewhere in her non-stop prattle, she innocently turned her attention to her grandfather's health. "Grandpa, after the doctor takes out your testins are you going to see God?" She gulped some milk while innocently waiting for an answer. Ellen nearly choked on her drink and spit a mouthful of coffee back into her cup. Avery halted his spoon mid shovel. And with that, the dark clouds were no longer limited to the other side of the glass. Jack squirmed in his seat, shaken from both the question and from sensing discomfort in his bowels. Seeing God was not on his to-do-list next week, at least not face to face. He stared into his daughter's eyes, wordlessly asking who should answer the question. Ellen released her gaze first and looked down into her plate. Jack realized then that they had never talked about that possibility. He saw her eyes grow moist and realized the answer could only come from him.

"Well honey, um...I, uh..." He stumbled over his words trying to find the right ones. The words he chose did nothing to satisfy his own needs, his faith having grown dim with age, but he knew they would comfort his loved ones. "No Brielle, but He will be there with me."

"Oh," she replied. "That's good." It was so simple in her mind, but the tone of the conversation had changed, ending the chatter. The din of the rain on the window, now falling with greater intensity, drowned the silence hovering about the table. The elephant now fully exposed, they became absorbed in the work of chewing and drinking.

Meanwhile, Jack's gastric dilemma grew.

It is said in folklore that when a group of gathered people become quiet at the same time it is because a spirit has passed through the room unnoticed. In what appeared to be one of those strange silences, the customers of the Parkside Diner all took a collective breath at the same time leaving the atmosphere of the room undisturbed. It was at that very moment Jack tried to stifle a gaseous release and failed. The rip of air, unfortunately for Jack both north and south respectively, rang through the diner. He was mortified and felt the heat rise from his neck up to his face. Then Brielle, who found the whole thing amusing, brought her hand to her mouth to try and stifle a giggle. The giggle was followed by a small laugh from Avery that grew louder the more he tried to deny it. Their eyes darted from one to another, finally landing on Ellen, wondering if they were in trouble. Other diners in the vicinity also reacted, though with greater decorum than the children. Jack couldn't help but get caught up in the moment; his gaffe was followed by an explosion of laughter that put everyone around him at ease.

They finished dinner, said their goodbyes to Jodi and walked out into the parking lot where they were assaulted by a sudden driving rain fueled by wind that seemed to come out of nowhere, a change in temperature, warmer than earlier in the day, apparently the culprit. Nearby trees tossed by the wind bowed to its mighty will. Leaves and branches fell in a wake of destruction. Ellen pulled Brielle close to her as they ran to the car. Above the din of the storm Avery said to Jack, "I hope it's not raining like this tomorrow."

Me too, thought Jack, aware of his limited time. Me too.

They saw it as soon as they pulled in the driveway. The half-finished fort was no longer tucked away in the corner of the yard as it had been when they left for dinner. Forces greater than the weight of the structure grabbed hold of the partially erected walls, using them as sails to drag and tumble it across the lawn. Avery was the first to jump out of the car. He ran to where the fort lay on its side, flailing his arms in frustration, not knowing where to begin the rescue, all the while crying, "No, no, no!" The walls were no longer at right angles to each other and barely connected to the floor at all. Several two by fours were splintered.

Jack was soon beside Avery assessing the damage. That's when he realized his fatal construction flaw: the fort was not secured to a foundation, no posts had been buried in the earth. The basic tenet of any building project, a firm foundation, had eluded their master design plans. Without it, the fort lacked the support needed in harsh weather. In a fraction of the time it took Jack to comprehend this, he also wondered if there wasn't a more powerful metaphor to be found in the situation.

Avery took hold of the felled wall and tried to raise it back up again, struggling against its mass and gusty winds. Jack, though older and infirm, was still stronger to the petite statures of his daughter and grandkids. It would be up to him to fix this and he had to do it now. Not tomorrow. Tomorrow was uncertain – a thing hoped for but not promised.

He ran forward and grabbed what was left of the wall and tried to right it. The weight and awkward condition of the piece kept him from getting a firm, supported hold on it. The wind continued to press in opposition.

"Get up there, you son-of-a..." he said behind gritted teeth. He struggled and fought against this new enemy to no avail. He changed positions, trying to push rather than pull it up. It raised slightly off the ground then fell back down again. He tried several times and several different ways to correct the overturned fort, each time failing. His anger boiled against the Controlling Powers. "Why are you doing this to me?" he yelled into the darkness, cursing the God he had earlier disclaimed. Still nothing budged and there was no answer to his question. Another attempt to pull down the uprooted far side of the fort yielded a loose and fractured two by four. He held it in his hand and stared at it. Then reaching back and holding fast to it with both hands he let out something between a grunt and a scream while flinging it as far as he could. It crashed with a dull thud in the driveway, barely heard above the roar of the storm. He stared down at his hands. A thin line of blood trickled down his left palm. He balled his hands into fists, shook them in the air, and dropped to his knees.

Brielle began to cry. Ellen had been standing to the side with her daughter watching the efforts of her father and son. She stepped into action. Turning to Brielle she said, "Come on sweetie, let's see if we can help." The girl hesitated at first then joined her mother as she walked to where the others were.

Ellen stood in front of her father, leaned down, and offered her hand. For the second time that night their eyes locked. A lifetime of missed opportunities and love electrified the energy between her outstretched hand and his. Could something so broken be repaired? His hidden metaphor became clear. Like the fort standing solely on its own strength, he too lacked the foundation needed in his time of trouble. His strength had been before him all along and he never knew it. He uttered an almost inaudible prayer except for the One for whom it was meant. "Thank you."

In a moment not of weakness but of meekness, Jack took Ellen's hand and rose to his feet.

When there is cancer in your body, time takes on new meaning. It becomes a thing chock full of possibility, not something by which we compartmentalize bits and pieces of our lives. It transcends beyond the passing of moments into opportunities: the chance to see one more sunrise, to hug your child again, utter one more, "I love you." Or maybe to hear a favorite song only to have the chorus reverberate in your mind again and again, hoping it will never be silenced, knowing better. It allows us to know that this chance, whatever it is, may never come again, so grab it now because there can be no delays. And know you will not go it alone.

When there is cancer in your body a new mantra is born: "Just once more."

JONI VANNEST

20
CONNIE ANDERSEN

Nurse Becky from way down South opened the curtains for me to gaze out the window. The sky looked appropriately menacing to go along with my prognosis. She chattered away while she checked my drips, and we had a mostly one-sided conversation before she moved on to her next patient. Jack came in shortly after she left. He was in bad shape: pale, hurting and slow to move. I just sat on the edge of the bed and we talked for a while. Every so often his face scrunched up from a painful spasm. "It won't be long now," he said. He did not define 'it', and I was too afraid to ask, fearing for my own mortality and that of his, fragility being equal partners to us both. It was unclear to me how we could survive one without the other. I did not want to find out.

"Jack, I need you. This can't be happening," I said with tears in my eyes.

"It's not our choice."

"Well then, whose is it?"

"The Author of all that is."

I thought about that. I did not have a great working relationship with the Author right then. He kept bugging me about my lack of forgiveness and I wasn't changing my mind on it. Not the best time to approach Him for a favor. I sighed. "He and I have some issues right now."

"That forgiveness thing, huh?" I looked away and he

continued. "We're always hardest on ourselves, aren't we? We strive to be perfect, and when we fail we kick ourselves for it, rubbing salt into the wound making it fester. And when it finally does heal we're left with a scar, a reminder of our guilt."

My scar, I knew, ran deep and hot. "My scar is on fire," I said. It always seemed right to share my innermost feelings with Jack like no one else I've ever known, even my departed husband, Bill. I felt like I was in a safe space when he came to see me. So I said it out loud and it was true. The scar of my guilt for having betrayed my family and my God by putting myself above them burned in my soul, keeping peace at bay.

He nodded. "Yes, but fires eventually burn out. When the ignition source is consumed the fire smolders and dies, the embers cool and are no longer a threat."

"What are you saying?"

"Don't be so blind, Connie." He was losing patience. This was the Jack I knew. "Look into your heart. You've acknowledged your crime against your family and the Almighty and it has left a painful wound. But," and here his voice softened and he spoke slower, "it is a healing wound."

A healing wound. Could that be it, was I mistaking a healing wound for guilt? I wanted it to be so. *Please God, let it be so.* I slid off the bed to my knees and prayed through tears. "Holy God, I'm sorry I did not accept your healing grace to bind my soul. Allow me to leave the guilt behind and move forward in your peace for whatever time I have left. Thank you for your mercy and unending love." I felt a warm hand rest upon my back and peace flood my soul just as volts of electricity shot through my chest and the sound of monitor alarms stabbed the silence, breaking my last hope for serenity.

21
ALL GOOD GIFTS

Prologue

On the whole, Brad Steele rarely picked up hitchhikers. But the couple he'd seen walking on the road that day weren't asking for a ride, they were simply walking... and walking... and walking on what appeared to be a long, labored journey. Brad and his wife, Ellen, passed them several times in their car while driving around that particular morning before stopping to offer a ride. That small gesture of kindness, they would later come to understand, was one that would set them all on a journey to understand the meaning of neighbor.

On the Road

Autumn sprinted past them on the other side of the windshield. Vibrant leaves of yellow and red lined the highway as they left North Carolina, until many hours and many miles later the foliage grew thin and lifeless, finally giving way to bare skeletons of trees lying in wait for spring. Dan's mind raced with excitement and anticipation as he drove

271

through each passing state, anxious to get to their final destination and wishing that bottled up energy could somehow propel them faster. Susan had already cautioned him about doing the speed limit. He was going home, and he couldn't get there fast enough.

Susan's head rested on a pillow against the passenger's side door, locks of hair had fallen across her face so that only her chin was visible. Dan noticed the grays now outnumbered the amber in her tresses. Life does that he thought, and theirs was certainly no exception and probably more so.

When the paper mill back home shut its doors for the last time, it left Dan and Susan without jobs and with barely any savings to lean on. Employment was hard to come by with so many out of work. Older folks like themselves were often overlooked in favor of younger new hires. It wasn't long before bill collectors were hounding them and the house payments got behind in their efforts to rob Peter to pay Paul. The mortgage company had their home up for auction before they were able to find a way to catch up. Dan's brother offered to put them up for a while until they got their lives back in order. That was May – six long months ago. But those days were behind them now: the past, past. Today they were on their way back home to Maine. And Mandy.

Dan's thought about how proud he was of his daughter - the first one in his family to go to college, and on a full scholarship at that. It was decided after the auction that Mandy would stay with her best friend's family until the fall when she'd go away to school. Saying good-bye to her was the hardest thing he'd ever done, knowing that everything in their lives had changed and not for the better. Neither he and Susan nor Mandy knew when they would be back together as a family. Dan watched helplessly as the women in his life clung tight to each other, not wanting to take that next step – the one that would tear them apart.

"Now don't cry, you'll make me cry," Susan begged of Mandy, trying to be strong for her daughter.

"But I don't know when I'll see you again." The tears flowed freely causing Mandy's mascara to run and Dan's heart to break. He wanted so much to be the father of his child's ideals. He wanted to scoop her up and tell her it would be all right, but he couldn't make that promise. Instead, he wrapped his arms around his small family to comfort them saying, "When the Good Lord wills it, sweetheart, when the Good Lord wills it." Then to himself he added, God, I'm not so sure what your plan is in all of this, but I'll hang in there. Just as he finished that thought, he noticed a bird swoop over the trees, wings open wide, floating gently on invisible currents. A scripture came to mind. "Look at the birds of the air; they do not sow or reap or store away in barns, and yet your heavenly Father feeds them. Are you not much more valuable than they?"

He stared after the bird and offered up one more prayer. Thanks for the reminder.

Yes, God was good, Dan thought to himself seeing the highway exit for Connecticut's Route 7. Despite their lives' turn of events Dan and Susan were still able to make that claim, the wellbeing of their spirits being the motivation for such words, not their material state.

Route 7. They weren't that far from Emmaus State Park, the place their truck broke down on the southerly trip last spring. It was there they met Brad and Ellen Steele who stopped to offer a ride upon seeing them walking at the side of the road. It was to their home they were heading, a little side trip before seeing Mandy. Dan had hoped the Steeles still remembered them when he called to ask if they could stop by to say hello. He remembered the surprise in Brad's voice when he answered the phone.

"Brad, this is Dan Deaton," he began. He thought he could sense the wheels spinning in Brad's head trying to place the name. "We met near Emmaus State Park some few months back. I had car trouble."

"Oh, yeah. Yeah! Of course I remember." Brad had ID'd him and now Dan was sure he sensed a smile on the other end. "Hey, how are you? Did that old truck get you where you were going?"

"Sure did. And it's still on the road."

"How about that... Good. Good. So, uh..." The unexpected phone call had Brad struggling for words, as the two weren't exactly friends, more like ships that passed in the night over a carburetor.

Dan picked up the discussion. "Well, uh, Susan and I are doing all right. We've been staying with my brother in North Carolina. Actually, that's why I'm calling. Seems we'll be leaving here and heading back to Maine in a couple of days and thought if you weren't busy, we'd like to stop in to see you and Ellen along the way." For the short time their paths had crossed, the two couples seemed to get along famously.

"That would be great, I'm sure Ellen would like that as well."

"We won't stay but a bit, just long enough to say 'Hey' and thank you for your hospitality the first time we came through."

"Oh, don't worry about that, I was just helping out where I could. But it would be nice to see you folks again. Must be time for an oil change by now."

Dan laughed. They spent hours together last spring rebuilding the truck's tired carburetor in an attempt to get it back on the road. Brad offered to help repair the truck as he dropped Dan and Susan off at the campground the day he gave them a ride. Dan never really expected Brad to follow up on the offer, but there he was an hour later, changed into an old pair of work clothes ready to climb under the hood. He could still hear Susan's mini-sermon after the truck was running again about his lack of faith.

"See, I told you: God provides. In His own good

time, but He provides."

A bobble-head turkey wobbled on the dashboard; it would be the extent of their holiday decorating. Susan stirred, slowly coming awake and Dan smiled at her the same euphoric smile he had been wearing since they decided to return north of the Mason Dixon line.

"Where are we?" she yawned.

"Just outside of Wheatfield Bridge." Saying the name out loud brought back a sudden rush of difficult memories for him. It was where they hit rock bottom. They had lost the things most precious to them and were carrying the spoils, like turtles, on their backs. Everything that was not sold or given away had been loaded into the truck and pop-up camper they towed behind it. Then the turtle said it wasn't going any further. Their lives had sunk lower than they thought possible. He had been thankful at the time for Susan's faith, which remained strong even as his waned. Without it he would have lost all hope. Her faith allowed him to believe hope would again rise. And it did, on the heels of a broken carburetor.

However, Susan was also practical. The whole time he and Brad worked on the truck she kept asking, "How can we pay him? We have nothing to spare, just enough gas money to get us to your brother's house." After the work was done, the problem of how to pay Brad for all his help became

Dan's last-ditch leap of faith. He remembered holding his breath as he turned the key to test the rebuilt carburetor, and then giving a loud, "Whoohoo!" when the engine turned over. He wasn't certain but he thought he might have also thrown in an Amen. He jumped out of the truck and gave Brad a high five. "Man, I can't thank you enough for all your help. Don't know what we would have done without you."

"Glad I could help," Brad replied.

Dan steeled himself with a deep breath before taking that leap. "You know, acts of kindness and earthly blessings come in many different sized packages. I think this one just earned you your angel wings in the next life." There it was, his faith laid out on the table like an offering.

"Like I said, Dan, it was my pleasure." Averting his eyes, Brad added, "I can see when a good man is down and needs a reminder there is still good in the world." Then looking straight at Dan he said, "Thank you for reminding me that's what this life is all about." The two men embraced, clapping each other on the back.

The truck slowed down as they turned onto Brad and Ellen's road.

"Number four-ten," he said. "A light blue house with black shudders and a birdhouse mailbox at the street."

With Humble Thanks

Dan was having second thoughts as he turned in the driveway. This was Thanksgiving morning. Most people were cooking a turkey and getting ready for crowds of relatives who would arrive later in the day to share in the feast. He suddenly realized they were about to impose at a very inopportune time. "We'll only stay for a few minutes," Dan said after he and Susan discussed it. "And then we'll be back on our way to Mandy. It's just a couple of hours now." She grabbed his hand and gave it a quick firm squeeze. This was the right thing to do.

Dan's right hand trembled slightly as he rang the doorbell while his left confirmed the envelope was still in his pocket. He slipped his arm through Susan's as they waited but it wasn't long before Ellen answered the door. He could see two children peeking out from behind her and a teenager standing off to the side. Brad strode across the room and took his place beside his wife. Dan's nervousness subsided when Ellen opened her arms for a hug and said, "Welcome. I'm so happy to see you. Come in out of the cold."

They ushered them into the warmth of the living room where the two couples shared greetings and more hugs like old friends. Ellen served mulled cider by the fireplace, sending the kids off to watch the parade on the TV in the family room. Soon they were reminiscing about their singular encounter and catching up on the months since, the conversation occasionally punctuated by the crackle of wood being consumed by the fire. Dan smelled the aroma of roast turkey wafting through the home and it brought to mind memories of better days. There would be more of those. He had to believe there would.

"Well, I told you we weren't going to stay long, so I'll keep to my promise. I'm sure you have family coming by soon; we won't get in the way." His tone sounded apologetic and self-deprecating. A habit picked up since their troubles began, he realized. He hoped that would get better as well.

"Please, you're welcome to stay as long as you'd like. That's what Thanksgiving is for, right?"

Dan thought it unfortunate geography separated what could have been a real friendship under different circumstances.

"That's sweet of you," Susan said. "But we're on our way to see our daughter, Mandy." Her face beamed.

"That's right," Dan said. "The family has been apart too long. Like they say, a heart can't live in two places." Silence hung on the air for just a moment then he continued.

"You know, back in the spring when the truck broke down we didn't know how we'd get 'er back on the road. Then you nice folks came along like a blessing from heaven. Gave us a lift, got 'er up and running and us on our way again. Even packed us a picnic lunch for the road." He smiled at Ellen. "I still say you folks got wings and halos hiding under those clothes." Ellen and Brad blushed, embarrassed by such praise. "Anyway, things have been looking up for us lately. Did some odd jobs in the Carolinas - put some money back in our pockets. Even had an offer for a factory job. That's when we knew if we stayed there permanent, we'd be missing out on the one thing that means more to us than anything else in this world (next to the Almighty, of course), our family." Dan reached for Susan's hand and they smiled at one another. "Now we know some day Mandy's gonna go out on her own, maybe even get married and have her own family. But for right now, we're all we've got, and families weren't meant to be divided. So we're going home again to try to make a go of it."

"Oh," exclaimed Ellen. "I'm so happy for you. I hope it all works out."

"God willing," Dan said sporting a grin. "Anyway, we felt it was only right on our way back home to come see you and once again say thank you for all your help when we needed it most." He reached into his pocket and pulled out the envelope, handing it to Brad. "Now it ain't much. But I think it should cover your troubles for all your hard work. Please take it with our sincerest thanks."

Brad put up his hands to refuse it. "Dan, Susan there's no need for..."

A humble, yet proud man, Dan cut him off. "Brad, please." Brad had no choice but to accept the offering. Without looking inside, he placed the envelope on the coffee table.

They chatted for a few more minutes then the travelers bid goodbye to their hosts, promising to let them know when they got settled in. "Who knows, maybe one day you'll come visit us."

As the Steeles waved from the doorway, Dan and Susan turned the pickup truck back onto the road. They were going home.

22
CONNIE ANDERSEN

The next think I remember I was standing behind Jack, who was still in the chair next to my bed, which was empty. Instinctively, I knew we had to leave so I put out my hand to help him up. He struggled despite my help and leaned heavily upon me as we walked out the door of the hospital room. Nurses and doctors scrambled past us to go in the same door without even a look in our direction, being too caught up in the emergency happening within. An announcement overhead repeatedly called out, "Code blue," and I thought I caught someone asking, "Have we heard back from UNOS? Do we have one or not?" The voices faded as we walked on and I couldn't hear the reply. But I knew the ultimate gift of love lay waiting in the balance.

23
CHAIN OF LOVE

The Designer

Alexis smoothed the fabric, noting how the nap of the material moved with each passing of her hand like the graceful ballet of field grass yielding to a breeze. The soft texture of the lavender fur would be perfect. She knew that in her skilled hands the fabric would soon undergo a transformation; she could feel it in her soul and could not wait to draw it out into being. This is how they always begin - with just an idea, one that would not go away and would gnaw at her until she made it a reality. She brought the bolt up to the counter for the clerk to cut.

This particular idea nestled in her head about a week ago and had been incubating ever since, rolling over in her mind, changing in shape and size, even in color. This week it would take shape. The design phase had created a fairytale-like character – cuddly, downy soft, gentle as a newborn. Of utmost importance, it must give the sensation of being so delicate as to wilt from a touch. It will be something a child can love and yet be a child itself.

"How many yards?" asked the clerk.

"Oh, about three of each," she said looking at the rolls of material lying across the counter. "I have to plan for trial and error, you know."

"So what is it going to be this time?"

Alexis was no stranger in the notions section of the department store. She regularly came in for supplies and, more times than not, it was this same woman who waited on her. Sarah, her nametag read.

"A bunny." The image in Alexis's mind placed a smile on her countenance and joy in her heart, her infectious bright spirit spilled over to Sarah who returned the smile.

"I see you in here all the time buying fabric for your dolls. What do you do with them all?"

"I make them throughout the year and sell them at craft fairs in the fall. I call the line *Alexis's Critter Comforts.*"

"Cute. Have you ever thought of putting them in stores? Like the toy shop in the village?"

"Oh, I..." She didn't know how to respond. The thought had crossed her mind. The little toy shop in town would be a great place to market her creations. However, the leap from craft fair item to store inventory seemed too great in her estimation. She loved her stuffed friends and they sold well at fairs, but mass-producing, even for just one local shop, seemed beyond her talents and abilities. At least that is what she told herself.

"You really should think about it," the clerk

pressed on. "American made is in these days. And handmade American made, well, it doesn't get much more chic than that."

To her surprise, the more the woman spoke, the more Alexis found herself considering the possibilities. "I appreciate the pep talk. I tell you what, I'll think about it."

"Good idea. And let me know because I'd love to look for your critters in the shop window."

Alexis bid goodbye, gathered all of her purchases and left the store dwelling on the newly sown seed of *maybe*.

The Shopkeeper

A wooden sign inscribed *Village Toy Shoppe* hung above the doorway and swayed with the wind. Alexis stood in front of the shop and took a deep breath trying to work up the confidence to go in. She felt a chill go up and down her spine and the cardboard crate in her hand grew heavy with her indecision. It was now or never. "Well God, this is it. It's in Your hands now." She pushed the door open and walked through.

A plump woman wearing glasses with half lenses was dusting a display of brightly colored racecars on the shelf behind the counter. Her gray hair led Alexis to believe she might be someone's grandmother, which she thought could prove to be helpful. The woman stopped dusting and welcomed her customer. "Good afternoon. Can I help you find a toy for someone?"

The friendly greeting did little to calm Alexis's nerves. She stuttered as she introduced herself and passed the woman her business card. "Hi, m-m-y name is Alexis Hunter. I am a toy designer."

"Well then, you've come to the right place. How can I help you?"

"Actually, I was hoping I could help you." That little spin on words was enough to give Alexis the boost she needed. Her well-rehearsed pitch began to flow, the words taking on a life of their own, much like her dolls. "I would like to show you some of my creations. I call them Alexis's Critter Comforts. They're a line of stuffed animals meant for pre-school age children. Each one is individually hand-crafted and no two are exactly alike."

"Is that what you have there?" The shopkeeper pointed at the container in Alexis's hand. "It looks sort of like an animal crate of some kind."

"Um." Alexis hesitated for just a moment. "It is. I couldn't just stuff them in a bag or a box without air holes. It wouldn't be right." She felt the need to explain further. "This seems more humane."

"I see." The woman's drawn out words and raised eyebrow told Alexis she may have gone a bit too far with her last comment, no matter how true she believed it to be. Thankfully, the woman seemed curious. "Well, let's see what, or rather who you have in there, shall we?"

Alexis opened the crate and pulled out several of

her friends, placing them on the counter. The likes of Monkey Mike, Ted Bear, Poofie Poodle and Lisa Lamb stared up at the owner. In a wave of anthropomorphism, Alexis could almost hear them pleading with the shopkeeper, Please let us stay.

"Oh, aren't they just adorable."

The merchant's words gave her hope.

"Oh, look at this one." The woman seemed to take an interest in her newest creation, Bonita Bunny. "Isn't that precious. And so soft, too." She picked up the rabbit and turned it over inspecting it on all sides. "Why it's wearing a housecoat. How original."

"She's dressed for bed, like a little girl would be."

"You really are very talented, but I'm so sorry I just don't have the room to offer them on consignment or otherwise."

Alexis's heart dropped. She cast her gaze to the ground in defeat and thanked the woman for her time, then quickly packed up her menagerie and left.

As she walked out the door, she nearly ran into a young woman who was opening the door next to the shop's entrance, not three feet away. It appeared to lead to a staircase, perhaps to an apartment on the second floor. Tagging behind the woman, yet holding tightly to her mother's hand was a little girl about four or five years old. The toddler turned her head toward the crate where tufts of lavender colored fur protruded from the air holes. The girl's eyes lingered on the toy-filled box in wonder as her mother gently pulled her inside and out of view.

Alexis sat in her car and wept for a dashed dream, allowing the tears to wash away her disappointment until she was ready to drive again.

* * *

Although the Village Toy Shoppe owner went about her business taking care of customers—both big and small—the rest of the day, she found herself repeatedly distracted by the thought of the little rabbit wearing a housecoat. It reminded her of her own childhood. As a little girl she, too, had a housecoat just like the one the rabbit was wearing that her mother had made. The memories took her back those many years. She remembered the comforting feel of the soft robe around her on chilly winter mornings, of her mother calling her to a breakfast of warm cereal or pancakes. She didn't realize until now how that simple robe provided a measure of wellbeing that as a child she didn't even know she had.

Well, it is getting near Christmas. Soon the toys will be flying off the shelf. And that bunny was so adorable.

She picked up the receiver and dialed. "Hello, Alexis? This is Caroline calling from Village Toy Shoppe and I was wondering..."

The Young Couple

It had been six months to the day - a beautiful wedding, the most wonderful day of their lives.

Dianne's memories of the occasion were just as vibrant on that cold winter evening as they had felt on that bright sunny morning. Recent comments from an older friend regarding their "monthaversary" still played in her mind. "Six months? Honey, you're still on your honeymoon. Come talk to me after you've had at least a decade under your belt." Dianne looked forward to that and many more joy-filled, and perhaps even challenging years ahead. On this particular evening, she saw the future in her husband Kenny's eyes, by candlelight at a small Italian restaurant in the village.

A waiter placed heaping bowls of pasta on the table; steam rose from them into the twilight of the room. As if by instinct or ritual, she joined hands with Kenny across the table while he prayed. "Thank you Lord, for six outstanding months and for the many years still to come. We ask you to bless this food to our bodies that we may be strong for you and for each other." A duet of "Amen" concluded the blessing. Their eyes met one last time before they turned their attention to the waiting food.

"Mmm. I think I died and went to heaven." Dianne savored the marinara sauce, letting the rich flavor linger in her mouth before washing it down with a drink. "So, have you thought about what we're going to buy everyone for Christmas? I have some ideas about my side of the family, but I'm at a loss as to what to get your Mom and Dad." Dianne loved Christmas. She had tempted Kenny with her visions of sugarplums since Halloween. The question was just one of the many things they had to work out for this, their first Christmas together, as they were still learning the finer details of how to create a family.

"You know, I really haven't given it much thought, but there is something I wanted to run by you."

Dianne put down her fork to give full consideration to her husband.

"I've been thinking, this whole year seems to have gone by in such an amazing whirlwind: the wedding, the island honeymoon, moving into the apartment together, getting that promotion at work. I just can't help but feel that I, that we," he corrected himself, "have been blessed beyond compare." There was no doubt, things were certainly going well for them - so well, in fact, they were even considering the possibility of starting their family earlier than planned. "So I thought maybe we could share a little of that blessing with someone else this Christmas. I know it sounds hokey and it doesn't have to be anything major, I just feel that I want to give back a little - you know, to make Christmas special for a needy kid or something like that."

Dianne sighed and looked at her husband with deep admiration. *This was why I married him.* "I think that's a wonderful idea. In fact, I saw one of those *Toys for Tots* barrels the other day. We could start with a donation there."

They finished off the meal with a tiramisu for two and decided to walk off the damage by going for a stroll around the green before heading home. Linked arm in arm they window shopped along the way. Village Toy Shoppe was just getting ready to close as they stood looking in the window.

"Oh honey, isn't that adorable? And look, she's got on pink bunny slippers." Bonita Bunny caught Dianne's eye and heart. "We *have* to get it *for Toys for Tots*. Come on!" Kenny was not given an option. She grabbed his hand and yanked him into the shop.

"Hi Caroline."

"Well hey, if it isn't the two lovebirds." Dianne's childhood neighbor and local toy merchant peered out over half glasses. She looked as if she'd had a long day and was ready to call it a night. The two greeted one another with over-the-counter hugs. "Gee, five more minutes and you would have missed me. I was just closing up."

"Oh, we won't keep you. We know exactly what we want."

"Dianne, let her close up. We can come back another time." Kenny then turned to Caroline. "Every now and then I find myself rescuing people from my wife's impetuous nature."

Dianne pouted in her husband's direction and implored Caroline, "*Please*. We need to buy that purple bunny in the window; it's for a special little girl."

"Well, don't let it be said that I'd ever keep a toy from a child." Caroline went to the front of the store and locked the door before pulling the rabbit out of the window display.

"Bonita Bunny. I have to admit, I thought she was something special when I first saw her." The woman carefully wrapped the little rabbit in white tissue paper, taking care not to cover its face. She placed her in a gift bag, feet first, so her head would stick out.

"So, who's the special little girl?" Caroline inquired as she rang up the sale.

"I don't know," Dianne blurted out, only realizing afterward how silly it must have sounded.

Kenny came to her rescue. "We want to give a gift to a toy drive. I'm afraid Dianne fell suddenly and madly in love with this doll. But I think it would be perfect as well." He smiled at Dianne and she in turn kissed him.

"Two hearts, one mind."

Caroline paused to look at Bonita Bunny before passing the bag to Dianne.

"This probably sounds silly, but I'm a bit sad at seeing this little rabbit leave the store. I've grown quite fond of her since her arrival. I suppose I'll have to be appeased knowing the doll will soon be in the arms of a deserving child." She finished ringing up the purchase and joined the couple's generosity by giving them a discount on the price.

As Caroline locked the door behind them,

Dianne and Kenny walked out into the crisp night air. Snow flurries filled the space between them but their love for each other and for a little girl they would never meet kept them warm.

The Marine
The ears first caught his interest. They were sticking out of the bag - one at attention, one having fallen over, weary from being on the alert for a child to love. The gift bag containing the rabbit sat atop a large brightly colored cardboard box labeled *Toys for Tots*.

Sgt. Joe Farrington was part of a crew of volunteers rounding up donations from various drop sites around the area. His truck had already made several trips to the warehouse from other drop-off locations. The magnitude of goodwill the toy drive created, and even more so, the generosity it produced still amazed him. Like that guy who showed up at the warehouse this morning.

"Are you in charge?" the man asked.

"No, just one of the volunteers," Joe replied.

"Then you're just the person I need. Can you give me a hand with these?"

Joe peered into the back of the man's pickup truck. Eight kids' bikes in ascending sizes filled the truck bed. "Looks like you cleared out some lucky bike store."

The man's face shaded a hint of red. He looked down at his booted foot and kicked it forward and back. "I just want to do my part to make sure no kid who wants a bicycle this Christmas will go without one."

Last year was the first time Joe took part in the program. It was enough to move his battle-hardened heart to melt upon seeing kids' faces at Children's Hospital light up when they handed out gifts. He believed that if no other good thing ever happened in his life again, the memory of those kids' smiles would more than make up for it.

Joe pulled the bag containing the bunny out of the drop box, and turned it around by its thin rope handle. It was completely out of character for him, after all, he was a marine—a lean green fighting machine—but he had to see what was attached to those ears popping out of the bag. He gently lifted the doll out of the tissue wrap to take a look.

The rabbit was small against his large, sturdy and callused hands, but still he could sense the fluffy softness of its form. Then he noticed the ribbons. Lavender ribbons of silk, just like the one's his wife put in their daughter's hair, were tied at the base of each floppy ear, and also in a bow above the top button of her outfit. It was like looking at a Beatrix Potter version of his own little girl. He wondered about the child who would soon be hugging the bunny and once again his heart turned to mush. *I must be going soft in my old age.* He wouldn't have it any other way.

The Mother

"What do you have there?" A tiny child with upraised arms holding a crayon drawing ran toward Pam Stilling at toddler warp speed.

"A 'smastree," came the excited answer.

For some reason Hope always overlooked the first syllable of Christmas tree and ran the two words together as one. Pam was glad to know verbal language was a fluid thing.

The child leapt into her arms for a hug. Pam hated the long days her little girl had to stay in daycare, but she had to make a living. Those outstretched arms running toward her at day's end were enough to temporarily quell the guilt of being a working mom and soothe her troubled soul. It was not as if she had an option. If she didn't work no one else would pick up the slack. "It's a very pretty Christmas tree."

Hope's eyes sparkled. "Sandy says Santy's coming."

Again, it's a fluid thing. "Santa, honey. And we'll see if he gets around to us, he's pretty busy you know." Pam tried to keep a low profile on the Santa Claus issue but found it nearly impossible this time of year. He was everywhere. Of course, the daycare workers were just doing their job. What kid didn't dream of presents under the tree? However, this would be Hope's first cognizant Christmas and it would be spare. If she had to spend money on the holiday, it was better to buy things her daughter needed. Pam was more inclined to think of practical gifts like snow pants and boots rather than toys.

"Pam, I'd like to talk to you. Do you have a second?" Sandy, the daycare manager, put her hands out in front of her indicating to Pam to let her take the child. "Hope, I need to talk to your Mommy. Why don't you go play with the blocks a minute?" The girl was easily distracted and did as instructed when Sandy put her down.

"Pam..."

"Look, if it's about the balance on this week's tuition, I get paid next Friday. I just needed to keep a little aside to get Hope a present."

"Actually, that's what I want to talk to you about; not the tuition, but a present. You, or rather Hope, was nominated to receive a gift from *Toys for Tots*. Are you familiar with the program?"

Pam was speechless. Yes, she knew of the program, she'd seen the toy drops around town. They were almost as common as the red kettles. But to be standing here having this conversation as an apparent recipient of one of the toys put her in unfamiliar territory. She had always worked hard to provide for herself and Hope. The public-assisted daycare was a godsend she couldn't make it without, and the rent on the studio apartment over the toy shop was manageable. It was usually the incidental things like car repairs and illnesses that sent the budget on a downward spiral, and Christmas was not doing them any favors.

"I don't understand," finally spilled from her lips.

"It's really simple. The daycare center is one of the agencies that helps to coordinate the distribution of donated toys. Hope's name came up."

Hope's name came up. Despite her hard work, despite her trying to be as normal as everyone else, she was still a statistic - one of the families that just wasn't making it. Pam swallowed her pride, for Hope's sake. A low, "Thank you," was all she could utter.

Pam looked around the apartment. Currier and Ives it was not. The small artificial Christmas tree in the corner wasn't even theirs. They borrowed it from a neighbor spending the holidays with relatives out of town. But Hope's handmade decorations of glittered pinecones and aluminum foil stars and bells graced the boughs making it feel like theirs. Last night, Christmas Eve, they strung ropes of popcorn from branch to branch adding the finishing touches. Outside the window, a fresh blanket of snow covered the street below without even so much as the imprint of a tire. The world was still slumbering in Christmas peace.

Pam had been in a good mood since receiving the Toys for Tots gifts two days earlier, and the spirit of Christmas filled her heart. Hope would have a toy under the tree. That was important to her but so, too, was the knowledge that someone somewhere thought to care for the happiness of an unknown child. Her child. She quietly uttered a prayer. "Lord, please bless the person or persons who provided this gift for my little girl. I am so grateful for their kindness. Amen."

Pam had gotten up early so she wouldn't miss seeing Hope's face as she awoke to Christmas morning and presents beneath the tree. She would make sure Hope opened the toy first. The practical clothes would take a backseat to the doll. She sat on the couch with a mug of coffee warming her hands and waited. It wasn't long before there was a stir and Hope stumbled into the hallway dragging her bankie in one hand while rubbing her eyes open with the other. In the twinkling of an eye, she saw.

"Mommy, Santy was here!" She never was able to get it straight – Sandy, Santy, Santa - it was hopeless. There was time for correction another day.

"Yes honey, he was. And look, he left you presents." Pam knelt on the floor and pulled the toy out from under the tree. Hope's small hands could barely hold the cumbersome package. She placed it on the rug, and at her mother's suggestion tugged at the wrapping paper until it tore off the box. She raised the lid.

The Child
"Ohhhhh..." A breath-filled sigh filled the room and Hope's eyes opened wide. A faint hint of memory—just outside their front door—flashed for a second then was gone. "Mommy, she's so pret-ty." Bonita

Bunny, her ears gently folded into the box, was ready for love.

Hope lifted the doll into her arms. The downy rabbit, the softest thing she had ever felt, even more huggable than her precious bankie, was dressed in lavender and pink from the tip of her floppy ears down to her bunny-slippered feet. Silk ribbons tied in petite bows at the base of each ear gave the impression that she was a gentle creature. Even the buttons on her robe were shaped like tiny bunnies. White whiskers emerged above pastel lips and lovingly, in her little bunny arms she held a teddy bear.

She squeezed the stuffed animal tight in an adoring hug. "Mommy, I love my dolly so much." Her eyes then abruptly filled with worry. "Is it OK if I love my new dolly as much as I love you?"

Her mother cleared her throat and stumbled over her reply. "Absolutely, honey, absolutely. Merry Christmas."

Hope threw her arms around her mother. "Merry Christmas, Mommy."

24
A LESS THAN SILENT NIGHT

It was cold, the sky overcast with threatening clouds and the parking lot a lake of remnant slush from the snowfall earlier that day. The jingle of bells was in the air. Kelly Loggins was tired of circling in search of a parking space - three times up and down the aisles and nothing. She even tried tailing a couple walking with packages until they loaded their bundles into the car then turned around to go back inside. A small unpleasant voice inside Kelly's head said to hit the gas through the puddles and douse them good as she passed. Luckily her conscience prevailed. Circling again, she spied white back-up lights advertising a spot and made her approach. Just as she was about to turn in, a Cooper Mini intercepted it and slipped into the open space with no apologies. "Aw, come on!" She hit the horn. "Boy, if I wasn't so desperate for this stupid doll..." She had to remind herself why she was going to the mall on a Friday evening just three days before Christmas. *I must be out of my mind. Certainly, the good Doc Ellen would have something to say about it.* She would have to remember not to whine to her about it later, or face the consequences.

Of course it was the Suntanned-Supermodel-Mollie-Dollie-on-Wheels, this year's **it** toy for every princess under four feet tall that had her at the mall despite her better judgment. Kelly could still hear the confidence in Tara's voice as her daughter shared the visions of sugar plums dancing in her head. "Mommy," she said, standing in the kitchen in her dress up tutu and magic wand. "I just know Santa will bring me a Mollie Dollie. And I'm gonna love her forever and ever."

Failure was not an option.

Backup lights again. Kelly was quick to squeeze past the exiting car with barely any air between them lest another micro car was lurking, and landed a much coveted parking spot. "Yes!"

She took a moment for a couple of deep breaths before heading out into the holiday fray. Then gathering her purse and wrapping a scarf around her neck, she opened the door and promptly stepped in an icy puddle that sent a sudden shock of cold through her body. At that instant she almost wished she were the type to use four-letter expletives. They would have come in handy. Instead, she raised her head tall and trudged toward the mall entrance, with each step producing a hideous sucking sound announcing her arrival.

The Dickensian décor of the mall's "Old Fashioned Christmas" which was supposed to evoke holiday cheer had little effect on her. It was her third trip to the mall that month—two too many times—and she knew decorations couldn't compensate for pushy shoppers, overworked sales people and elves with attitudes, making it the last place she wanted to be. But she was hot on the trail of an elusive doll that every other parent of a fairly princess was looking for as well. So she girded herself against the throngs and began her search, one soggy foot in front of the other.

Stores of every genre hawked their wares, which, of course, no one should be without this Christmas. She wondered how it ever went from a cradle in Bethlehem to a blue light special on Main Street. How did she allow herself to fall for all the commercialism? *Ninety dollars for a Mollie doll,* she lamented, *if you can find it.*

As she entered the toy store, Kelly heard the unmistakable voices of Muppets singing "The Twelve Days of Christmas". Miss Piggy particularly insulted her ears with a doleful, "Five Golden Rings." She scanned the nearly empty shelf and saw one last Suntanned-Supermodel-Mollie-Dollie-on-Wheels just about to walk away with a shopper who couldn't contain her happiness at nabbing the last one in the store and did a little happy jig. Kelly audibly whimpered. The next toy store was also out. When she got to the specialty doll shop, they were just putting a sign in the window: "Sorry, we are out of Mollie Dollie, but come in for her cousin, Pollie

Dollie." Everywhere she turned, store after store, there were cries of children and droning music but no Mollie. It was getting late and she felt a headache coming on.

Kelly sat down In the food court to rest her feet and every other over-worked body part for a few minutes while she regrouped and tried to come up with Plan B. A young couple strolled by with clasped hands, moving along in gentle synchronized strides oblivious to the ruckus around them. Kelly assumed they were childless, which afforded them the peace and quiet of their own little world.

Her headache grew stronger and she decided to get some aspirin at the drug store upstairs. Boarding the escalator that rose out of the food court to the second floor, Kelly became aware of the soundtrack to the shopping mayhem as provided by the vendors. Each oblivious to the other broadcasted their favorite Christmas music out into the center of the food court. From the Chix-D-Lux on the left came, "Grandma Got Run Over by a Reindeer." The McDonald's on the right was blasting something about, "All I Want for Christmas..." In front and behind, respectively, were a resounding, "O Come, O Come Emmanuel" and "Joy to the World." It was an auditory assault, truly a Nightmare on 34th Street. *Is there no such thing as peace on earth?*

Then, as if rising to heaven in her ascent to the floor above, the cacophonous medley from below faded the higher she rose, replaced by a gentle, sustained melody. The music graced her ears like a salve for her state of mind. The strain of an organ crescendoed to a sweet, tender lullaby as she neared the top, enveloping her with the resonating sounds of "Silent Night." Kelly savored the music, allowing it to fortify and move her spirit. *"All is calm, all is bright."* The lyrics she heard in her mind offered hope. Every stressor, every pressure of the season was extinguished in its beauty. She stood before the Piano & Organ Store drinking it in, becoming one with the moment, purging herself of the holiday so that only the holy remained. Her mission forgotten, Kelly's thoughts were drawn once again to the cradle in Bethlehem: a Savior born to die for a hurting world. She closed her eyes and for the first time in a long time received the gift of Christmas.

With renewed peace in her soul she walked on, having made a resolute decision: Next year, we'll write that letter to Santa in August!

JONI VANNEST

25
ANGEL BRIGADE

Good morning, Lord. I sure could use some last minute inspiration. My sermon for tonight is as stark as those branches out there.

Reverend Paul Hemphill looked over the front yard from his bedroom window as he did most mornings. The trees were bare, the grass dry and brittle, having long since given up the suppleness of summertime. He noted plump silver clouds casting gray shadows, perhaps a sign of things to come or maybe snow. The possibility of snow on December 24th lightened his mood a bit. He should have been filled with the joy of Christmas, and to some extent he was. But a large part of his joy was still to be poured out of his pen in the form of a sermon for the Christmas Eve Service. When Runilla asked for the title of his message to put in the bulletin he was at a loss. Being the creative secretary she was, she improvised: "Christmas Surprise!" Not unlike something out of the church cookbook - Tuna Surprise or Meatloaf Surprise. He hoped his sermon turned out to be more fulfilling than a form of mystery meat. So far, the message comprised only five words, an opening befitting the season, "Rejoice, for He is born!" Everything between that and Amen remained a mystery.

He heard Hannah rolling over, waking with a yawn. She was the love of his life. Twenty-three years a pastor's wife and not one time had she complained. Not even about his long hours or the many calls in the middle of the night from parishioners needing comfort, nor the vacations cut short by some crisis or another calling him home. But she wouldn't trade it for the world, of that he was certain. He recalled the night she made that clear. It was the end of a week filled with far too many church obligations causing him to delegate the family's needs to the back burner. With uncommon understanding, she was able to assuage his resulting guilt. "Hey handsome, don't you know you're the love of my life? If I have to share you with three hundred or so other folks well then, so be it." She had sealed her proclamation with a kiss.

"So, what do you see outside there, Rev. Hemphill? If it's not the Second Coming, then come on back to bed for a minute or two. It's good to snuggle on crisp mornings like this, especially if it's Christmas Eve."

Paul continued to stare out the window. "No, The Almighty doesn't seem to be appearing in His glory today, unless you count the wonders of His creation. In that case, the neighbor's dog just chased one of His cats up a tree." He turned to face his wife. "Good morning, sweetheart. Sorry, I've got too much to do to linger today."

"That old sermon for tonight still eluding you?"

"Yes, it is." He sat on the edge of the bed. "The trouble is, I so want to bring something new to the message this year. Tradition is a good thing, but I can't help feeling a new angle on the nativity could bring greater meaning and significance to the congregation's celebration."

"Paul, it was good enough for the angels and shepherds. Leave well enough alone and come back to bed."

Hannah's generosity to share her husband on most occasions was indeed a blessing, but there still were those times when she wanted him all to herself. He leaned over, kissed her on the lips and said, "Sorry, my love, The Spirit and duty call."

"Fine. Don't forget we're having a family dinner at four o'clock so schedule your day accordingly."

"How could I forget? You've been planning this meal for weeks." Paul had grown weary of seeing mouthwatering delights coming out of the oven for the last few days only to be told, "They're for Christmas Eve."

Hannah rose from the bed and retrieved her robe, wrapping herself in soft terrycloth. "No sense lounging in bed all alone. Besides, I still have more cookies to make for refreshments after tonight's service."

"If you need me to taste test anything, you know where to find me," Paul said with a hopeful smile.

"Glued to your computer, I suppose."

He sighed. "No, my dear, praying for a revelation."

"Twenty-three years and you're still full of surprises."

"Well, if I don't get inspired soon, the sermon will be full of surprises, too. Catch you later." He closed the door behind him as he left the bedroom.

*　　*　　*

Ellen Steele reviewed her long to-do list in a panic.

1. Finish wrapping

2. Make punch for refreshments

3. Hem Brielle's costume

4. Pick up present

5. Glue cotton balls on sheep costume

6. Check on Dad

And there was so much more that didn't even make the list.

Nine-thirty a.m., less than ten hours 'til show time. Of course, she knew it was improper to think of the children's Christmas pageant as a performance. "The children's pageant has long been considered an integral part of the Christmas Eve Service. As such it should be presented with reverence and decorum," the head of the Sunday School Committee had told her. *Right.* **She** *probably never* *tried to get a room full of children to listen, let alone obey instructions, this close to Christmas.* Still, as the director, she was aware the children's part of the service was the highlight of the evening and every parent expected his or her child to shine.

Ellen was still doing the breakfast dishes when she heard the house phone ring. *Is there ever enough time in a day?*

Avery appeared in the doorway, interrupting her thoughts. "Mom. Phone."

"Take a message, please." she said, up to her elbows in bacon grease and soap bubbles.

"It's Mrs. Cavanaugh, she says she has to talk to you. It's important."

Of course. Isn't it always? One thing she'd learned as director was that every pageant parent became a stage mother, even at this level. "OK."

Ellen caught her breath before taking the handset from Avery. "Hi Monica, Merry Christmas."

"Oh, I wish that it was," came the reply, sounding almost like an apology. "I really hate to tell you this." Ellen dreaded whatever Monica was going to say next. *Nothing good ever starts with those words.* "The triplets came down with chickenpox; they won't be able to be in the pageant tonight."

Ellen grabbed a chair to steady herself then flopped onto it. She wanted to scream. Instead, "Oh dear," was all that came out. "Oh. Dear." she repeated, spitting the words out in staccato bursts. The triplets had been cast in vital roles as the three wise men. Three missing angels or shepherds could be overlooked, but three wise men gone AWOL, no way.

"Ellen, I'm so sorry. I waited to call until I was absolutely certain. There's just no way they can be there tonight." Ellen could not form a response through rising panic. Her end of the line went silent. "Ellen? Ellen?"

In a daze, Ellen Steele hung up the phone without even saying goodbye. Her day just got as bad as it could possibly get, or so she thought.

* * *

A hard knock on the office door preceded his son popping his head in without waiting for an answer. Paul thought Jim was wearing his hair a little longer than usual, probably to cover up the Hemphill ears, a curse his own father had passed on to him. He too wore his hair on the long side as a teenager. Despite that one mistake of heredity, Paul believed his son to be quite the catch for some lucky girl.

"Dad, Ellen Steele is on the phone for you. Says it's urgent."

"Don't you mean, Mrs. Steele?"

"*Dad.*"

Jim seized every opportunity to assert his maturity these days. His latest efforts involved bypassing the more formal surnames of his elders, who to him had always been Mr. or Mrs. and instead call them by their given names. Paul wondered how stodgy old Mr. Caldwell would take to that. After all these years, even he didn't dare address him as Eustace.

"OK, OK. I'll get it in here, thanks."

Jim started to close the door then opened it back up again saying, "Oh, one more thing before you pick up. Do you want a rematch of Guitar Hero to try and redeem yourself after last night?" Jim had beaten his father in the first of what would probably be a full-blown tournament before the holiday break was over.

"At some point. Let me get through this evening's service first, ok?"

"Sure, but plan on getting another sound beating." He played a strong downward strum of air guitar and left.

A little humility would go a long way for that boy.

Paul turned his attention to the phone. Few people called him on the house phone these days, as most people had his cell number. Usually it was the older folks who still used the landline, they had for years and they weren't about to change. Old habits were hard to break. Ellen Steele on the other hand wasn't old, but she was set in her ways which had the same effect. He picked up the phone with some trepidation, hoping it wasn't bad news about Jack. Ellen kept him apprised on her father's illness, calling each week to make sure he stayed on the prayer list. Last he'd heard the treatments were rough but he was doing okay. He made a mental note to try to visit him between the holidays. "Ellen, this is Paul, what can I do for you?"

"Oh Paul, it's the pageant. I don't know what I'm going to do. It's a catastrophe. Never in a million years did I think a thing like this could happen. So of course, I have no contingency plans. And at the last minute like this. It's a nightmare I tell you, a nightmare!"

"Whoa, slow down. What's a nightmare? It's a children's pageant, Ellen. It can't be all that bad."

"Oh, if you only knew, pastor, if you only knew."

"Well then, why don't you tell me all about it?" Paul found himself speaking as if to calm a child in the midst of a tantrum.

"Monica Cavanaugh called to tell me the triplets have the chickenpox and won't be able to play the three wise men in the pageant tonight. We have no understudies. How can we depict the nativity without the magi? It would be a travesty."

"Certainly, there must be some children you can move into the roles. Upgrade them, so to speak."

"You don't understand. There are lines to memorize, stage directions to get straight. Believe me I know those kids. There is not one child who can step up to the plate at the last second like this and get it right, let alone three. Oh, what are we going to do?"

We? Paul spent the last week confounded by the elusiveness of his sermon; he didn't need to add this to his troubles as well. Surely, this was more up the alley of the Sunday School Committee. He was also sure Ellen wouldn't want to hear that at this moment. A quick solution was necessary. "Look, if there are no grade school children capable of playing the parts, then what about aging the magi a few years?"

"What do you mean?"

"How about contacting some of our high school youth to see if any of them would be willing to step in?"

"Hmmm. I hadn't thought of that."

Paul was a firm believer that goodness and clear heads will always prevail. Right now Ellen seemed to be running on empty in the clarity department.

"Got any ideas?" she asked.

Paul closed his eyes and took a deep breath. All my trials, Lord. "Well, the first one who comes to mind is my Jim. Why don't I put him on the line and you can see if he and some of his friends are up for an adventure tonight?"

"Paul, that's a great idea. Jim and the other boys have been helping as stagehands and with props so they probably know the play by heart. I'm sure they could do it."

"See Ellen, problem solved, and in less than five minutes."

"Praise the Lord!"

"Amen."

*   *   *

Jim Hemphill rocked like a hurricane on Guitar Hero to the point of excluding all else. He became aware his little brother Bobby was trying to get his attention only after the boy worked himself up into a frenzied tantrum and resorted to yanking on the hem of Jim's shirt. "Please let me play. Please. *Jiiiiim.* Come on." Jim elbowed Bobby away like an annoying bug without missing a note. *Yeah, I'm good,* he thought right along with the melody.

"Jim. Jim. James Matthew Hemphill." His father's voice drowned out the Scorpions and ruined his concentration. *James Matthew Hemphill. Uh oh.* His dad had resorted to using his full name. *Not good.* He wondered how long he had been oblivious to him and decided to play it safe and sweet and innocent. He turned down the sound and looked directly into his eyes. "Yeah, Dad?"

His father sighed. "Jim, it's not good you get so involved in that game you ignore everything around you. You're brother has been trying to get your attention and so have I."

Jim gulped. He really couldn't help it. It was his ability to totally immerse himself into the game that made him so good at it. Should he have to apologize for excelling at what he does? Something told him his father wouldn't buy that angle, so instead he said, "I'll try to listen out for others from now on." His father's scowl morphed into a more tolerant expression. The quasi-apology worked.

"Jim, Mrs. Steele is on the phone; she'd like to

talk to you. And I suggest you may want to consider the Christmas spirit when you hear what she has to ask."

The cloaked warning made him nervous. He got the feeling that whatever it was Mrs. Steele wanted, she was going to get. Two hours later Jim had his friends, Sean, Denny and Tyler gathered in his living room. "You mean you said yes for us without even asking? What if we had plans? It is Christmas, you know." Tyler always took the defensive stance, even if just for the sake of arguing.

Jim was quick to return. "You don't. You were going to be there doing props anyway. Now you'll just be there in a different capacity."

Sean tossed in his two cents. "But I get stage fright. I mean totally; I clam up. Remember the bumble bee thing?" In the second grade spring play, Sean had to "buzz" across stage to the waiting flowers of Mary Jones and Alex Hurlbutt. He refused to go beyond the curtain and ended up buzzing from the wings.

"That was years ago. I should hope you've matured since then." Jim was rarely without an answer. In this instance, he was able to cover all the bases without even trying. The one thing he didn't have an answer for was when Denny brought up the caliber of the play he had so quickly gotten them involved in.

"It's the three wise guys. We know the lines already, how bad can it be?"

"But there's four of us," Sean reminded him. "And it's so boring," added Denny.

Tyler leaned forward when Jim mentioned the three wise guys as if a light bulb had gone off in his head. "Hey, I think you've got something there, Jim." Tyler had an idea.

*   *   *

Lunch that day at the Hemphill's was just a light snack. Paul stood at the counter piling cheese and crackers on his plate, still trying to pull several ideas together into one cohesive sermon as the family milled about. "Save room for dinner," Hannah reminded him. "So, how's the sermon coming along?"

"I'm afraid the only perspective I can get on the nativity is the same one they've been playing for two thousand years."

Jim grabbed a bottle of water out of the refrigerator. "If you ask me, it's all hogwash anyway."

"Jim!" his mother objected.

Paul saw the twinkle in his son's eye upon making the comment. The boy enjoyed playing devil's advocate. Being on the debate team had taught him to look at a situation from all sides before drawing a conclusion, which encouraged the impish trait in him.

"What?" Jim tried to look innocent again, or at least affronted. "Don't you think it's just a little unreal? I mean a virgin birth, angels and all that. Come on? Besides all the Gospels don't even agree on what actually happened." He took a quick sip of water before continuing. "What if Jesus was born like every other baby since the beginning of time? No virgin birth, no heavenly choir. Just a kid in a cradle, a son of man. Would the world still be in awe?"

A concerned Hannah defended her beliefs. "Certainly the *Son of God* would make Himself known. He couldn't help but reveal His true nature while doing the Father's will."

"But did we need the fairy tale to get things started?" Jim was being incorrigible.

"Jim, stop being such a jerk." Bobby may not have understood the bantering but he made it plain he did not like the way his brother was speaking to their parents.

"I'm just trying to spark intelligent conversation on an age old theme."

His father gave him a firm glare. "You're going to give your mother a heart attack. Just tell her you haven't walked away from the faith so we can have a pleasant Christmas."

Jim went to where his mother was standing, her face now an ashen color, and put his arms around her. "Don't worry, Mom. God is still my co-pilot."

She hugged him back, relieved to hear his convictions were still intact. "Maybe you should let Him be your navigator as well."

Still concerned for his sermon and looking for any inspiration he could get, Paul decided to ask for input from his opinionated teenage son. Maybe Jim could come up with something he could use. He only had a couple of chances a year to reach the 2x4s and this was one of them. Paul had always teased that a vast number of Christians were actually a lot like 2x4s. Their pastors saw them twice a year – Christmas and Easter, and at four other times in their lives: when he'd hatch 'em, match 'em, patch 'em and dispatch 'em. He didn't want this Christmas to be a lost opportunity. "So tell me," he began. "Has the nativity story become insignificant, succumbing to the popularity of the commercialized Christmas?"

Jim shook his head. "Un uh, leave me out of it, lest I be branded an infidel."

"No son, I'd really like to hear your opinion."

The boy hesitated at first, then took the opportunity to be heard and regarded. "In that case, Christianity has been marginalized by the mainstream media and televangelism with its zealous preachers and CEO's. Whether or not the nativity story has been marginalized is not nearly as significant as the perversion of the religion supposedly born from its story."

"How interesting." Paul picked up his plate and started walking toward his office. He tossed his head in that direction to indicate his son should follow. "But don't you think that in today's society..." His intention was to move the conversation out of Hannah's earshot. No doubt, it would have given her hot flashes.

*   *   *

The small church could have been a model for Currier and Ives or Thomas Kinkade. Built in 1807, the original structure saw several additions over the years as the needs of the congregation changed. The white clapboard sanctuary, the oldest part of the church building, stood above a dirt basement that provided its share of heebie-jeebies to the curious or the daring. The steeple and bell added in 1837 for the expressed purpose of "calling all to meeting," was paid for with funds raised from a covered dish supper put on by the ladies social circle in that same year. To this day, public suppers were still the preferred method of fundraising for special projects. It was the joy of every child to be the one to ring the bell ten minutes before the service began and again when it ended, the rope raising the smallest of them clear off the ground in its oscillating cycle.

On this night, two pine wreaths, elegant in their simplicity, hung illuminated on the double front doors facing the street. At 7:10, ushers opened the doors to welcome those who had come to worship. Mellow candlelight softly illuminated the church and reflected off the tin ceiling and muted colors of the stained-glass windows lining either side of the room, greeting those who entered with a brief glimpse back into history and how a Christmas Eve service would have looked in earlier times. Pastor Paul Hemphill met all who walked through the doors with a handshake and a hearty welcome. It would have truly been a tranquil scene, if not for the shrill voice heard coming from the parish hall on the opposite side of the sanctuary.

*   *   *

"Children, can I have your attention? *Please*, can I have your attention? I NEED YOU TO TAKE YOUR PLACES." Ellen Steele was losing her already frazzled patience.

Mothers were making last minute adjustments to costumes or taking pictures of their children, getting in the way and being more nuisance than help. Ellen wished she had the nerve to take the shepherd's crook and farm them all out of the hall. She was thankful Kelly and Bill were helping out. It was not a one person job. They moved among the kids, placing in their assigned spots those who were still out of place. Ellen came upon Jim, Sean, Tyler and Denny who were now wearing makeshift kingly robes and talking to some of the children.

"Boys," she said, placing her hands on Sean's and Denny's shoulders and speaking to all of them not as children, but as the young adults they were. "I can't thank you enough for your flexibility in stepping up to take on these roles. You really saved the day. I owe you one."

"Think nothing of it," replied Tyler.

"Are you ok with your lines?"

"Got it all under control," said Jim. "Improvise is our middle name."

Ellen thought that was a strange way to put it, but she supposed it was applicable. She thanked them again and continued rounding up her angels, shepherds and other barnyard critters.

*   *   *

Back in the vestibule, Paul shook the hands of his congregants as they arrived, keenly aware that even yet he had no definitive sermon to offer this evening. After much thought and a lot of prayer, a new angle on Christmas never materialized. At such a late hour, he had only two choices: he could try to wing it—which was not advisable—or recycle one from a few years back and hope no one noticed. He opted for the second choice.

He was shaking Eustace Caldwell's hand and praying his memory wasn't as good as he always claimed it to be, or else he'd get an earful tomorrow about resurrecting a sermon. "Good evening Mr. Caldwell, and Merry Christmas."

"Evening Pastor Paul. A chilly night to be out, for certain. But we're sure the children's performance and your sermon will warm our hearts."

Paul's relative calm skyrocketed to sheer panic with just those few words. "Let's hope, Mr. Caldwell, let's hope." He began praying for wisdom and/or a miracle while continuing to greet his flock by name and with a handshake.

"Tom, Sheri. I'll have to stop by the diner for some of your apple pie before I make my annual New Year's resolution to lose weight. Merry Christmas."

"Merry Christmas, Andrew. How wonderful to see

you here tonight. Welcome." He gave Andrew's handshake an extra pump or two. He was thrilled to see the young man had finally accepted his invitation to join them in worship, and what better time than Christmas Eve. Andrew gave a quick, nervous smile then ushered in two younger boys and a heavyset woman, presumably his mother, who came in behind him, without introducing them. Paul stretched his hand in the woman's direction anyway. "Welcome. Nice of you to join us." Her hand felt limp and sad in his. "Merry Christmas."

"Merry Christmas, Helen. How is your sister Louise doing in Georgia? Be sure to send her my regards."

"Joe, good to see you. Dragged yourself away from the store to be with us, eh?"

Joe Whitmire smiled and wished Paul a merry Christmas. Karen Tanner, his young associate was with him. The last Paul heard from Hannah was that their romantic entanglement had phased out but they remained good friends. "Wouldn't want to miss the pageant. After all, Tara's in it this year you know."

"Yes, I saw. A sweet angel if ever there was one." He reached his hand out to Karen. "Welcome."

He caught a glimpse of Jack Priestly coming up the steps leaning heavily on his son-in-law Brad Steele's arm, with his granddaughter, Jodi, on the other side for extra support. The two younger Steeles, Avery and Brielle, were in the parish hall preparing for the pageant. "Jack." Paul clapped the elderly man on the upper arm and held fast to his hand. "How are you doing?" Paul was a regular visitor during Jack's recuperation after the surgery. It was then he discovered Jack was never one for long, drawn out conversations; he was usually brief and to the point, making visitations difficult.

"Treatments are rough. Keep me alive, though. So far."

"And the journaling?"

"Helps."

"So glad to hear it. You know you remain on the church's prayer list and I look forward to the day when we can celebrate that you're healthy enough to come off the list."

Jack started moving his lips to say something then either changed his mind or found himself unable to speak the words. He nodded and started walking away with watery eyes. Brad looked at Paul and uttered a sincere, "Me too."

Seeing Jack at church rather than in a hospital bed gave Paul hope that there really were such things as Christmas miracles. He bid, "A blessed Christmas to you all," as they walked on.

And so it went. The good people of Wheatfield Bridge converged on the little white church, filling it to capacity as the bell in the steeple echoed on the cold night air, calling all to meeting.

When the time arrived, Pastor Paul processed up the aisle behind the choir singing *Joy to the World*.

He stood in the pulpit and looked out over the fold through the ensuing verses. The pews held a mixture of young and old, visitors and members, the well-to-do and the struggling, newcomers to the community and those home grown.

The Order of Worship called for the pastor to welcome everyone to the service then turn the program over to the children for their pageant, after which, he would give a short message on the meaning of this joyful occasion. All of this would be interspersed with hymns and carols of the season.

Knowing he had no new revelations to share, Paul was at least determined to make up for his lack of originality with unbridled enthusiasm. His planned five-word greeting Rejoice, for He is born! would still stand. As the choir finished the last verse of the processional with the director holding the last note for effect, Paul's mind searched, even yet, for some new insight to add to his message. Nothing. Maybe, he hoped, something would strike him while the children were performing. His mind was still wandering when he took hold of the pulpit and in a loud, excited voice proclaimed, "Hallelujah, for He is risen!" It took a second, but then everybody in the church, including Paul, realized the great faux pas he'd made. A mixture of surprised giggles and guffaws spread like a wave. Paul's face turned red as he quickly attempted to correct the error. "Uh, uh, and He will... some time in spring. But for right now, REJOICE, for He is born!"

The service was off to an inauspicious start.

Just as Paul was about to regain enough composure to welcome the Christmas worshipers, 2x4s included, a nervous Ellen Steele jumped the gun and hit the button on the stereo system starting the karaoke music. A flock of sheep, complete with cotton ball wool, sang and "bahhed" their way through the sanctuary. They were joined by a cow with an unusually large set of udders hanging from the front of her costume, as well as an assortment of odd, if not adorable, farm animals. By the end of the first song they were assembled on the altar which now substituted for a stage.

There was no going back. Paul sat down and let the pageant roll on.

*   *   *

Ellen took her place in the aisle seat of the first row where it was easy to direct the young ones and prompt the older ones in case they missed a line. She signaled for Mary, Joseph and the donkey to walk up the aisle.

Taking small and deliberate steps, they slowly approached the "inn." About halfway up the aisle the donkey, played by brothers Jacob and Allen Taines sharing a costume for two, began to lose control of its rear portion. Every two steps or so, the hind legs kicked out behind it in what appeared to be a seizure. Step, step, kick; step, step, kick. Gyrations and grunting sounds started coming from the donkey's middle. They had almost made it to the inn when the legs gave one final kick that pulled the front and back sections apart. Allen Taines' head appeared and, in a great gasp, he sucked in air as if his life depended on it. Ellen jumped up to piece the costume back together again and whispered, "What happened?"

Louder than she expected so that the whole assembly heard his response, Allen said, "Jacob farted." Laughter erupted from the congregation. Ellen, too nervous to appreciate the humor, tried to be calm and keep things moving. She motioned for the innkeeper to make his entrance.

"Hark! Who goes there?" The innkeeper was right on cue.

"Please sir, my wife is with child and we've no place to stay."

Ellen was glad it seemed things were back on track.

Suddenly, the newly patched donkey began seizing again. In the fray, Allen lost his balance and fell to the left, pulling his brother with him. The donkey tumbled into poor Mary who promptly gave birth to the pillow that had been tied up under her blue garments. She quickly stuffed it back under her costume and held it in place with her hands as if carrying a heavy load.

Ellen started to lose it. The script started to shake in her hands. The brothers uprighted the donkey and the children broke into their second song, No Room at the Inn. The song came off without a hitch.

Then it was time for the blessed event, at least the one written in the script.

The Narrator proclaimed, "And she brought forth her first born child and laid him in a manger because there was no room for them at the inn." Another signal from Ellen and the angels appeared in procession from all corners of the church. The congregation provided a plethora of toddlers and pre-school children to wear the white robes with strap-on wings and shimmering silver halos. A unified, "Awwww" escaped from the adults as dozens of precious angels made their way to the stable. Shepherds soon joined the angels in bowing down to worship the newborn King. It was truly a Kodak moment and Ellen knew it.

She enjoyed it while it lasted.

*   *   *

Jim and his friends had taken their positions at the back of the sanctuary, ready to make their entrance. His little brother, Bobby, and two other children were prepared to enter behind them dressed as camels.

Before they started to make their way into the room, Tyler turned to the children and said, "Now you remember what we told you about camels?"

Three heads bobbed in unison.

The Narrator spoke. "Behold, there came three wise men from the east."

*   *   *

Karaoke music once again played and the

children broke into a jazzed up version of *We Three Kings of Orient Are* as the magi and their dromedaries made the journey to the stable. Ellen, looking toward the stage to direct the singing, feared one of the kings might miss a line, having to learn them as fast as they did. As it turned out, her worries were justified, but for a different reason.

Every couple of bars Ellen would turn her head to observe the royal entourage. Then something caught her eye. The camels seemed to be making strange faces, as if puckering their lips. From just her stolen glances, she was not able to see what they were doing. But she did hear some of the people in the pews make grumbling noises and even caught an occasional, "Ewwww" and "Gross." Paul, sitting next to her, turned to face the children. She knew there was trouble when she caught a glimpse of his eyes nearly bulge out of their sockets at what he saw. She turned around to get a better look, even as she still directed the singing. Three costumed children who appeared determined to be the most life-like and realistic animals of the whole bunch were spitting into the congregation. She quickly jumped up and reprimanded the children, asking them in hushed tones, "Why are you doing that? It's not nice."

"But it's what camel's do," one of them said.

Ellen got firm. "Well, not tonight they don't. Understand?"

The children looked contrite and refrained from

live-action camelry for the rest of the evening.

Paul, on the other hand, gave the teenage kings a stern look, which Ellen did not understand, but did notice that it stopped the snickers they were trying to contain. She was suddenly concerned there might be something more to this than met the eye. Still, she prayed the boys would be able to salvage what was left of the show.

Jim was the first king with a line of dialogue. Ellen slunk down in her seat as she heard him announce to those gathered at the stable, "We are three wise guys from the east: Moe, Larry, and Curly. And this is our servant boy, Fred." He pointed to Sean who was dressed in a toga and holding onto the camel's reigns. The congregation giggled and the boys looked pleased.

Ellen, in a prompters whisper said, "NO, that's NOT how it goes."

Jim, not losing a beat asked, "Would you prefer Manny, Moe, and Jack?"

The people in the pews who had no idea this *wasn't* part of the script burst into peals of laughter. Ellen put her hands to her head and slunk even further into her seat.

Then it was Tyler's turn to get a laugh. He broke from where he was standing and sidled up to the cow whose costume prominently displayed its udders. With great exaggeration and hunkering down in his best Groucho Marx impersonation, complete with an invisible cigar, he examined the cow up and down then turned to face the audience saying, "Why that's udderly ridiculous." Then, in a flash, he was back in form with the magi.

"Look!" shouted Denny. "We bring gifts."

He dug into a pouch wrapped around his waist and pulled out the first of the three gifts: Gold. And as those particular boys were wont to do, it wasn't the expected gold spray-painted styrofoam that had been used in every pageant for the last twenty some odd years. No, Denny pulled out and raised up long chains of bling that would look more appropriate around the neck of a rap singer than in a Christmas pageant. From one chain hung a cross and from the other a Star of David. "Gold," Denny announced. "And symbolically, very appropriate, I may add."

Next, Tyler produced his version of Frankincense, in the form of a perfume atomizer. He sprayed fragrance in the direction of the baby while declaring, "Chanel #5. Only the best for my Savior!"

Jim then produced his gift. "Myrrh, the finest of oils." He held the bottle he'd taken from the kitchen pantry high for all to see - a bottle of olive oil. "Extra virgin, of course."

The laughs weren't uproarious, but they were consistent. The congregation found the boys' irreverent take on the nativity humorous, unaware that it was all unscripted.

By this time, the altar was bursting with nativity characters: animals, shepherds, angels, kings. Ellen kept telling herself they had just one more song to get through and then it would all be over. The end was near. *Thank God.* It was then she noticed Kelly and Bill's little girl, Tara, tugging on the neck of her costume and waving her hand like a fan. She remembered seeing Tara before she donned her costume, dressed in a turtleneck sweater, corduroy jumper and warm woolen tights – appropriate attire for a cold winter night but not for standing in a warm, crowded stage. Ellen noticed some of the other kids seemed to be squirming as well. The lights, the heat and the close proximity of her fellow angels had then proven too much for Tara's endurance. She began to disrobe.

First, she untied her wings and dropped them to the floor. Then, with a great deal of wiggling and struggling, she pulled the costume over her head until she was free of it. A couple of other little angels decided it was a good idea and did likewise, so that before Ellen could do anything about it, two dozen angels were undressing on stage in the midst of her Christmas pageant. She wished there was a hole nearby into which she could crawl and never have to show her face again.

Finally the children, costumed and un-costumed, wrapped up the pageant with their closing song, *Glory to the King*. They smiled and took their bows amid camera flashes and applause. Ellen was also supposed to take a bow at this time but remained seated, unable to move, and just stared straight ahead wondering how it could have gone so wrong.

What had become of my lovely pageant? She felt Paul take her by the arm and pull her up against her will to face the congregation. The applause grew louder as they showed their appreciation for a job well done. Even still, she remained in a semi-catatonic state. It took a couple of minutes until she became herself again. The first words out of her mouth to Pastor Paul were, "Next year, get someone else to direct." She also made the executive decision that later that evening, after the kids were in bed and she and Brad were through playing Santa, she would relax in a warm bubble bath while sipping eggnog, which under the circumstances would require a little extra holiday cheer.

As the children left the stage, Paul grabbed the attention of the three "wise-guys".

"My office. After the service. Be there."

*   *   *

Once again, Paul Hemphill took the pulpit and faced the congregation eagerly awaiting his learned interpretation of the second chapter of Luke. Somehow, after the presentation of the most discombobulated Christmas pageant he had ever witnessed, the recycled sermon printed on the pages in front of him seemed out of place. It was, to the best of his abilities and opinion, an outstanding elucidation on the famous scripture, but he deemed it unsuitable in light of what had transpired that evening. In a leap of faith, he turned over the pages and spoke from his heart.

"Friends, tonight the children have given us more to think about than my mere words could ever hope to express. For days I have struggled with the question I had hoped to answer for us in my Christmas message: Is there a place for the nativity in our modern world? Well, the children in all their innocence, and yes, even their mischief, clearly answered my query.

"You see, Jesus came into this world as our King just as the children showed us. But He also came into the world as a Savior, a Savior for our most imperfect world. For we, even in our greatest efforts to please an Almighty God, will fall pitifully short of being able to do so. Our imperfect nature can't compare to His perfect nature, so we need a Redeemer. And God the Father in His infinite wisdom and love sent us that Holy Deliverer in the form of a baby. Someone just like us—someone who had to learn to crawl before he could walk, and who probably skinned His knees in the process—someone who knows what it is to be human, yet overcame His humanity by the grace of our Father, and thus, can lead the way for our salvation.

"So my friends, when those who would criticize or seek to commercialize and destroy this Holy Season ask, is there a place for the nativity in our modern world? You can feel confident in answering. Yes! Yes, my Savior reigns!

"A blessed Christmas to you all. Amen."

"Now," he concluded with just a touch of

exasperation, "let's sing our final hymn and get out of here and go home." Paul walked from the altar and joined Hannah in the pew. She reached for his hand and held it tight.

In soft, hushed tones the organist played *Silent Night* while the ushers handed out small candles. The Light of the World passed from one to another until the room was aglow only by candlelight. The song ended and, as was tradition, the worshipers spilled from the sanctuary into the night in silence. A light snow was falling.

Paul was in his office hanging up his robe and stole when he heard, "Good night, Pastor Paul. Merry Christmas." The three wise guys and Fred didn't ignore the pastor's directive, but they did try to escape the coming retribution with a quick goodbye and head out the door.

"Not so fast you guys."

"Rats!" cried Denny. "We were so close."

"Get in here." Paul ushered them into his office, reserving a stone cold stare for his own son, Jim. He was certain they were behind the impromptu camel antics that nearly ruined the pageant, in addition to hijacking the script. "What on earth did you think you were doing out there tonight?" The boys' silence confirmed their guilt.

Then Tyler spoke. "The pageant was so boring; something had to be done to rescue it."

"And you thought you had the answer, huh? How do you think Mrs. Steele felt watching all her hard work go out the window? Do you think those people enjoyed being spit on?"

This time even Tyler didn't have an answer.

"Lucky for you most of the people watching didn't know any better, but others were very much aware. You boys need to find a way to make it up to the people you hurt tonight, starting with Mrs. Steele."

The boys looked at each other; perhaps hoping one of them would defend their actions. No one did, and they replied in unison, "Yes, sir."

"Think about it and you can be sure we'll talk more about this in a couple of days. Now get home and have a Merry Christmas."

Later that evening the Hemphills enjoyed each other's company in front of the Christmas tree while a roaring fire burned on the hearth. Paul made the conscious choice to defer his anger at Jim until after the holiday. He also made the executive decision to pass the torch onto his eldest son as the official reader of the Christmas story. He needed a break. Jim opened the well-worn family Bible and read from Luke. "And it came to pass..."

*   *   *

Some time in the wee hours of the morning, when most of the town was fast asleep, Jim and his friends quietly slipped out of their beds, pulled on warm outer clothes and met in front of his house. The gentle snow that fell earlier had changed over to near whiteout conditions for several hours, covering the earth as if in a blanket. His brother Bobby had toddled off to bed satisfied that Santa would be able to land his sleigh on the roof and bring him toys. But at this hour, though the snow had dissipated, the streets were empty save for the occasional plow truck clearing the roads.

In those wee hours, Jim and the boys took it upon themselves to make good on his father's request to make amends to those they hurt with their antics at the pageant. However, they opted to start with the reverend rather than Ellen Steele.

* * *

Christmas morning the sun rose in a clear blue sky, denouncing the winter storm of the previous night. As he did most mornings, Paul Hemphill looked out over the front yard from his bedroom window. A shimmering blanket of snow sparkling like diamonds in the morning sun spread out before him, leaving him in awe of the tiny miracles God grants us each day. Then he noticed the broken continuity of the snow. Paul thought his eyes were playing tricks on him in the bright light until he realized what he was seeing was not a trick at all but a message of sorts left behind by four boys hoping to atone for the stress they had caused their favorite man of the cloth. A broad smile came over his face and there was no doubt in his mind who left the gift laid out before him. For there on the lawn, side by side, were four snow angels just about the right size of the three wise-guys and their servant boy, Fred.

26
CONNIE ANDERSEN

As I sit here surrounded by pastel peonies, hollyhock and butterfly bushes near the watchful eye of an ancient oak, the oldest character in my garden, I tap away on my laptop bringing to conclusion the odd story of how it is that I'm still here.

No one was more surprised than me when I awoke to a second chance at life, being the grateful recipient of someone's generous and painful gift of love. I pray every day for the original owner of the heart that now beats in my chest, and for the loved ones he left behind. I am humbled by the gift, as I am humbled by God's continued mercy toward me, a sinner. I marvel at His grace that sustains and keeps me, refreshing me anew each day and soothing my healing wound.

And so it is that I remain among the living. Jack said it's because my work here is not yet finished. "The Author of all that is still has a plan for you," he said the last time I saw him, which was months ago. It's hard to reconcile the doubt that I will ever see him again. I grieve for something that was impossible in the first place and will probably never experience again. I don't know why I'm so certain of this. Intuition? Maybe. Prophetic knowledge from the universe? Perhaps. It's as good an answer as any, I suppose. The one thing I do know is that his leaving was as if a page had been torn from the story of my life, the sheared paper leaving a fresh new wound in its place. But that, too, I know my God can handle.

Jack also got a second chance. And although our paths may never cross again, I am comforted knowing that he has a renewed relationship with Ellen and that there is peace in his heart.

I know our fixes, my heart and Jack's remission, are only temporary. Someday I will be called home and someday his cancer will find a new place to invade and destroy. But temporary is OK because we are but one player in a long line of characters playing out one scene after another. Life, the never ending story, will continue until The Author has closed the final page.

I will leave you with one more thought.

A week after the surgery I was visited in my hospital room yet again by the little dancer in a tutu. She looked as if she had been playing dress-up. A feathered headband with a butterfly in the middle of it pulled back her hair and she wore plastic pearls around her neck. Her plump little lips had just the barest hint of rosy coloring on them. This time I knew who she was. "Come closer," I said. "Don't be afraid." She was just as shy as the first time I saw her, pressing her finger against her lip as she approached. "I'll bet your name is Tara," I said. Her eyes grew wide in a "How did you know?" kind of way. "I'm sorry I don't have any more Jell-O to share with you like last time." She shrugged her shoulders. It was all right.

"Do you want to see me dance?" she asked.

"Of course, I'd love that."

Tara lifted her foot to the front and then the back. Then she spun in a pirouette several times with her arms circled out in front of her. For the finale, she stood on her toes and raised her arms overhead and began to turn again and again and again, until she grew so dizzy she landed on the floor giggling. I laughed right along with her.

She didn't stay long, but before she left she came to the

bed and gave me a hug. Her little headband got caught on my cannula and nearly fell off in the process. We untangled and blew kisses to one another as she danced out the door. The short time she was there she gave me hope for the never ending story. I saw my own granddaughter, Frannie, in her eyes and new the future was in good hands however the story played out.

After she left I noticed that one of the feathers had fallen from her headband and landed on my chest, from when she had hugged me. I slipped it in the drawer with my personal things, where it stayed until the day I came home. As William and Molly were packing up for me to leave, he came across the feather and was curious. He held it up and waved it. "What on earth is this?"

"I believe it's called a feather," I replied, teasing him.

"Yeah, I know that. Where did it come from and why do you have it?"

I thought about Tara, Ellen and Kelly, and the other characters who saw me through my illness. And Jack. Dear, dear Jack. I answered William's question the only way he could possibly understand. "You would never believe me if I told you."

Yes, one thing I can vouch for with unwavering certainty: that now and some other time aren't the only planes of existence.

THE END

[1]Scarborough Fair/Canticle lyrics by Paul Simon and Art Garfunkel

ABOUT THE AUTHOR

Joni VanNest lives in the suburbs of a large city but her heart resides in New England where she and her husband raised their two sons. Not surprising then, most of her stories center on the simplicity and charm of small town life. It is Joni's sincere hope that you, the reader, enjoyed the characters of Wheatfield Bridge as much as she enjoyed creating them.

Made in the USA
Middletown, DE
22 December 2016